Under the Suns

A Novel By
Ches Smith

Library of Congress Control Number: 2014912275
Printed in the United State of America, Charleston, SC

First Edition, 2014

ISBN 10: 0692241590
ISBN-13: 978-0692241592

ACKNOWLEDGMENTS

I feel like I wrote this book in a vacuum. Each bit of feedback I squeezed out of someone was like a precious drop of water in the desert. I would like to thank the following for reading various drafts or bits and pieces of drafts: Lanena Berry, Karen Blakeley, Della Cooper, Mark Dostert, Janet Gray, John Harkey Gibbs, Tom Harper, Susan Keller, Leif Masrud, Blake Pitcher, and Margret Robles. Every bit of feedback helped. To one of the world's great librarians, Cindy Dinneen, I'm grateful for your infectious love of reading! Rodney Woo and Jonathan Williams, fellow authors and two of the most committed pastors I've ever known, we may not agree on spiritual matters, but you'll never know how much your concern and friendship has meant to me. I feared stones and you gave me grace. Daniel Han, the two of us have been conjuring up stories since middle school. You're one of the few people who understands my creative life and your longstanding friendship is precious to me. I would also like to thank my parents, Roger and Susan Vernon. My gratitude for your support of my family and me can't be understated. Finally, I want to thank my wife, Silvia, and our amazing kids, Sarah, Cristian, and Max. My frailties haven't made easy waters for you to navigate, but you've stuck by me, always offering unconditional love. One of these days, I swear I'm going to get it together.

1

Nodi wasn't sure what he expected of the temple scriptorium, but whatever it was, this wasn't it. An oblong room with mildew spotted walls and candlelit writing desks cordoned off in wood cubicles. The cubicles reminded him of the forced labor cells of Kan Ludo, but this was no prison, it was a place dedicated to the word of God.

Red and green-skinned scribes, seated at their desks, noticed him as if his presence lit a fire of contemptuous stares. They didn't care for blue-skinned folk in the capital city.

An akigo in a black robe entered the room, his flesh pale pink and desperate for sunlight. His dreadlock-like tentacles were clipped back in a ponytail that wobbled when he walked. "Nodi of P'Aa?" he said, in English.

"Just Nodi."

"Ashamed of your roots? It's not like you can hide it. You're as blue as the east ocean." He surveyed Nodi's untethered tentacles. "Tie them back. Are you a savage?" He looked him in his bulbous purple eyes. "How well do you speak English?"

"Completely fluent."

"I'm chief scribe here and we only speak English in the scriptorium. It's the holy tongue. Set apart. None of your P'Aanian gibberish here. Understand?"

Nodi nodded.

The chief scribe grunted and measured him with his eyes. They were an unsettling shade of blue that might have made one think he was blind if his stare wasn't so penetrating. "Before you meet the chief high apostle, he's instructed me to take you before the Lord so that the holy countenance might look upon you." He smirked. "Maybe he'll strike you dead."

"I'll stand before the Lord? Today?" Nodi was weak-kneed, queasy at the thought.

"In mere moments." The chief turned to an akigo on his right. "Fetch him a robe."

Nodi changed into the ragged robe they gave him. It dragged on the ground and smelled like urine. The chief led him down a dank passageway into the temple cloister. Columns, like majestic arms, held the overhangs around the perimeter against the sky. A tree was in the middle, an old twisted hardwood covered in pink flowers. Two stone doors stood on the other side with an engraving above them that said,

WHAT THE HELL IS GOING ON HERE?

Nodi followed him toward the doors but stopped short. He wished he'd had time to mentally prepare. "*Now?*"

"The righteous have nothing to fear in this place." The chief smiled as if this nasty business might end soon. He gripped a brass ring on the left door and pulled, leaning under its weight. "Remain quiet and reverent while inside," he said, straining. The door grumbled like thunder.

He dusted his hands after it was open. "Hinnoben will join

us in a moment. Show respect or I'll have you arrested for blasphemy."

Blasphemy against the Lord or Hinnoben? Nodi wondered.

The chamber was round, the floor smooth with granite tiles that radiated out from the center. Fire cracked on sconces and slivers of light shone through the windows of the dome high above. A tall case stood in the center atop a golden altar. A chain ran from it to a loop in the ceiling and back down to a hook on the wall. The case had a clear shell hewn and polished out of petrified tree sap. A figure was inside, suspended in the middle.

Both of Nodi's hearts beat fast, he was short of breath. He fluttered his eyes and bowed, enough to be reverent, but not annoying, and looked up at God in the flesh.

The Lord was more than twice Nodi's size with gray flesh stretched like old leather. His mouth was open in a toothy grin, olive eyes rolled toward heaven. Wisps of long gray hair poked out of his head like threads of a weave come undone. His extremities hung limp like a marionette. The holy jumpsuit he wore was a shade of orange so bright it glowed. Maroon splotches were around his neck and torso, probably blood, though scholars debated it. His left sleeve was long with diamond patterned stitching on the cuff, but his right sleeve was missing, torn away for some reason. On the right side of his chest was a pocket that said,

TIM

A small hole in Tim's chest exposed a still-beating heart that emitted a spectral light that glowed divine. It echoed in the chamber.

Bdump ... bump ... Bdump ... bump ... Bdump ... bump ...

It had beaten for two hundred and forty-three years. It was hypnotic, terrifying, glorious.

The Akigi Bible

The Gospel According to Hinnoben the First, 1:1-11

1 In the tenth year of the reign of Queen Julizob, God sent forth his chosen one, Tim, foretold by the prophet Zuzi to Selidin, the greatest nation on all Akigol. ² As it is written,

"ONE WAS SENT FROM HEAVEN AND RULED THE LAND WITH GREAT POWER, UNITING ALL AKIGOL, SHOWING THE AKIGI HOW THEY OUGHT TO LIVE."

³ On that day, a great light burst forth from heaven and illuminated the fields of Pluro in the central province of Selidin. ⁴ From amidst the center of the swirling clouds and light, heaven gave birth to a star that fell upon the ground with great power. ⁵ Tim stepped forth from the fires of the star, unharmed and shining, tempered by the fires of heaven.

⁶ When the akigi of the city of Gloo saw the star, they went out and found the Lord walking through the fields. ⁷ Seeing that He had the appearance of a God, they fell before Him and worshiped.

⁸ When Tim saw them worshipping, He spoke to them in English saying, "What the hell is going on here?" ⁹ When He saw that they did not understand, He held out His hand to Grilo the Plucker and a light shone forth from a talisman he held within it. Grilo stood up and spoke the language of the Lord and everyone marveled. ¹⁰ Tim repeated this miracle to

all that were there. They were about fifteen in number.

[11] When they understood Him, they remembered that he said, "What the hell is going on here?" and knew they provoked the wrath of God. They were lost and even God did not know what they were doing for they were in darkness.

The Gospel According to Hinnoben the First, 2:6-14

[6] Tim chose thirteen disciples. [7] The first was Klum the Zealot who snuck up behind Him. When He turned to see Klum so close to Him, He said, "Jesus! Where did you come from?" [8] Thus the name of Klum was changed to Jesus and he was made the first disciple. [9] Many akigi names were changed to Jesus, so they called themselves things such as "Jesus of the City of Gloo" and "Jesus, Son of Sally."

[10] Tim gave most of His disciples new names [11] and they were called Jesus the Zealot and his brother Hinnoben, Kluki the Tax Gatherer, Pickles and his brother Runs with Scissors, Bill, Kilgore, Dumbass, Puffy, [12] Thomas the Banker, Doug, Dammit, and Judas the P'Aanian, whose name was changed for reasons known only to he and the Lord. [13] Judas was also the one who betrayed the Lord unto death.

[14] They stayed in Gloo for many months and whenever a new convert would join them, the Lord would change their name unless He did not have trouble pronouncing it.

The Gospel According to Hinnoben the First, 7:1-9

7 One day, the constable of the city of Mo brought two prisoners before the Lord while he stood on the cliffs of Mobi.

² The constable said, "Lord, we caught these akigi having relations with a Wild Furry Beast of the Ubar Plains. ³ We put the beast to death for enticing them, but what should we do now, set them free or punish them?"

⁴ TIM turned to His disciples and said, "You shall not tolerate deviant behavior. It rots the very fabric of society."

⁵ He looked at the prisoners and said, "Can you fly?"

⁶ The prisoners said, "No, my Lord, we don't think so."

⁷ TIM said, "How will you know unless you try?"

⁸ He pushed one of them over the cliff and it was made known to all that he could not fly.

⁹ The other prisoner held onto a tree and would not let go. TIM grew angry and called fire from the talisman in His hand. He burned the prisoner until the prisoner fell, headlong and burning, to burst upon the rocks below.

2

Looking up at Tim, Nodi thought about his conversion. He was just a youngling sitting alone on a rock in a clearing up the hill from a village in Pasica. His father was a missionary there. It was dusk. He was on his haunches, arms across his shins, perched like a bird, and could hear his father's thundering sermon even from there.

Pale green light from an aurora pulsed through cracks in the ceiling of thick clouds as if some silent war was going on above them. The glow made the shadows jitter on the forest floor. The air was crisp with the smell of rain, the rock warm beneath the pads of his feet. Four days' worth of heavy storms had taken pause. Willows drooped around the clearing and water dripped from their airy appendages and tapped the dead leaves below.

A small orange light flitted on the ground to his right. He hopped from his perch to look. An orange zolar, a rare species of phosphorescent bee, struggled to escape the clutches of a puddle. It kicked its legs back and forth, spinning in vain until Nodi scooped it up. Its fat abdomen was like a burning ember and it wobbled in the halo of its own luminescence on the palm of his hand. Four antennas crowned its head and it had needly mandibles beneath its chrome-colored eyes. Those eyes refracted honeycombed images of Nodi in them.

What could make such a fascinating creature? Noi thought. *Only an artist. Only the great architect.*

The zolar's iridescent wings fluttered and it flew away in a streak of orange between two trees. Nodi watched until it disappeared and then looked down at his dim, waving image in the puddle. He could barely make out the features of his face in the creeping dark.

He so rarely saw himself.

In his reflection, in one resonating second, Tim appeared behind him radiant with spectral blue. He looked at Nodi as if he loved him.

The vision was sudden, like a waking dream. Nodi turned to look, fell on his back, and Tim was gone. He lay there, covered in mud, looking up at heaven.

The Lord whispered on the breeze. "Seek."

Now, in Tim's chamber, Nodi stood before the Lord and couldn't reconcile what he'd seen that night with what he saw before him.

The doors opened on the other side of the chamber. Three guards shoved an akigo in, hands bound. A robed silhouette stood behind them in the doorway—the chief high apostle, Hinnoben the Eighth. The guards threw the prisoner down. He wore nothing but a cloth diaper, green flesh scored and broken, blood eeking out of the gashes.

"It's all a joke. We've been tricked!" he said.

A guard pushed him. "Say one more thing and I'll unhinge your jaw."

The prisoner lunged at Nodi as if to tell him something. Nodi stepped aside, confused. The akigo fell to his knees, sobbing.

The chief grabbed Nodi's shoulder and pointed him toward Hinnoben.

"The word can't be trusted!" The prisoner yelled as the guards dragged him into the cloister. It was a penetrating, desperate yell. Nodi got the impression the temple authorities weren't interested in letting him hear what the poor akigo had to say.

He stepped into the adjoining room, the Great Hall of the Chosen. The chief left, closing the doors behind him. Hinnoben spoke in hushed tones with one of his guards. Another guard stood close, staring at Nodi. She reminded him of his betrothed, Aenna. Aenna was a soldier once. All akigas were, at one point or another, being taller and stronger than males. The highest positions of power, however, belonged to akigos. Tim favored males, one of many ways he disrupted the accepted order of things.

The hall was a semi-circle along the backside of the Lord's chamber. Thick, spiral columns stood along the far wall. The floors were coral, rough like sandpaper, and a long mud bath was in the middle of the room that smelled like potter's clay.

While Nodi waited for the chief high priest, he surveyed the artifacts encased in wood cabinets between the columns—petrified remains of Tim's first meal on Akigol, fragments of his star, some crude sketches. The final case held a sample of his writing, the only one in existence, scribbled on tattered parchment. Most of it was scratched out as if done in a fit. Only one phrase remained:

SAME SHIT, DIFFERENT SOLAR SYSTEM

"My timing was unfortunate," Hinnoben said from across the room.

One of the guards left through a door at the end of the

hall. The other continued to watch Nodi.

"How so?" Nodi said.

"A group of P'Aanians set fire to three temples on the west side of town a few nights ago. Dissenters Guild operatives. I can't imagine you've had too warm a reception in Prontis because of it."

"If it hadn't been that, it would have been something else."

"That's true. I wonder why so many seek to collect the debts of the dead from the living. Judas was a P'Aanian like you, but that's as far as the similarity goes … I hope."

"The moment Judas betrayed the Lord it set a self-fulfilling prophecy in motion. I can't deny that my region is fertile ground for treachery, but most there are simple TIMian folk."

"Yes." Hinnoben nodded. His eyes, like puddles of oil, went distant for a moment. He wore an ornate robe with gold patchwork that glinted in the candlelight. He had a pleasant face, grayish green with age. He'd cut off his tentacles, thought to be the seat of sexual desire. Their stubby remnants remained, swelling up and down on his scalp as he breathed. Nodi tried not to stare.

Hinnoben approached, guard remaining close as if to prevent some phantom threat she'd dreamed up in her head.

"What do you think the pure word of God is like?" Hinnoben said.

"What do you mean?"

"The actual word of God, untainted by the crudities of language."

"Reality itself, no distinction. He speaks, it is."

"That's what I think too. God doesn't need to speak the name Nodi. God speaks and Nodi is. But how do you speak to that which has been spoken into existence? How do you speak to the words themselves?"

"You give the words words of their own so they might understand." Hinnoben was drawing on the wisdom of Rolitin, a theologian.

"TIM was God made word," Hinnoben said. "And his word is gospel. There's an alarming trend on the rise, an emphasis on the *experience* of God over his word. But you can't experience God apart from his word any more than you can see without knowing what you're looking at."

Hinnoben turned toward a spiral staircase in the far-left corner and motioned Nodi to follow. The staircase was chiseled out of a giant orange conch shell with pink steps embedded in it.

The guard followed.

"You're known to be good with words, Nodi."

"My father was a missionary. He studied all the languages of the kingdom. I learned from him and also studied in Forwo."

"I knew of your father. Known for his integrity. Are you coupled?"

"Promised. Her name is Aenna. We'll be coupled in eight months."

"That's unfortunate. Scripture allows for it, but I prefer my scribes not to be distracted by such entanglements. Do you love her?"

"With both my hearts."

"Then what room is left for God?"

Nodi said nothing. He was already failing the test. He followed the old apostle around the staircase.

"Would you leave her for the Lord?" Hinnoben said.

"If God willed it."

Hinnoben nodded. They walked down a cramped hall. "I'll be honest with you, you were something of a last resort. Having a P'Aanian work in the temple comes with … complications. At least you're from a moderate border town like Kan Ludo and not Sigate or someplace like that. Your lineage works in your favor, too. The truth is there aren't many akigi that have your broad linguistic skill set."

"Which languages am I to translate scripture too?"

"Oh, we don't translate into other languages, anymore. I put a stop to that. No. We only produce English texts."

"I mean no disrespect," Nodi said, "but *why?*"

Hinnoben stopped at his chamber door and opened it. Nodi looked back at the guard who just stared at him. They followed Hinnoben inside. A harvesting festival was going on outside. Nodi felt the bass drums, could hear the hypnotic chants of the crowd. A preacher was crowing somewhere about the end of the world. He followed Hinnoben onto a balcony while the guard waited inside and watched.

Nodi held on to the railing and looked out. The sky was spotted with daystars and a red-orange aurora glistened in waves from east to west below the suns. Pale purple cliffs were on either side of the temple that opened into the valley beyond. Cone shaped towers peppered the canyon floor and blossomed into a booming city past the River Hyxl. The towering cerulean blue palace of King Jesus the Fifteenth was in the distance, thin and jagged, on the north side of town.

"Beautiful, isn't it?" Hinnoben said. He turned to the guard and nodded. The guard went to the desk in the corner of the room. She brought back a scroll and handed it to Nodi.

Nodi looked it over. "It's a gospel forgery. Only a fragment. It suggests TIM never existed, that it's all a hoax. Pretty convincing, but the syntax is too modern."

"You *are* good," Hinnoben said. He took the scroll, rolled it up, and clenched it in his fist. "Do you realize how many documents like this have been produced? It's all lies. Thousands of them in every language of the kingdom. The Dissenter's Guild produces them."

"They're trying to undermine the authority of scripture. Confusion works in their favor."

"Yes. And it's succeeding."

"So you're trying to set standards? One language, one word, no variations?"

"Exactly, but I didn't bring you here for that. We've charged apostles throughout the kingdom to gather up as many of these documents as they can, using their discretion, of course. Anything we might need to see. Paying good money for them, too. And what isn't given willingly, is taken by force. You will receive the most problematic ones."

Nodi watched the crowd, a mass of red and green dots like course gravel flowing in the streets. This was a bad deal, not what he was expecting at all.

"The kingdom is bleeding misinformation, Nodi. We need someone like you to help put a stop to it."

Hinnoben directed his gaze up and to the left. The prisoner Nodi encountered in TIM's chamber was rising on a platform to the top of the cliff closest to the temple.

"He was one of our scribes," Hinnoben said. "He came across this fragment about a year ago and was deceived. It's lies consumed him. He lost faith in scripture and slipped this excerpt into the works he produced. Several of them made it into circulation before we discovered the error."

The guards dragged the scribe off the platform and onto the edge of the cliff.

Nodi understood what was about to happen and wasn't sure how he felt about it. He could justify it scripturally, but his own constitution resisted. Pushing deviants off cliffs was based on a passage of scripture in which TIM pushed two akigi, caught in the act of bestiality, to their deaths. Was it intended to be a prescription for *all* deviant behavior? If so, what qualified? Some scholars argued that *everyone* was guilty of one form of deviant behavior or another and deserved to be cast from the highest precipices in the land. Ultimately, those same scholars, realizing the peril their own interpretation put them in, decided the punishment should be carried out as deemed necessary by the temple, as long as none of *them* had to go jump off a cliff.

Hinnoben grabbed Nodi's upper arm and squeezed. "This is the fate of all who question the Lord."

The drumming stopped. The crowd became still. Hinnoben waved and the guards pushed the scribe over. He fell head first, appearing to float a moment until hitting the floor with a crack and splash of viscera. Nodi clenched his eyes shut.

The crowd observed the proper amount of somber reflection ...

... and then cheered.

The Akigi Bible

The Gospel According to Hinnoben the First, 6:9-18

⁹ Later that day, Tim showed His disciples a book that He carried in His satchel. They had never seen a book before. ¹⁰ It was called *Holy Bible*.

¹¹ He spoke to Dumbass and Hinnoben and Kluki, His inner three, saying, ¹² "This book contains the pattern by which you shall write scripture. ¹³ You must read it and write my deeds in like manner so that all who come after you will know the truth."

¹⁴ His disciples questioned Him saying, "Lord, what is this book?"

¹⁵ He answered saying, "It is a book of hope and desolation, having the sound of truth, but no truth in it. ¹⁶ When you understand how to write scripture in like manner, you must burn it."

¹⁷ So Dumbass and Hinnoben and Kluki read the book and learned how to record the words and deeds of the Lord in like manner and then they gave *Holy Bible* to Judas to burn it.

¹⁸ But Judas secretly kept it.

The Gospel According to Hinnoben the First, 12:18-23

[18] Judas kept *Holy Bible* because he saw there was a disciple in it whose name was also Judas. [19] According to the myth of the Messiah called Jesus, Judas was a tool of salvation in that he delivered Jesus unto death. [20] Jesus had to die to appease the wrath of their God.

[21] When Judas the P'Aanian saw this, the evil one, that creature of old called Duvoi, spoke to him and they reasoned together and decided that Tim changed his name to Judas because He wanted to be killed by him. [22] This was so that Akigol might be saved.

[23] But Tim never said He wanted to be killed by Judas. That was the reasoning of the evil one.

The Gospel According to Hinnoben the First, 13:12-16

[12] Sometime during the night, a villager who was lost in the woods wandered into the camp. [13] Tim was drunk in the spirit and was surprised by him. He held out His hand to burn the intruder, but He was not wearing His talisman.

[14] When Judas saw that Tim did not cast flames from the palm of His hand as He had done many times before, he reasoned that Tim was powerless without the talisman. He plotted to steal it and kill the Lord.

[15] But in truth, God was the source of Tim's power, not the talisman. [16] Judas was made to think these things so that God's plan of redemption might be carried out.

The Gospel According to Hinnoben the First, 14:9-15:5

⁹ One night, while the other disciples were on leave in Forwo, Judas seized Tim as He slept. He tied His hands and feet and removed His talisman.

¹⁰ Tim was strong, but could not break the bonds. Judas took a log and placed it on the ground and tied the Lord to it. ¹¹ He hammered nails through Tim's hands and feet as it was in *Holy Bible*, and also so that the Lord would not fall off the log. ¹² He lifted Him up with ropes and dropped the end of the log into a hole.

¹³ After Tim hung there for several days, Judas became impatient because the Lord did not die. ¹⁴ In his anger, Judas hit Him on the head with a rock and heard a great sound that hurt his ears. Tim still did not die.

¹⁵ Now Hinnoben was fasting and praying in a cave when God came to him in a vision and showed him what was happening. ¹⁶ He went and told the other disciples and they gathered up their belongings and went out to where they had seen the Lord last.

¹⁷ They found the log with the nails in it and the ropes were on the ground, but Tim was gone. They wept for they realized Judas had murdered the Lord and they did not know where he put his body.

¹⁸ They said to one another, "Come, let us kill the betrayer, Judas," but when they went to look for him, he was gone.

15 Many months later, a farmer was having relations with a wild furry beast on the cliffs near Prontis. ² He looked down below and saw the transfigured body of Tim and realized he was sinning before the Lord. He cast himself down and burst on the floor of the canyon.

³ When his brother came out to find him and saw what had happened, he killed the wild furry beast for enticing his brother and then went down and marveled at Tim.

⁴ When he heard that Tim's heart still beat, he tore his tunic and cried out that Tim still lived. ⁵ He went and told the villagers about what he had seen and they came out and worshiped and sang hymns and tore their tunics, but not unto nakedness so they would not offend the Lord.

3

Isu Kru was stark raving mad, a P'Aanian, purple instead of blue, with arms twice the length of her legs. She knuckle-walked across a splintered obsidian plateau that glinted in the sunlight like a black jewel. To the north, the port city of Sigate shimmered in the heat, its piers reaching into the sea. Black columns of smoke rose from its shipyards. To her left, waves crashed against the cliffs, foam splashing over the edges and blowing back at her in the wind. A few boats with red masts sailed along the coast. Beyond them, an indigo darkness loomed on the horizon, an eternal storm that never came.

She climbed to the bottom of a shallow fissure and found a cave entrance filled with debris. She dug it out and stuck her head inside.

"Here?" she said to her imaginary friend as she clapped dust from her fingers. Her companion always remained outside her peripheral vision. Sometimes, she spun around to catch a glimpse but never did.

Yes, he said.

"Papa?"

Maybe.

She went into the cave, came to a narrow opening, and turned sideways to squeeze through. The draft blowing from inside was cool, but it smelled like stale droppings. Daylight glowed around the bend ahead. She followed it around to find it ended in a cozy cavity. The lesser sun shone down on the floor from a hole at the top of a long, stone shaft above her. On the ground at the edge of the light, was the ash gray skeleton of a dead akigo, sticking out of the mud. Its skull was cracked and its thick boned arms clutched a worn leather pouch.

Him? her companion said.

"No."

She pulled the pouch away and opened it. Nothing was in it but a piece of old cloth, torn in half, with writing on it. She was disappointed. She pulled one of the pieces out, threw the pouch down, and moved into the light to get a better look. The writing was crusty and faded. She had no use for it but held onto it mainly because she forgot to let go.

She hadn't found what she was looking for in that cave. "Sigate," she said.

Home.

Isu lived in the alley next to the temple and was back by sunsdown, crouching beneath the overhang of the roof. The temple apostle came out to give her some bread as he did every evening about that time and noticed the cloth. He gave her the bread and took it when she put it down to eat. He held it up in the fading daylight. The writing was P'Aanian to be sure, but some lost dialect he didn't recognize.

"Where did you get this, Isu?"

"Cave."

"What cave?"

She chewed her bread.

"The temple pays for documents such as this. Would you sell it to me?"

She nodded.

"Here." He handed her a coin.

She took it, popped it in her mouth—

"No. Isu."

—and swallowed.

He shook his head.

He took the fragment inside and put it on a stack of documents bound for the scriptorium in Prontis.

4

Nodi held the word of God in his hearts in much the same way he held the words "I love you" when Aenna spoke them softly in his ear. The spark was lit as he sat on the floor of the parsonage in an arc of sunlight that shone in through the window. He was a youngling, his skin still slate gray because his color hadn't come in yet. *The Sayings of Tim* was splayed out before him. He read chapter 13 verse 13:

> [13] When TIM saw Judas and the other disciples watching him from afar, he called out to them saying, "Curiosity killed the cat."

Nodi's father, Nodol, sat at his desk writing a sermon. The window was open and a draft rustled the pages. He looked around for something to put on top of them so they wouldn't blow away.

"What's this mean?" Nodi said, and read the verse aloud.

Nodol put his quill down and turned. "When Tim

introduced English to us, there were words we couldn't comprehend. We lacked the context. 'Cat' might have been such a word. But what's interesting about that particular passage is that Tim may not have been using an English word at all. There's a lot of controversy about it. In P'Aanian, an old first-century word sounds very similar to 'cat.' It means 'ignorance.' However, in Selidinese it means 'faith.' Tim was speaking to Judas, a P'Aanian, but in the presence of Selidinians, so either is a possibility. Now, in English, 'curiosity' means "a desire to know," so depending on the translation of 'cat', it either means that the desire to know can kill *ignorance* or *faith*."

"Which do you think it means?" Nodi said.

"I don't think it matters. What about you?"

"Both?"

"I hope not. Put it on your list." He referred to a list of questions Nodi hoped to ask God in the hereafter. Nodol turned back to his sermon. As a passing thought, he said, "Some theologians think the discussion is pointless. Sometimes Tim used words that had no obvious meaning. They're called gibberisms."

That's when it occurred to Nodi that scripture was a puzzle to be unlocked, an enigma, a roadmap of the very mind of God. If he could decipher the riddle, could he discover the answers to the grandest questions of all?

After serving in the scriptorium for four months, it was a riddle he cared less and less about. Bitterness was seeping into his soul. The other scribes wouldn't sit near him so he had a corner to himself near a fire pit used to burn refuse. They hung a crude sign from the rafters above him that said Department of P'Aanian Affairs with an arrow that pointed at his desk. The chief scribe refused to let him remove it.

During his time there, he'd uncovered Dissenters Guild messages, heretical copies of scripture, and documents encouraging religious dissonance. They listed names and places that the temple could act on, but the majority of stuff that came across his desk was either mundane or ludicrous. He hated going there every day and counted the minutes until he could go home each evening. He hadn't seen Aenna since he'd left Kan Ludo. Everyone despised him and he was beset with such a foul attitude that nothing could quell it. He suspected it was his attitude that kept him in the mire, but he couldn't deny his own feelings.

He prayed for forgiveness, mentally flogged himself for being so negative, and tried to keep the faith. He kept it most days.

This was his last day before a brief leave. He was close to going home to Kan Ludo, to Aenna. The anticipation of seeing her again carried him through. She was God's favor in the flesh.

Just finish the day.

"Anything of interest?" the chief scribe said on his midday rounds.

"Nothing actionable," Nodi said. He pulled a few of the more curious items out of his stack of documents. Tossing them on his desk one by one, he said, "This is a list of ingredients for an infertility cure that is probably lethal. This is an invitation to a midnight rendezvous between two lovers, both eunuchs. And this is a tract from a Timian death cult. If the admonitions in it were heeded, they're all dead now."

"I'll put it in the fire." The chief picked the stack up, put another in its place, and walked away. Nodi resisted the urge to shove it off his desk. He closed his eyes and held his head in his hands.

Why did you send me here, Lord?

Heaven was silent. Either God had abandoned him or he'd lost the ability to differentiate the holy voice from his own train of thought. He looked at his fellow scribes and saw arrogance, self-righteousness, false humility. He hated them but hated himself more.

This is a test. Forgive me, Lord, for failing.

He thumbed through the stacks of pages. They'd been sent from the temple in Sigate according to the strap that bound them together. As the stiff parchments flipped under his thumb, one didn't feel like the others. He removed the strap and pulled it out.

It was half a letter written on a piece of cloth, tattered around the edges. It was very old. He handled the fabric with care, spread it out in front of him, and brought a candle in close. It was an extremely rare dialect of P'Aanian, written in blood. Akigi blood was known for its permanence and was often used by the ancients when no ink was available. He studied the hooks on the vowels and the jots at the ends of the sentences and knew he could translate it, but it wouldn't be easy. A signature was at the bottom:

JUDAS.

That name was like a magnet for his eyes. It was like finding the childhood toy of a genocidal maniac or the parasol of some viral whore. Could the great betrayer have actually written this?

It has to be a forgery.

The volume of the scriptorium turned down, the whole world might as well have disappeared around him. He translated it, piece by piece, scribbling his translation on a piece of parchment. When he finished, he looked around the room to see if anyone had taken an interest in what he was doing. No one cared. As usual.

He leaned forward and read it:

THE LORD WAS BADLY HURT BECAUSE OF THE CRUCIFIXION BUT STILL HAD ENOUGH STRENGTH TO

ATTACK JACKASS. THEY STRUGGLED MIGHTILY, BUT THE LORD OVERTOOK HIM AND KNOCKED HIM DOWN. HE TURNED THE VESSEL AROUND AND STOPPED IT IN THE AIR AND OPENED THE DOOR. A GREAT WIND BLEW IN. I HAD TROUBLE BREATHING. THE LORD KICKED ME TOWARD THE DOOR AND I FELL THROUGH BUT HELD ON TO THE EDGE SO THAT I WOULDN'T FALL OUT. HE FORCED MY HANDS LOOSE. JUST BEFORE I FELL, I SAW JACKASS RUN UP BEHIND HIM, BUT I SAW NO MORE.

I LANDED IN THE WATER OFF THE COAST NEAR SIGATE AND SAW THE VESSEL FLY BACK THE WAY WE HAD COME. I SWAM AWHILE AND MADE IT ASHORE. WHILE I SAT ON THE BEACH, THE VESSEL FLEW BACK OVER ME, GOING TOWARD THE ISLAND I HAD SEEN ON THE MAP. IT DISAPPEARED ON THE HORIZON. I NEVER SAW IT, OR THE LORD, AGAIN.

I DISCOVERED WHAT I BELIEVE TO BE THE CAVES OF HIJOON AND HAVE HIDDEN THERE EVER SINCE. IF YOU HAVE FOUND THIS LETTER, YOU WILL HAVE FOUND MY BODY FOR I WILL BE DEAD SOON. THE TALISMAN OF THE LORD IS BURIED HERE. *HOLY BIBLE* TOO, THOUGH I WAS INSTRUCTED TO DESTROY IT ALL THOSE YEARS AGO.

THAT BOOK BROUGHT ME NOTHING BUT PAIN.

THE LORD CHANGED MY NAME BECAUSE I TOLD KLUKI THAT THE LORD WAS THE ONE WHO ATE HIS SUMMER BERRIES. THE LORD CALLED ME "JUDAS" BECAUSE HE FELT BETRAYED. SO TRIVIAL A THING.

BUT WHEN I READ ABOUT THE ONE CALLED JUDAS IN *HOLY BIBLE*, I CAME TO BELIEVE THAT THE LORD CHANGED MY NAME SO THAT I MIGHT FULFILL A ROLE IN THE SALVATION OF AKIGOL.

I FAILED.

NOW I WILL FOLLOW THE PATH OF MY NAMESAKE AND PUT AN END TO MYSELF. I WRITE TO YOU MY FINAL GOODBYE.

PERHAPS THE LORD HAS RETURNED TO YOU ALREADY, BUT IF NOT, KNOW THAT HE MAY NOT BE WHO HE SAYS HE IS. I CANNOT TELL WHAT THE TRUTH IS ANYMORE, SUCH IS THE CURSE GOD HAS PUT UPON ME. I HOPE THAT SOMEDAY, SOMEONE MIGHT FIND A WAY GO TO THE PLACE MARKED ON THE MAP I'VE DRAWN ABOVE.

SEEK TRUTH.

DO NOT TRUST HINNOBEN. THE SCRIPTURE HE IS WRITING IS FULL OF HALF-TRUTHS AND SELF-INDULGENT DECEPTIONS. HE SEEKS ONLY POWER FOR HIMSELF. HE, ABOVE ALL, MANIPULATED ME IN SECRET. HE WAS THE TRUE BETRAYER.

NO ONE WILL BELIEVE ME.

I ONLY HAD AKIGI INTERESTS IN MIND.

WITH REGRETS,
JUDAS

Nodi laid the translation down and smoothed it out with his hands. He wanted to wipe away what he'd read. His mind was an open tap of questions, thoughts teetering the line between divine revelation and damnable blasphemy.

It's a fake, he thought.

He picked up the cloth and cradled it between his blue fingers. The oddly shaped swatch had torn stitching along the wide end of it. He turned it over and rubbed his finger across a corner to remove some dirt. It was faded orange, familiar, diamond patterned stitching on one end—

He rolled it long ways and knew exactly what it was. Tim's missing sleeve.

The letter was authentic.

He looked around. No one was watching. He opened his desk and slipped it inside, struggling to breathe. He wanted to sob, to turn his desk over, to laugh hysterically.

Hinnoben the Eighth can't know about this. He'll suppress it. He'll have to. It speaks ill of his forbearer. He'll eliminate anyone who knows about it.

Not if you turn it in, he countered. *He would see it as a show of good faith.*

The risk would be too great.

Be loyal.

Loyal to who? Hinnoben or God?

Is there a difference?

"We're closing," the chief scribe said from down the aisle. "What've you got?"

The sudden intrusion startled Nodi. He picked up some materials he'd translated earlier and held them out.

"For the fire?" he said, hoping the chief wouldn't comment on his shaking hand.

The chief grunted and looked them over. "If I'm not mistaken, you've got leave time coming to you. Going home to P'Aa, I suppose?"

"Yes, sir."

The chief walked away.

Nodi pulled the cloth back out. He could be arrested for withholding it, probably killed, no, *definitely* killed, but he couldn't let it go. He put it back under a stack of unfinished documents, slid them inside his desk, and locked it. He clutched his translation and stared at the fire pit. He read his copy once more and threw it in the fire on his way out.

The Akigi Bible

The Gospel According to Hinnoben the First, 4:1-20

4 One day, while the priests of the Temple in Gloo were sacrificing animals to God, Tim entered and spoke to them saying,[2] "I have been sent from heaven to show you the path to redemption.

[3] "You shall no longer offer sacrifices to God for it is grotesque and I am not pleased by the smell coming from my temples.

[4] "And akigos shall no longer go into akigas unless it is to create offspring. [5] The horrible sounds of fornication are not pleasing to the Lord.

[6] "And you shall not drink ale unto drunkenness for it leads you to the path of violence. [7] Surely you will try to kill me and I shall add your number to those who are in hell.

[8] "And you shall wear clothes when you are in public, for your genitals are offensive to the Lord."

[9] When the apostles heard these things they said to Him, [10] "Lord, these things you say are like nothing the prophets that came before you said. [11] It is as if you know nothing of our history or our teachings."

[12] So Tim answered them with a parable saying, [13] "An upright akigo built a temple to God on a hill and went away for a while.

[14] "One day, a villager came along and saw the temple, but believed it to be the mansion of a wealthy akigo. [15] A second villager said, 'That is not a mansion, but a bar and I am very thirsty.' [16] A third villager said, 'You are both wrong, for that is a brothel. Come, let us go in and see.'

[17] "When the builder returned and saw the villagers there, he said to them, 'Do you not recognize a temple dedicated to God when you see one?'"

[18] And then Tim said to them, "You see and you hear, but you interpret it on your own accord. [19] I see and hear and understand because I and God are one."

[20] Then the apostles said to Him, "Ah Lord! Forgive us for not trusting you. We are tainted and imperfect, but you are truly the Messiah sent from heaven!"

The Gospel According to Dumbass, 8:6-7

[6] And the Lord spoke to them saying, "You shall build temples devoted to me and you shall worship me on the first day of each week and again in the middle of the week. [7] You must have someone to lead music and someone to preach the gospel and make you feel guilty about yourselves and promise you hope even if there is none."

5

odi had only been in Kan Ludo for a few hours. It was early evening and he was crossing the central bridge with Aenna on their way to midweek worship. The old wooden bridge shook underfoot from rickshaws and wagons passing over it. Aenna pulled him to the side to make way.

They stood there awhile and held each other. She cradled his head against her chest, her tentacles tickling the back of his neck.

God, he'd missed her.

He let go, leaned on the railing, and looked out at the city. Kan Ludo was spread across egg crate hills peppered with lime green trees, weed flowers, and boulders that looked like they sprouted right out of the bluegrass. It always smelled like citrus because of the orchards to the east. A web of tributaries cut through the tight, low-lying valleys so that a network of bridges was necessary to connect the hills together. Most of the buildings were clay and swamp-wood igloos built on platforms that clung to the hills like tree fungi.

"Our favorite tree is gone," he said, nodding at a stump by the stream below.

"It was infected. They had to dig it out."

"Remember how we used to meet under it in the mornings before temple?"

"You'd always bring Ru with you."

"We were what, eleven, twelve?"

"Younger, I think."

"I haven't seen Ru in ages. He's still up North."

Aenna had a scar that cut across her right temple. She wasn't bothered by it and it reminded Nodi of how strong she was. She made him feel safe.

"What's it like in Prontis?" she said.

"I'm not happy there. It's nothing like I thought it would be. I trust God and I still believe it was his will for me to go there. I'm just not sure why. I shouldn't be so negative."

"Have you made any friends?"

"God, no. They hate our kind in Prontis."

"That's not very reassuring. I'll be with you in a little over four months."

"*Humph.* The P'Aanian scribe's companion. You'll be like a pimple that pops up on top of a pustule." She didn't think that was funny. "I'm sorry," he said. "It'll be fine."

She nodded and looked down at the stream bank below. An old gray akigo was gathering up his fishing gear for the evening. They stood there a while longer and watched the suns go down behind the mountains. The coral streaked sky glistened with stars that grew brighter as night approached. Finally, they continued, unhurried, up the sloping bridge to the town square amid scattered groups of akigi herding to their respective temples.

"What do your hearts tell you?" she said.

"About what?"

"God's will."

"They don't tell me anything. I've always sought a deeper understanding, turned to scripture for that, but now I feel like I understand less than ever."

A small group of Hillers, a cultish assembly of robe-clad akigi, passed by. They exchanged uneasy looks.

"Maybe there's a reason you feel that way," Aenna said, watching the Hillers whisper to one another. "Maybe God's testing you."

"He must be."

"You have to stay true to God, Nodi. He'll show you the way."

"I can't feel the presence of God anymore. I believed I was called to Prontis for a purpose. I was sure the Lord would reveal himself to me, but he hasn't …" He stopped and let his emotions simmer. As they crossed the threshold of the bridge he said, "I've only been there for four months. I'm being silly. God's timing."

Aenna nodded. She was tense.

The main square was just ahead. Gravel crunched under their feet. Four extravagant temples were around the square, surrounded by dense marketplaces. A bonfire in the middle lit everything in stark shades of orange.

Nodi wanted to tell her about the letter, he had to tell someone. "Speaking of God's will," he said but thought the better of it.

"What?"

"Nothing." *Maybe later.*

Various factions of akigi siphoned off into their respective temples, acting as if the other factions didn't existent. Nodi and Aenna went into the smallest one, which was more of a benchless amphitheater with three skeletal spires at the back and a raised pulpit in the middle. They stood near the back and loosely held hands while their fellow congregants flowed around them. Out of respect for God, their denomination didn't believe in sitting during the service. This also created more room for akigi, which was favorable for reasons of prestige and finance.

A large akiga stood in front of them, fashionable with her tentacles in reeds that made them stand on end. Nodi felt like a multi-limbed weed was obstructing his view. A youngling kept knocking the back of his knees and the akigo to his right wouldn't stop talking about the weather.

Nodi didn't want to be there.

The service began.

Unlike Aenna, he never cared for the music much. The songs lacked originality, they weren't profound or thought-provoking, just simple, cryptic phrases repeated over and over. Sometimes Nodi wondered if simple repetition could lead to belief. They sang-chanted verses filled with colloquialisms and grotesqueries about the way of suffering. Would an outsider glean anything from them at all? Would they find meaning in their traditions? Their vernacular? Their scriptures?

Maybe that was the point. Us and them. You're either part of the tribe or you're not. Was there any end to the bands of tribes to which one might be a part?

The music apostle, an old akigo who shook when he spoke, launched into a feverish prayer. The congregation cocked their heads to the left, the customary posture for prayer. The only difference between their temple and the temple to the left of it was the other temple prayed with their heads cocked to the right—a seemingly negligible difference, but of monumental importance between them.

So absurd.

Nodi couldn't concentrate, couldn't connect—felt like he was outside himself. His mind was out of alignment, jaded even, and no matter how hard he tried to succumb to the spirit of God in that service, it drifted toward the letter. Its contradictions infected him.

When the apostle finished his prayer, he said, "What the hell is going on here?" and the congregation repeated, in unison, "What the hell is going on here?"

Indeed.

He excused himself. The akiga in front of him turned and her reed-sheathed tentacles almost poked him in the eye. He batted them away as if they were vile serpents. She was outraged, but turned back around and seethed. Aenna followed him down the aisle and outside.

"There's something you're not telling me," she said, calling after him.

He stopped and turned towards her. "Let's go to Relovo's."

———— ‡═►❖◄═‡ ————

Relovo's was a mid-sized tavern with an open-air courtyard. A stone fireplace and torches burned in the middle, flames pulling and cracking in the breeze. Nodi went to the bar to buy them some juice while Aenna got a table. It was crowded. One table had five ixaquoi at it who were being bawdy. The only free table was next to them.

Nodi watched them as he waited for his juice. Ixaquoi were a different species originating on the island of Gologa off the southwest coast. They were two heads taller than akigas with blood red, sinewy flesh and bald heads. The akigi discovered them sixty years prior, flooded their island with missionaries, and influenced their leadership to adopt Timianity as Gologa's official religion. Some ixaquoi rebelled and lost. They were exiled and, along with akigi sympathizers, formed the loose network that became the clandestine group known as the Dissenters Guild.

Nodi took two clay bowls of cider from the bartender and went to the table. As he passed by the ixaquoi, one of them reared back in laughter and almost knocked the bowls out of his hands. He finessed them side to side so that he didn't spill anything. The ixaquoi said, "Sorry, sport," in Selidinese and started laughing again.

Nodi sat next to Aenna and set the bowls down on the knotted wood table. She raised her brows as if to say, "I've waited long enough, now tell me."

He looked over at the ixaquoi then back at her. He spoke quietly. "I discovered something just before I left the scriptorium. I don't know what to make of it ... I probably shouldn't tell—"

"What is it?"

He drummed his fingers on the table, searching for the best way to put it. "They've had me translating these asinine, inconsequential letters and fragments since I've been there. At the end of each day, I give the chief scribe the stack of translations and he usually just burns them."

"I thought you were translating scripture into kingdom languages."

"I assumed that's why they summoned me there, but I was wrong. They don't even do that anymore. It's English only now. Instead, they have me looking for anything related to the Dissenters Guild because I'm fluent in so many languages. They don't even *want* me there. I was the last resort—Hinnoben the Eighth told me that himself."

"Well, that explains your discontent."

"I received this stack of letters and there was one—"

"What?"

"It was written by *Judas,* Aenna. *After* the betrayal."

She pursed her lips. "Judas was taken by the Lord for his sin. No one ever heard from him again after the betrayal. It's a forgery. You *know* that."

"That's what I thought too ...," he said. He stopped and watched as all but one of the ixaquoi got up from their table.

They patted the remaining one on the shoulder saying, "See ya, Mal," as they left, stumbling out of the tavern, single file. The final one tripped over a step and fell over. The others struggled to help him up amidst raucous laughter.

The remaining ixaquoi held up his hand. "One more, barkeep." He was dressed in black with a hood over his head. His back was to them.

Nodi looked back at Aenna and leaned into her. "That's what I thought, but what if I told you it was his suicide note. I saw it with my own eyes and it's *not* a forgery."

"How can you be so sure?"

"When I was in Tim's chamber, Tim was missing his right sleeve. This letter is written on the missing sleeve, Aenna. I swear it! How else can you explain that? Who else would have had it?"

Aenna was stiff, uncomfortable with the conversation. "That doesn't necessarily prove it, but suppose you're right. What difference does it make? Judas betrayed and killed Tim. So what if he committed suicide?"

"It was the second half of the letter. The first half was missing. It mentioned Judas' location, some sort of vessel, a map, it spoke of someone called 'Jackass,' and it said he buried the Lord's talisman and *Holy Bible* there … If one were so inclined, they might be able to find Judas' body, those priceless artifacts, the first part of the letter, the map, whatever the map leads to—"

"If one were so inclined," Aenna said, implying that Nodi was not the one.

He took a drink and tried to calm down. Aenna stared at the fireplace.

"The scariest part," Nodi said, with a renewed whisper, "is that Judas closes it with a warning that Tim might not have been who he said he was. It also implicates Hinnoben the First as a co-conspirator in the crucifixion. What do you think that means?"

"It doesn't mean anything. Even if it's authentic, a long shot, it just confirms what we already know about Judas. He was given over to darkness. It's the ravings of a lunatic."

"I once knew a ravin' lunatic," the inebriated ixaquoi at the next table said. He turned around and leaned into them, "who hit his best friend with a brick. He whacked his head, until it bled, and cleaned it all up with a lick."

"Do you *mind?*" Aenna bit back.

"Sorry, sorry." The ixaquoi turned around to nurse his ale.

"Keep your voice down," Nodi said to her.

"What did the chief scribe say when you told him about it?"

Nodi looked away. "I haven't told him yet. The letter accuses Hinnoben the First of being manipulative and power—"

"Are you *crazy?*"

"He'll never know. The letter is locked inside my desk. Even if he finds it, he'll just assume I didn't get to it yet. I burned the translation so there's no way he'd know. I just didn't want to see it destroyed too hastily. I needed time to reflect on it."

"They can *execute* you for this, Nodi."

"They're not going to know." He met her eyes. "What if everything we believe is based on a misunderstanding ... or worse, a *lie?*"

"I can't even entertain that thought." She leaned away.

"What if God wants me to look into this further? What if he set this cup before me? It *can't* be a coincidence."

She held his face in her hands. "I agree. It's not a coincidence. It's a test. If you fail this test, if your search for truth takes you *away* from Tim, you've sacrificed truth on the altar of self-exaltation. It's hubris to think these things, Nodi. Think of your faith. Of your career. You want to quit these menial tasks at the scriptorium, maybe this is the path to do it. Turn it in. *Immediately*. And then forget about it."

"I know what it says. What if that fact alone gets me into trouble? The letter, as an object, isn't what's dangerous, it's the information it contains."

She took her hands off his face and picked at a splinter on the table. "Maybe you tell them you didn't translate it. Maybe you say you saw the name and wanted to alert them immediately … Maybe you just trust God."

Nodi leaned back. Two paths were before him, one easy, one arduous. She recommended the easy one, the one he wanted to take anyway.

He was resigned to do the *right* thing. The easy thing.

The resolution was freeing, as if he'd been released from a debt.

At the back of his mind, however, he wondered when in his life the easy road had ever been the right one.

The not-quite-as-drunk-as-he-led-them-to-believe ixaquoi at the next table, Mal the Dissenter, restrained an almost uncontrollable smile. His burnt orange eyes crackled with excitement at what he'd overheard. He left the pub, stumbling for show, but after rounding the corner, he ran down the street, full stride, to fetch his things.

6

Mal the Dissenter was in Prontis four days after overhearing the scribe in Kan Ludo. He woke up on the floor early evening to a spinning room and a foul taste in his mouth. When he sat up, four empty jars rolled off his chest. The shrill clank made his head feel as if it was being crushed between a rock and a pillow.

He didn't remember much about the evening before, was sure he hadn't gone to bed alone but had no idea who'd been there or where they went. The small room had a bed of hay strewn about, rotten food caked on the floor, a little on the wall. He wondered if he'd had the kind of night he wished he could recall or one he was glad he forgot. A bottle was on the floor next to him with a little ale swirling around the bottom of it. He suckled it like a desert refugee.

The deep orange of the setting suns pierced the greasy gossamer curtains, burning his retinas as he got up. He retreated to the far wall and shielded his face. A few new tattoos had appeared on his forearms. He couldn't remember how they got there. His markings were a mazelike tapestry of cogs, swirls, and swoops in phosphorescent red ink. He loved the way the glowing patterns stood out against his deep red flesh. He thought it made him look savage and intimidating.

The trouble with glowing tattoos, though, was that they were an impediment for sneaky, trickster folk like Mal. He usually wore thick black clothes that covered them, but at the moment, he had no idea where they were. He scanned the room to no avail. Frustrated, he peeked through the curtains and saw his favorite outfit, the one that made him look like an assassin, strewn on the ground, trampled by passersby. Whoever had been with him had either a grudge or a sense of humor.

He took a deep breath, opened the door, and strolled out onto the street, naked and unapologetic. Some of the onlookers were aghast at the sight, while others found it amusing and pointed at him in support of his grandiosity. He dressed in the middle of the road.

He went back inside and collected his satchel. It had a fair bit of money in it, a shiv, some red paint, and a brush. He pulled out the shiv, concealed it in his belt, and cleaned his face with some linen. He threw the satchel over his shoulder, took a final look around the room, and decided he had no chance of getting his deposit back.

He left the burrow, one of the walled-in slums of Prontis, and headed east toward the temple quarter. The greater sun was taking its bow, the shadows long. A cacophony of clanking metal, crowing vendors, and sizzling meat played in the streets. He slipped through alleyways and behind buildings, keeping to the shadows, occasionally avoiding a second story purge of raw sewage.

He'd caught a break in Kan Ludo when he overheard that conversation at Relovo's. It presented an opportunity he couldn't pass up. He hoped he'd beaten the scribe back. The scribe said he wouldn't be back for a week.

It was twilight when Mal arrived down the street from the temple. He peeked around a corner and saw the scribes leaving for the day. The P'Aanian wasn't among them.

The scriptorium would be inaccessible, but the temple was a different matter. He knew a turncoat guard once who'd assured him the way in was to scale the wall by way of its thick mortar cracks and enter through the roof. The cracks were too far apart for akigi to scale, but they didn't know about the taller, long-armed, ixaquoi when they built the place.

He hid between two bungalows on the back side of the temple. Six guards were posted evenly around the side. He waited until the closest wandered off to converse with the next one down the line and launched a rock toward the front of the building. A crack echoed throughout the area and as the guards turned to look, Mal ran full speed at the wall. He scampered high enough to wedge his fingers into one of the crevices between the bricks and then scuttled up until he could press against the wall. He waited and held his breath. The wall was pale in the moonlight, the crevices black gouges on the face of it. It felt cool against his body.

The guards hadn't noticed.

He climbed to the top and over the edge, knocking mortar down as he did. It crumbled in a tiny rain of cement pellets. He rolled out of sight quickly. The guards asked each other if they'd heard anything and waited to see if they would hear it again, but Mal lay still and soon they went back to their posts.

He jumped up. A warm wind rustled his clothes such that he was afraid it might betray his position. He pulled them taut and kept low, slinking further in. He came to the precipice of the wide overhang above the cloister and sidled around to the edge of the temple for a better look. The scriptorium was inaccessible save two entrances, the guarded one facing the street outside, and the one down there in the cloister. He looked for a way to it. There was the tree, but the jump was too risky, especially in the dark. He looked behind him at the oxidized copper dome that sat over Tim's chamber, shining in the moon glow. Perhaps there was a way through one of the windows around its circumference. He'd have to go through the temple, a risky move.

The roof was fashioned out of logs and smelled like pitch. He had to be careful not to trip, or worse, fall through. He slinked to the dome. He could climb in, but it was a long way down. The only other way was through Hinnoben the Eighth's chamber, which had a candlelit window facing him. He stayed in the shadow of the dome, careful not to step into the moonlight. Hinnoben was probably in there. Mal considered an assassination but as tempting as it was, it would just strengthen the resolve of the Timians against the Dissenters Guild. In a matter of months, Hinnoben the Ninth would spring forth like a vile little weed.

The way to bring down the Timian faith wasn't by the power of the blade, but by the power of an idea.

The idea that Tim was full of shit, to be exact.

Mal peered through one of the small dome windows. The dead villain was down there, bathed in murky light. Even from there, Mal could hear that dreadful heartbeat. He squirmed through the window and was able to reach the chain that connected to the top of Tim's sarcophagus. He descended hand over hand on the cold metal links until dropping directly on top of the wicked bamboozler.

Tim's eyes appeared to look up at him. Inconspicuous stitching secured wood rods around the back of his shoulders and neck—slipshod support to aid the illusion. Mal jumped down to the floor and turned around to confront the fiend.

Where the kingdom of Selidin saw life, he saw death. This thing, this dead character, had changed the course of history. It had become the national crutch to the masses, the big stick

of the powerful. He couldn't fathom what it was, maybe a
deformed ixaquoi or some other rare creature. Most likely, it
was just an elaborate fabrication. It certainly wasn't a Messiah.
Anything but that. Mal lacked the capacity to believe in
ghosts and Gods and mythical beasts. He couldn't understand
how *anyone* could believe such things. He often thought the
supreme irony of his life was that his greatest enemy was
already dead. Dead, yet alive and unkillable.

He observed for a moment, seethed, and kicked the case
with all his strength.

It barely made a sound. Tim didn't budge. The heartbeat
stayed true.

Mal was disappointed. In a rare moment of clarity, he
wondered what he was doing there. The truth of it was that
he was addicted to chaos, intoxicated by the challenge of
picking at the Timian foundation until it collapsed. More than
anything else in his life, he wanted to see what might emerge
from the rubble.

He kicked and shoved the sarcophagus some more, but
got no satisfaction. He thought about painting things on the
case, genitalia perhaps, limp and unremarkable, but there
wasn't time for that. He slipped over to the doors that led to
the cloister. Was that a faint cracking sound behind him? He
looked back only to see that horrible grin goading him.

He pushed the doors open as quietly as he could, but they
creaked loud and long anyway.

The cloister was empty. He ran across it and tried to open
the door to the scriptorium. Locked. Metal armor jangled
down the corridor to his right, getting closer. He ducked
behind a column and waited. The orange light of a torch
painted the concrete around him, intensifying as it drew near.
His jostling shadow would give him up.

A rock was near the tree in the middle of the yard. He
kept low and rolled over to it. He'd been waiting all night for

a moment to use that move. He was satisfied with his execution of it, but the guard standing a few paces away wasn't impressed at all. She tried to let out a bellow, but Mal grabbed the rock, threw it, and hit her between the eyes. She was even less impressed by that and dropped the torch to charge him. Her tentacles were rigid, teeth bared like some kind of demon banshee in the firelight.

He rolled to the side, but she snatched him by the back of his shirt and pulled him to her. She hit him on the side of the head, sending him crashing to the ground and kicked him on the back of his legs to hobble him. After that, she struck him in the face three times, kicked him in the chest, and managed to shoehorn a few fingers under his diaphragm and pull so hard it broke two ribs. He was taller than she was, but she was stronger and, as if showing off for her finale, picked him up by his feet and slung him into the tree trunk. He doubled around it like a wet rag, sputtered some blood, and curled into a fetal position, groaning.

Mal had never been good in a fight.

As she stepped up onto the retaining wall around the tree, he kicked her feet out from under her. She fell back and hit her head on the ground. He crawled on her back, bloody, aching, and winded. He pulled out his shiv, cut her cheek, and then put it to the base of her skull, a deadly anatomical soft spot. Her serpentine tentacles felt creepy against his hand. He threw her long sword and battle hammer off to the side and examined her dagger. He decided to keep it. He tossed the shiv and used the dagger to pierce her soft spot a little to let her know he was serious.

"You're tryin' to kill me." He spoke to her in Selidinian with a genteel Gologan accent. His breath was labored. "You had *three* weapons and you tried to kill me with your bare hands, you savage."

"Just trying to scare you a bit," she said. Her lips were

mashed into the ground.

"Well, it worked! And now I guess I'm scarin' you a bit."

"A bit," she said and tried to spit bits of dirt out of her mouth.

"I'd like to get into that scriptorium over there."

"Why?"

"We ixaquoi need more of the gospel. You wouldn't want to deprive us of that would you?"

She didn't answer.

"Do you have the key?"

She nodded.

"Would you be so kind as to open the door for me?"

The dagger dug deeper. She was probably growing faint.

Mal stumbled off her and reached for the torch on the ground. She got to her knees then slowly to her feet. The murky shadows of the episode danced wildly on the walls. The two of them went over to the door. She fumbled with the keys, hands shaking, until she located the one she needed. They went down the hall and into the moonlit scriptorium.

"I think the gospels are over there." She pointed at the back corner cautiously.

"Hold this," Mal said and handed her the torch.

He observed the cubicles, trying to decide where to begin. It would take a while to open them all, especially if he had to force the locks. He wasn't sure how long he would be able to keep the guard under control.

He heard the jingle of keys outside. The lock on the door to the right of them, the one that led to the street, clicked.

"Lie or I'll end you," he said, slipping behind the slowly opening door.

A second guard poked her head in. "Who's in here?"

"It's just me. I saw a koboo run in here and was trying to chase it out."

"Oh, okay."

As the door closed, a patch of light briefly illuminated a sign hanging in the corner: Department of P'Aanian Affairs.

Mal didn't speak English, but he recognized the word P'Aanian.

"Over there," he said, staying behind her.

When he got to the desk, he made her sit on the floor facing away from him. He pried the lock open with the dagger and grabbed the torch to bring it close. It was obvious which document he wanted. He placed it in his satchel and patted it for luck.

"What's your name?" he said to the guard and put the dagger back on her soft spot.

"Xoja."

"Xoja, we're goin' back to the cloister and I'm goin' to leave you there and take your keys."

"Are you going to kill me?"

"If I was goin' to kill you, why would I go to the trouble of takin' you over there?"

"That's true."

Mal hooked his finger through the loop on Xoja's keys.

"It was nice meetin' you," he said and shoved her into the cloister.

"You too, uhh ... what's your name?"

"Nice try, Xoja."

He closed the door behind her, locked it, and doubled over from the pain. It wouldn't be long before she could scramble through the side entrance and around to the front of the temple for help. He hobbled back into the scriptorium to the corner where the completed copies of the gospels were stacked. He lit them on fire. The orange haze in the windows was enough to cause the guards to burst in.

As they scrambled for water, Mal slipped down the street unnoticed.

The first thing the next morning, Mal took the letter to an associate of the Dissenters Guild, a P'Aanian and trustworthy translator. The place was long and narrow, cramped with shelves full of writings and ancient artifacts from around the kingdom. The curator was an odd, twitchy little fellow, a half-breed the color of a bruise.

"Mal!" he said. "You look terrible."

"I've had worse. Good to see you again, Vasillo," Mal said. "Don't have much time."

"I hear they had some excitement at the temple last night."

"I brought you somethin'."

"What is it?"

"Have a look."

Mal laid the cloth letter out on the counter in front of him.

"It's lovely. Very, very old. Never seen anything like it." He leaned over and sniffed. "Smells like barbecue." He smiled mischievously.

"What's it say?"

"No idea."

"What do you mean?"

"I can't read this."

"You're P'Aanian. It's written in your native tongue, how can you not be able to read it?"

"It's an ancient dialect of P'Aanian. I recognize some of the letters and I can guess at the meaning of a word here or there, but hell if I know what it actually says. You're gonna have a tough time finding *anyone* who can translate this."

Mal dropped his head in exasperation. He looked around at the books on the dusty shelves for a minute and then back at the curator.

"I'm goin' to need that scribe."

7

Nodi stuffed his pack with clothes and other provisions for the journey back to Prontis. He was cutting his trip short, nervous about the letter and wanting to be done with it. He took a last look around his father's old parsonage. It was empty now. Everything he had was either in Prontis, at Aenna's, or in his pack. The temple let him keep the place awhile after his father's death, but someone new would move in soon. Another chapter of his life closed. He wondered what his father would have said about the letter. Maybe he would have been just as curious. Nodol loved a mystery.

The deep blue of morning was just making an appearance. Feathered newts belched along the banks of the tributaries, their hideous croak announcing the day's approach. Aenna was half-asleep when she let Nodi in. She left the front door open behind him so no one would think something unsavory was going on between them. He stood in the rounded entry of her home and looked at a clay tablet with a crude charcoal drawing of the two of them together. She stood nearby and watched him. Her face said she wished he didn't have to leave.

"I'm sorry," he said.

"I'm relieved that you're going to resolve this," she said. "I know it's been weighing on you. It's been weighing on me, too."

"Just think, next time I'm here—"

"We'll be coupled."

He smiled.

She held his hand. "Everything's going to be okay."

"I can't shake this feeling—"

"You're going to miss the caravan. You've got to go." She caressed his face. "This is the last time we'll have to be apart."

They hugged, rubbed their faces together, and said their goodbyes.

He ran down the street, lugging the heavy pack over his shoulder. He'd paid an exorbitant sum to procure a spot on the caravan. Had he waited, the temple caravan would have taken him free, but this was too important.

He sat on the back of a wagon that shook and rattled. Kan Ludo grew smaller and smaller then disappeared behind a swamp bend. He feared he might never see it again.

———————

He arrived at his hovel in Prontis late at night several days later. He wished he'd made it back before the scriptorium closed, but a stampede of yellow goliataurs prevented the caravan from moving forward awhile. He didn't sleep much, but what sleep he got was rife with nightmares. He kept seeing that ixaquoi's face, the one from the tavern, frightened that he might have been a member of the Dissenter's Guild. Nodi wondered how he could have been so stupid, talking about the letter out in the open like that.

It'll be okay, he thought. *God will protect me. He knows my hearts.*

He left early the next morning to go to the scriptorium. It was raining and he trotted down the street, hopping over puddles while trying to hold the hem of his robe off the slushy ground. A few blocks away, he ducked under an overhang for a brief reprieve from the downpour. Freshly scrawled graffiti was on the wall across from him.

tHE tROotH CANt BE StoPPED

He marveled at the poor spelling and punctuation, the vandal clearly didn't know English well. He stepped back out onto the street. An unusually somber crowd was near the entrance of the scriptorium. Wisps of smoke escaped the door and the wall around it was scorched black. Guards stood by, eying everyone with intense scrutiny.

Nodi went down the street and pushed through the onlookers. The floor inside was drenched. Soot covered everything, the smell of fire overpowering. Part of the roof had collapsed and many of the cubicles were crushed under angular masses of burned wood. He looked for his desk. It was intact, but its drawer was open. Four scribes stood next to it staring at him, bewildered.

"Stop right where you are!" The chief scribe said from across the room.

He came over, took a firm hold of Nodi's arm, and led him to the cloister. Water dribbled off the overhangs of the roof, pooled on the ground, splashed under hurried steps. A guard sat on the retaining wall around the tree, soaking wet and staring at the ground. Another guard stood over her.

Hinnoben was under the overhang wearing an unkempt robe dusted with ash, eyes trained on Nodi. An unease lurked beneath his glassy disposition. He stopped and looked at the guard a moment.

"Would you know," he finally said, talking to Nodi, still

looking at the guard, "why someone would go to the trouble of breaking into the temple, just to rifle through your desk?"

Nodi looked down. *Judgment. This is judgment.* He wasn't a liar. He was a good thinker, a thorough thinker, but a *slow* thinker. Lies were too fast-paced and haphazard. "I ... I know what they were looking for," he said and told the chief and Hinnoben everything. He hoped his honesty would be a credit to him, that he might find God's favor again, but Hinnoben's eyes spoke only of horror and embarrassment.

"If you knew about this letter, why didn't you give it to the chief?" Hinnoben said. "You kept it from us. *Hid* it. You've made possible the very thing I brought you here to prevent. Can you imagine the damage this will cause? It doesn't matter that it's full of deceit or that it's written by the great betrayer. Akigi aren't interested in truth, they're interested in what's sensational, to feed their worst selves, to revel in the sin that Tim died to save them from. Too many in this kingdom *want* to believe that Tim was a fraud, that my predecessors and I are power hungry hate mongers. It's easier for akigi to tear down. Salvation is too costly, peace too hard, righteousness too trying. The Guild will reprint this. They'll disseminate it to every corner of the kingdom. This is the kind of thing that could cause riots in the streets. We're close enough to that already. We can't hide what happened here last night—"

"I meant no harm," Nodi said. "I came back to Prontis early to turn it in. I'm sorry. I couldn't have known—"

"You might not have known this would happen, but it happened all the same. It couldn't have happened without you. Who else did you tell about this?"

"My companion, Aenna, back in Kan Ludo, but there was a group of ixaquoi at the next table. They were drunk. Couldn't even walk straight. They left before us, but one of them stayed behind and I think he might have been listening—"

"Didn't you say the thief was an ixaquoi, Xoja?" Hinnoben said.

She nodded.

"They're *laughing* at us." He paced awhile as if trying to solve a complicated riddle. He looked at Xoja. "For the crime of failing to forfeit your life in the service of the Lord, you shall forfeit it anyway."

He nodded to the guard standing over her. Xoja tried to move forward, but the guard stuck a blade into the base of her skull before she could. She fell to the ground with a quiet rustle. The pool of rainwater quaked under her body and turned pink. Some of her tentacles writhed like dying serpents.

Nodi's eyes stung, his knees were weak. He tried not to look at the body, tried to find the words—

Hinnoben waved a disinterested hand at any plea he might offer. "According to apostolic tradition, you may go before the Lord and ask for mercy and forgiveness. You will receive neither from me."

Nodi looked at him. He wouldn't look back. The chief scribe turned away, too.

Is it death, then? Nodi thought. *Death for so small a thing as curiosity?*

Curiosity killed the cat.

He stood there awhile looking down at his reflection in a puddle. A small bug struggled to escape the water, legs pumping back and forth.

I've done nothing wrong. He held his head up and walked across the yard in the rain. He pulled the doors open and went inside. They slammed shut behind him with a startling boom. He walked into the light around the Messiah. The rain pattered on the dome above.

He closed his eyes and listened to the heartbeat.

A guard pulled the door open a crack, peeked in, and

closed it again. Tim just stood there with that sick grin, full of death. In that moment, Nodi didn't give a damn about him.

Hated him, even.

Almost.

Not really.

The heart kept beating. He closed his eyes again.

What are you up to? He prayed. *To what end? Have I been chosen ... or cursed?*

He kept his eyes closed and concentrated on the beating ...

... and then the beating stopped.

He opened one eye, afraid of what he might find. Everything looked normal, but the heartbeat was gone. Silence reigned. He opened the other eye to initiate a full investigation.

"Oh no, no, no, no, no, no." He paced back and forth. "I can't go down in history as the one who canceled the heartbeat. Oh, God. Oh, God." He wrung his hands. "One P'Aanian tries to kill him, another finishes him off. If I thought I was dead before, I'm definitely dead now. They'll torture me first. Publically. I'm just ... so ... so ... *dead*."

He shuffled around the case looking for any clue as to what was going on. He thought it couldn't hurt to bang on it. He knocked a few times, gently at first, then with desperate conviction.

To his abject terror, Tim's jaw came unhinged and fell to the floor of the sarcophagus with a thud.

"This can't be happening. This is one of those nightmares, it's not happening."

In an effort to convince him that it *was* happening, Tim's head rolled back and tore off to join the jawbone on the floor.

Nodi ran like hell.

The Akigi Bible

The Teachings of Hinnoben the Second, 3:8-14

[8] For Tim was sent to Akigol to challenge the akigi. [9] He did not come only to teach right from wrong through strict adherence to the law but to empower us to decide for ourselves. [10] He was a trickster, an enigma that we might never understand, nay, we shall never understand, but we have made our choice through faith in Him and it is to follow God with strength and honor and integrity. [11] He gave his life for us, died at the hands of an akigo with a cruel and sinful heart, but sometimes the act of dying has far more power than the act of killing. In Tim's death, Judas was defeated, aye, the evil one too. [12] The akigi must rise above that which has enslaved them and conqueror sin, yay, even death itself. [13] For just as Tim died, we shall all die, but just as His heart still beats, so shall ours. [14] As long as the heart of the Lord beats, we have hope, for we know that God is with us forever, even beyond death.

Amen.

8

Amidst the chaos of the fire and the confusion over Tim's collapse, the guards were ill-prepared to stop a crazed akigo running amok in the temple. Nodi ran past Tim and tripped over the hem of his own robe. He shuffled back up and fought the heavy doors into the Great Hall. He had no idea how he was going to escape, but running to the left seemed as good as to the right. He got to the door at the end of the hall that led to the front gates and tried to shove it open.

Locked.

He whirled up the spiral staircase that led to Hinnoben's quarters, burst in, and ran out onto the balcony.

No way down.

Guards coalesced at the gates below, alarm horns were blowing. He went back in, ran across Hinnoben's bed, and opened the window that led to the roof. The dome over Tim's chamber was out there, the cloister beyond it. He climbed out. The wind blew through him; the rain fell sideways. He tripped again, got up, and ran to the far edge, looking for a place to go. Guards rushed into the temple below while others climbed out of Hinnoben's window behind him. His only chance was a wild leap to the tree. Hinnoben stood near Xoja's body, looking up, mouth agape.

Nodi ran back to get a head start and then leaped right before one of the guards could tackle him. He grabbed branches on his way down. They tore his robe to ribbons, tree bending under his weight. He hit the ground, landing on his right shoulder. The pain seared, his vision went white, but he got up and limped toward the arched exit that led to the temple gates at the front. Hinnoben just stood there, watching him run by. Nodi knocked him down with a disoriented shove.

A light was at the end of the tunnel. The front gates were open, but they were open for a reason. Guards were standing there, waiting. He stopped and held his hands up in front of his face. He was soaking wet, tentacles dripping. A splotch of blood glistened on the dark fabric over his shoulder. The guards stood wall to wall, shuffling forward. He backed up.

Someone shouted, "That's not him! Look! He's in the cloister!" It was shouted with such conviction, such absolute certainty, that none of them questioned it. They rushed past. When the way was clear, the ixaquoi from the bar in Kan Ludo was left, bruised and wild-eyed.

"Come on," he yelled and plunged into a crowd of akigi running for shelter. He bowled a few of them over, mud sloshing as he scampered by. Nodi watched his bobbing head as it broke for a side street. Hinnoben was yelling at the guards, telling them to go back. Nodi followed the ixaquoi and spotted him rounding another corner. He was sore and having trouble breathing, but his will to survive propelled him. He caught up to the ixaquoi when he stopped to crouch behind a stack of crates. They waited as three guards ran by.

When the path was clear, they took off, crisscrossing

between huts and buildings, carts and trees, careful to stay out of view. Their pursuers ran parallel to them without realizing it. They kept cutting in the wrong directions, getting farther away. The ixaquoi and Nodi ran down an alley and stopped on the backside of a building. A small crawl space was near the ixaquoi's feet. He bent over, looked inside, and reared back from the smell. He slipped in anyway, tapping Nodi on the foot to prompt him to follow.

They scuttled into the shadows and crawled under a moldy tarp draped over some crates. Dust covered everything, black mildew on the walls. It smelled like ammonia and wet fur. The stench was so strong, Nodi's eyes watered and his nostrils burned. Footsteps splashed outside, getting louder. Nodi coiled into the shadows and waited. A guard's head popped in for a moment, but the smell was so overpowering, she withdrew and ran off without noticing them. They waited until the footsteps trailed away and then relaxed.

Nodi wriggled out of the tattered robe. The shirt and pants he wore under it were soaked. His shoulder ached. The energy left his body. He breathed deep and tried to slow his hearts. He thought he might faint. He looked over at the ixaquoi and muttered, "You're the one from the tavern in Kan Ludo."

The ixaquoi stared at him, squatting, panting.

"You stole the letter," Nodi said. He was outraged, filled with righteous indignation, but the pain and exhaustion overtook him.

⸻ ◆◗●◗●◗◆ ⸻

Nodi had a nightmare.

He floated in a void and a blood red tent was out there in the dark, standing over a gray threshing floor. It was made of sinewy, skinless muscle, pulsing in and out as if alive. His father, Nodol, was at the edge of it, motioning him forward.

Nodi was pulled in.

There was no sound, no smell, no taste, no touch. It was as if all but his eyes were dead.

Two golden piles of ludberries were on the threshing floor, nestled in their husks, one pile large, the other small. The ixaquoi appeared next to the small one, dead-eyed and wearing black. He drove a wooden pitchfork into the pile and tossed it up. The chaff blew away and the ludberries fell to the floor. Tim appeared next to the large pile, shining blue with burning eyes. He shimmered in the light, a trick of perception so that Nodi couldn't focus on him. He drove a golden pitchfork into his pile and began threshing, too.

As they threshed, Nodi shrunk and became a husk in Tim's pile. He was lifted up on the pitchfork, floated into the air, and was caught in a wind that blew in circles around the tent. In the middle of it was a gray, featureless figure, an extension of the floor. The chaff blew and all but Nodi was consumed by the gray figure. The wind blew Tim apart, his pieces tumbling into the mouth of the gray. A blade carried on the wind ran the ixaquoi through and he, too, fell forward into the gray.

Nodi knew that the wind was chaos, the gray figure, indifference.

The figure rose up, crushed the ludberries beneath its feet, and made a fine purple ink that congealed into a set of words Nodi didn't recognize. The words formed texts that intermingled and recombined to put forth infinite combinations of speculative answers to life's grandest questions. Every one of them faded into gray. The figure dissolved and nothing was left but the threshing floor, the tent, the wind, and Nodi blowing in it.

He swirled until the tent collapsed and drove him through the floor and back out into the void. All was gone. Absolute nothing.

Before he blinked out of existence ...

...he woke up—

9

Nodi tried to focus. There were voices.

"Where you from?" someone said.

"I was born in a volcanic vent in the southern seas," the ixaquoi said. "My father was a flatfish, my mother an eel. Now shut up. He's awake."

Nodi supposed the fumes in that dank little room made him loopy. A blue akigo with a cleft palette sat across from him. He looked out of the hole in the wall. It was night now. Shadows crossed back and forth in a box of moonlight on the floor. Hurried footsteps made the ground tremble.

"What's happening?" he said.

"What's your name?" the ixaquoi said in Selidinese. He was lying on his stomach looking out at the street.

"Nodi. What's happening?"

"I'm Mal. This is … I forget."

"Ougith," the akigo said with a lisp.

"Ougis says the city's up in arms over what happened at the temple," Mal said.

"Yeth," Ougis said, nodding his head. "I came in here ta

hide. They thay Tim wath dethecrated."

"What happened before I found you at the temple?" Mal said.

"Tim wath dethecrated."

"Your lisp is makin' me insane," Mal said. "Let me talk to my friend, now." He sat up and crossed his legs. "Is it true? A desecration?"

Nodi rubbed his shoulder. One of them had wrapped it with a torn strip of robe. He looked at his hands. "I didn't desecrate him ... He just ... fell apart. On his own. I didn't do anything ... I was alone when it happened and ... I don't know."

"And the heartbeat?" Ougis said.

Nodi dropped his eyes.

Ougis groaned and bumped the back of his head against the wall.

Mal got down on all fours again and looked back outside. "They're on the verge of riots out there. This works in our favor. We gotta get out of town."

"I'm not going anywhere with you."

Mal popped back up on his haunches. His golden eyes shone in the shadows, electric and weary at the same time. Nodi guessed he was at least twenty years his elder. "You've already gone somewhere with me," Mal said. "What are you goin' to do? Turn yourself in? Neither of us wants to get caught. If we can't trust each other on anythin' else, we got that. Let's get out of town. We'll sort out the rest later."

"I'd lithen to'em," Ougis said. "Get outta the city. They'll be riotth thoon."

"That's enough out of you," Mal said and turned back to Nodi. "You've been out all day and this guy's been here for the past three hours, praddlin' on and on. I can't take it anymore. You ready to go? The crowd is thinnin' now."

"Can I come?" Ougis said.

"No," Mal said. "Farewell, Ougis."

He slipped through the hole like a rodent. Nodi looked at Ougis for counsel. Ougis shrugged. Mal's head popped back in and he raised his eyebrows expectantly as if to suggest he was in charge and Nodi, by God, had better follow.

The sky was clear, three moons out above a purple aurora that wobbled back and forth. Crisscrossed shadows streaked the streets. Torch-bearing akigi ran to and fro, some up to no good, others trying to stay out of their way, a few here and there trying to restore order.

"Are the guards still looking for us?" Nodi said.

"They don't know what they're lookin' for at this point. They're fueled by rumor, and that guarantees they don't have the first damn idea what's goin' on. There's a burrow that shares a border with the temple quarter. It's over by the northern cliffs, just before the river. We need to go there. We can't cross the river. They'll catch us if we try."

"If we can't cross the river we can't escape the city."

"Not true. I know a place."

Perhaps it was the dark and the chaos or the less than desirable neighborhood, but Mal walked through the streets with an arrogant swagger, apparently unconcerned about getting caught. Nodi trailed behind him, cautious and wild-eyed.

"Shouldn't we be trying to be a bit ... sneakier?" Nodi said.

"You're new to Prontis, aren't you?"

"Been here four months."

"Well, you don't get out much. On the streets, they call this pagan alley. Leads to the burrow I mentioned. Everyone here is runnin' from somethin'. It's not like we stand out."

They turned a corner and saw four half-naked akigos on display, dangling from horizontal pillories suspended by ropes above the sidewalk. They were dead, rawboned arms locked in a V over their heads. A sign declared them blasphemers.

Nodi looked away. "Oh, merciful God! As I said before, we should be sneakier."

"They've probably been hangin' there a week now. Don't worry, the temple likes to make a big show of it to scare the locals."

"I may not be local, but it's certainly scaring me."

Nodi tripped over a dead soldier's leg and did his best to pretend it was just a log. "This is terrible!"

"The temple's power is slippin' away, my friend. These are historic times. Your scriptures make it sound like Timianity, the organized religion, swept over Selidin peacefully, but it didn't. It came about through much travail. Welcome to the *new* travail. Soon, *they* will be the hunted."

"By 'they' you mean me."

"Not anymore, no?"

Nodi wasn't sure. What he believed about himself and what others believed about him were quickly becoming two different things.

They arrived at the back wall on the outside of the burrow and Mal led him to a small hole behind a thicket. They fought through the jagged limbs, wiggled through the hole, and popped out of the other side behind an old cart. They crawled under it and scurried down a narrow corridor to the main street.

"Do you travel like this exclusively?" Nodi said, trailing behind.

"Not exclusively."

No trees were in the burrow, just a web of stone streets and alleys arranged around an oval midway. The buildings looked like stacked crates in a warehouse—cheap architecture streaked with multi-colored, phosphorescent swirls and streaks that reflected off the wet streets.

"Come on," Mal said and led Nodi down the street to an

unmarked club built off a wall that faced the cliff. The floors of the club were covered in mud and a phosphorescent ceiling created a purple haze that was as depressing as it was disconcerting. The tables were wood barrels arranged in clusters with tree stump chairs. It reeked of alcohol. An akigo played a flute in the corner surrounded by a few customers singing folk songs out of tune. The words were unintelligible, just basic sounds like *ba ra fa ka* that might have been *real* words had any of them been sober.

A huge bartender, an ixaquoi with a scar-pocked face, stood behind the counter. He held a jar of ale in his meat-anvil hands and served up a patron who didn't appear to be capable of consuming anymore. When he spotted Mal, his eyes got wide.

"Mal! I didn't know you were in town," he said in Gologan. He set two cups of ale on the counter. "I thought you were in Morlaj."

"I was. Briefly. Tyin' up loose ends." Mal reached into his satchel and slipped the bartender a stack of coins.

"I knew you were good for it," the bartender said. He laughed. He looked at Nodi. "Who's this?"

"This," Mal took a gulp of ale, "is Nodi. Got involved in Guild business today.

"*Involved?*" Nodi said in perfect Gologan. Mal and the bartender looked at each other in wonder. "More like *ensnared.*"

Mal laughed and said, "Got a table?" to the bartender.

"Yeah," the bartender replied with a head shrug to the right.

Mal took Nodi to a table near the storeroom door. The bartender stood on the other side of a curtain that shielded them from view. Mal plopped his satchel on the table and pulled out the letter. He laid it neatly in front of Nodi. The purple light illuminated the orange fabric; the words on it looked like black slits.

Mal tapped it with his finger. "What's it say?"

He was speaking Selidinese again.

"And if I tell you? What then?"

"I don't know. I—"

The music stopped. The bartender reached through the curtain and waved. Mal scooped up the letter and forced Nodi into the storeroom. They heard a muffled exchange outside and then the bartender came in and locked the door behind him.

"The guards are looking for you. You better go," he said. "Someone will turn you in soon. They're offering a reward."

He pulled up a hidden hatch in the floor to reveal a staircase beneath it. They scuttled down to a clay-walled basement lit by a single candle. The bartender pulled back a tapestry. An entrance to a tunnel was behind it. The tunnel was wet with wriggling tendrils around its circumference like some demon birth canal.

"They've got detailed descriptions of you both and you don't blend in," the bartender said. "Be quick. Be careful."

"Thanks," Mal said.

"Anything for the Guild."

The bartender went back upstairs and Mal took off his shirt exposing his glowing red tattoos. "Let's go."

"What? In there? I'm not going in there."

"You'll be fine."

Nodi didn't see that he had much choice. Where would he go? He shook his head and entered, afraid to touch the tendrils. He shuffled through the winding tunnel by the ghostly red light of Mal's tattoos. The walls felt like the inside of a cheek.

"What is this thing?" Nodi said.

"Tubeworm. Very rare. Very big. Very old. They grow through rock over many centuries. Stay in it long enough, it'll digest you. The slime is slightly acidic. Smugglers've been using this thing for years. Ever since they started chargin' temple tax on the bridges into town."

"Is it safe?"

"More or less."

"That's not reassuring," Nodi slung slime off his hand. "You mentioned a Guild. The Dissenters Guild?"

"Yeah."

"So you stole the letter for the Guild."

"For the Guild, for myself, whatever."

"There was graffiti down the street from the temple. Was that you, too?"

"Yeah."

They crept around and up the giant corkscrew in the red-tinted darkness.

"Your English is terrible. Just so you know."

"I don't even speak English. Just learned a few phrases here and there. Gologan and Selidinese. That's all I know. All I *need* to know."

"Well, whoever taught you those phrases doesn't speak English very well."

"You understood it, didn't you?"

"Yes. But that's no excuse for poor grammar."

"Look, less talk, alright? We can only be in here so long."

• ⬥━❦⬥❦━⬥ •

When they were at the foot of the final incline, Mal stopped to put his shirt back on. Nodi fumbled up the last bit in complete darkness. They exited the tubeworm and were in a chamber of solid rock. Mal pounded on something above them, cursing. Nodi heard a bang and a creak and then milky blue moonlight poured over them. Nodi looked up. It was like peering through a skylight into God's domain—one of the moons, an aurora, and stars innumerable.

He climbed out and fell on his back into the soft embrace of the grass around the entrance. A warm breeze blew, bugs chattered, leaves rustled. It smelled like wet peat. They were in a clearing on top of the northern cliffs and a long line of trees was behind them, just black cut-outs against the night sky. The distant rumble of a mob was somewhere below. Nodi was afraid to see what was happening down there.

Mal fought the thick wooden hatch back into place and plopped down on the other side of it. The hatch had a layer of sod and a stubby bush growing out of it. Nodi wouldn't have known it was there had he not just crawled out from under it. He summoned all his strength, rolled over, mindful of the shoulder, and got up to go to the precipice.

Along the streets of the temple quarter, akigi, mere insects from that distance, shuffled in clumps, mostly toward the temple where a crowd was amassing. Three fires burned in the streets like glowing towers of smoke and spark. Nodi wondered if it was a riot. He couldn't tell for sure. The thought of it was disheartening.

He'd betrayed his kingdom, but more importantly, his faith. He would be hated forevermore. He felt a newfound sympathy for Judas. It was as if he'd just been inaugurated into some dark brotherhood with him.

He wanted to blame Mal for everything, but that felt disingenuous. He knew it was his own fault, he just couldn't understand why God let it happen. This was too big, too important a change in the course of history for God to be cheated out of his own providential plan.

As if such a thing was possible.

He sat down with his feet hanging over the edge of the cliff. He thought about jumping, but not seriously, not without seeing Aenna one last time. Besides, if he'd *really* wanted a cliff dive, he never would have run in the first place.

Mal got up and stood near him.

Nodi closed his eyes and took a deep breath. "This is all part of God's plan," he whispered

"God's plan?" Mal said. "*Humph*. If there's a God, he's indifferent. He doesn't make plans. The rules are set—the game just runs its course. Which is to say he's an *irrelevant* God."

"You're wrong," Nodi said. "God's hand is in all of this. Finding the letter was a sign. What happened to Tim was a sign. The fact that we're still alive is a sign. It *has* to be."

"It's not a sign," Mal said. "It's chance. Religious folk have a sick need to put God in everythin'. Just because you *want* that to be true, doesn't mean it is. Things go your way, 'it's a sign.' Things don't go your way. 'It's God's will.' You mine everythin' for meanin'—make it mean whatever you want."

Nodi shook his head and looked away. Mal stepped into his peripheral vision and took a long look at him. He relaxed and looked out at the mountains to the south.

"I knew a three-eyed akigo back in Kulof." He rubbed the top of his bald head as if it might refresh his memory. "That's one of the port cities that ships out to Gologa, y'know. Anyway, ever heard of such a thing? An extra eye? It was just to the right of his nose. His mother thought it was a gift from God. Told everyone it was. 'It's a sign,' she'd say. Said he was a seer. A prophet. Never mind the fact that he was almost blind. To hear him tell it, his vision was skewed such that everythin' looked like it was swayin', like under the sea." Mal emulated the waves with his hands. "Poor bastard couldn't walk a straight line. Kids used to tease him, run him in circles and such. He was dumb, too. God, he was dumb. It was like the cost of producin' that extra peeper was deducted from his powers of reason. The local apostle got in on it, validated the prophetic claims as apostles do. I'm surprised he didn't charge admission, but he *really* believed it, I guess. One day, they helped him up to the roof of the temple so he could address the village, y'know—impart words of wisdom. They were so sure God would speak through him that day. *So* sure. He fell off the roof. Got impaled on a fence spire. Spent the next hour moanin' in agony. He bled out while the townsfolk tried to find a way to get him down. An old akiga stood at the bottom and dabbed his blood up with an old dress as if the sight of it wasn't proper. He died. Had to cut his body in half to pull him down."

Nodi looked up at Mal, appalled.

"You know what he said before he died?" Mal said. "What his great prophecy was?"

Nodi almost shook his head but was too confused to follow through with it.

"No one remembers. But they *all* said he died for a *reason*. Just couldn't agree on what that reason was. Some said it was a sign. But a sign of what? Some said he was evil. His death was judgment, y'see. Some said his death was a message—non-specific, varied interpretations, of course. Some said he was too beautiful to live amongst us—mostly his mother said that one."

Nodi rolled his eyes and looked away again.

"They all needed it to mean something," Mal said, "but the truth is … there *was* no meanin'."

"And a meaningless life is worth living to you?"

"Does it matter? It is what it is. You make the mistake of assumin' that if somethin' is true it should also be comfortin'. Besides, it's only meanin'less on the grand scale. On a personal scale, it's not meanin'less at all, not as far as I'm concerned. That three-eyed akigo—I can't remember his name—his life meant nothin' to *you*, but it meant somethin' to *him*."

Nodi wondered if Mal spoke exclusively in half-riddles and tall tales. He doubted the truth of the story and refused to be baited into an argument.

He sat in silence awhile and then said, "Now what?"

"At first light, you're goin' to translate the letter for me."

"And then?"

"Depends on what it says. I'll probably go look for the other half. See where it takes—"

"What happens to *me*?"

"Oh. We'll go our separate ways. You can go wherever you want. Stay off the main highways. Maybe head for the border regions. You *might* be okay. I wouldn't go back to Kan Ludo, that's for sure."

"Kan Ludo is the only place I *can* go," Nodi said. "I have to go back for Aenna."

"Who?"

"My companion. The one from the pub."

"Look, as long as you translate the letter for me, I don't care what you do."

"And if I *don't* translate it?"

Mal bristled and pulled his dagger out enough to show Nodi the hilt. It glinted in the moonlight, savage and beautiful. "You don't have a choice."

Nodi was disgusted. He fumbled to his feet, careful not to fall, and walked along the cliff's edge. He could try to run, but was too tired and in too much pain. He looked at the mountains to the south. He had to think if it *was* south. Maybe it was north. Kan Ludo was northwest. He knew which road out of Prontis to take, but he couldn't take that road or he'd be captured. So what then?

He needed Aenna. He had to reunite with her, but was that what God wanted? Was Aenna his idol? His mind was a maelstrom of questions like that. The will of the Lord was as elusive as ever, the still small voice a lying bastard. This path was *set* before him. It *had* to have been.

Mal walked up behind him.

"I'll make a deal with you," Nodi said.

"What deal?"

"Help me get to Kan Ludo and make sure Aenna is safe. Do that, and I'll not only translate *this* part of the letter, I'll go with you to find the rest of it."

"I don't *want* you to go with me?"

"Who'll translate the other part?"

Mal hadn't thought about that. He grinned, plopped down on the ground, and spread out in the grass.

"I need sleep."

The Akigi Bible

Chronicles of Selidin, 10:24-26

24 Hinnoben was revered among the akigi and they declared him the wisest and most righteous of Tim's disciples. 25 Since Queen Kuzli and her line were smitten by the Lord, the akigi proclaimed Hinnoben their king and he vowed to uphold the word of God in the kingdom. 26 He also proclaimed that he would bring the great betrayer, Judas, to justice, but to this day, the betrayer has not been found.

The Gospel According to Hinnoben the First, 15:8-112 (Selected Passages)

15 One night, the Lord Tim appeared to King Hinnoben in a dream saying, "You shall build a temple where my holy and transfigured body was found 16 because that is where I descended from heaven. 17 And you shall make the temple 120 widbits long, 53 widbits at its tallest point and 42 widbits wide …

… 32 There shall be a front gate that is 30 widbits tall 33 and above it, you shall inscribe the words 'WHAT THE HELL IS GOING ON HERE?' 34 so that you shall always remember that the Lord is wondering what you are doing …

… 53 And in between the Great Hall and the cloister, in the center of the temple, you shall place my holy and transfigured body so that the apostles of Selidin might come and see and hear the glory of the Lord …

...[76] And you shall also require a tithe of the akigi that shall be designated for the temple and its apostles because it is the duty of the faithful to provide for their leaders.

[77] Anyone who does not pay the tithe shall have their heads dashed against a rock and their younglings burned unless they can pay double the tithe in restitution. [78] And the tithe shall be paid every week and shall not be late lest a curse of the Lord come upon thee ...

... [104] And you, King Hinnoben shall be made the first Chief High Apostle of the temple and you shall make your brother, Jesus, the new king.

[105] The Lord Tim hath spoken."

[106] When the king awoke from his dream, he wrote these things down and stepped aside as king to give the throne to his brother. [107] He declared that the temple should be built in the place where Tim was found. [108] They built the temple and encased Tim there so that all might see and hear and remember that Tim had saved them from destruction.

[109] To this day, Tim watches over the kingdom and the akigi [110] and His heart beats for them, such is the love of the Lord for His younglings. His forgiveness goes out with every beat. [111] Because of this, faithful akigi who believe in Tim are reconciled unto God [112] and will live in eternal glory with Him when they die.

Amen.

10

Persecutor Shirka stood at the edge of Morlaj. She never wore a helmet, but the crisscrossing scars on her green face made one wonder why. They extended up the right side of her head and cut a single jagged row into her tentacles. She tugged at the collar of her flat black armor and started into town, walking away from the small regiment that had accompanied her.

Morlaj was a sad little beacon of civilization in an otherwise barren, rust faced wasteland. With the exception of the stone brick temple on the outskirts, the city consisted of nothing but clay domes that looked like boils on the face of the desert. Sand dunes in the distance shimmered in the heat, and the cloudless sky offered no relief from the suns.

A courier rode up next to her and handed her an urgent message. She took the parchment, nodded, and sent him back. It was a summons to Prontis from Hinnoben the Eighth. She slipped it under her thigh plate and looked at the temple wall to her left. In red graffiti it said,

GOD IS INDIFURENCE

She'd seen this sort of thing all over Selidin, not always in the same hand, but usually the same pitiful English.

A maroon akigo, an apostle, stood behind her in a sweat-stained robe that flapped in the wind. Shirka walked around to the front of the temple and went inside. The apostle followed her like a frightened youngling.

The wood coffers lay open on the floor near the stage. Empty, of course. The statue of Tim, the one that hung above the altar, was upside down in the middle of the sanctuary, lewd diagrams painted on it. On the plaster wall behind the stage, another message read,

THERE IS NO GOD

A trail of red footprints led away from it, across the sanctuary, and outside. The back door, the one the vandal used to enter, banged open and shut in the wind. The old wood roof creaked. She took a last look around and said, "Clean it up."

"I will. I only left it like this so you could see." The apostle shuffled out of her way.

A chorus of singing came from somewhere in town. She tried to discern where it was coming from. She followed, listening. The apostle trailed behind.

"Did you get a description?" she said.

"I saw him down by the well before I knew what he'd done. He was an ixaquoi, dressed in black. Had a pleasant disposition."

"Did he speak to you?"

"Yes. Said he pitied me. Asked me about my dreams as a youngling."

"Your dreams?" the persecutor said. The singing was

getting louder.

"Yes. Strange isn't it?"

"What were they?"

"What?" the apostle said. He tripped over a pothole but managed to keep his footing.

"The dreams. What did you tell him?"

"Well, I always wanted to be a painter. Or an inventor. Maybe even a gladiator in the Crispilan games—probably too scrawny for that, though. That was before Tim saved me, of course, and led me to stay here to look after his flock."

"What did the vandal say to that?"

"It's not too late."

"It's not," she said. "Maybe you should look into it."

"Into what?"

"Following your *dreams*," she said as if it was a dirty word. "You've failed to look after the Lord's house, after all."

The apostle stopped and stared as she walked away.

A fire smoldered unattended behind a saloon. It had an empty barbecue spit over it and a gutted animal carcass off to the side. She went around to the front doors. The chorus continued unabated. The drunken performers didn't know she was outside. A blue curtain was over the door, a shoddy, illegible sign next to it and the wood canopy over the porch was collapsing. She looked back before going in. The town appeared empty, every business closed.

The revelry stopped when she went inside. Most of the patrons lowered their heads to avoid eye contact. Every lopsided table in the place held portions of meat and nuts. Coins were strewn on the bar. It was clear where the money from the coffers had gone. These akigi weren't the culprits, though. She'd seen enough of this kind of nonsense to know that. She took a jar of ale from an old akigo to her left, poured it out on the floor, and swept the remainder of the money into it.

"Is this all?" she said to the bartender. The bartender froze, trying to muster the courage to lie. He thought the better of it and handed her three small pouches. The persecutor put them in the jar and turned to look at the customers. Thirty, maybe forty akigi were there, all red skinned locals. They sat around the tables doing their best to look befuddled.

"Any information about your benefactor would be appreciated."

No one spoke up.

"You call yourselves people of faith?"

A few nodded, others looked at the walls.

"I know you think this money is about you, about what your religion *takes* from you, about how little it leaves you with, about lost freedoms, and oppression. But who among you can stand before God, unblemished and worthy to challenge His wisdom? Is it not clear in scripture that you are to tithe?"

A few of them rolled their eyes, but most stayed still.

"There is no God, it says down there at the temple. God is indifferent. Who among you would put your money on that?" She held up the jar. "Who would put God's money on the bet that he *doesn't* exist? That he is *indifferent?*"

No one dared answer.

"Speak up!" she screamed and they jumped. She had their attention ... and their guilt.

She pulled the curtain aside to go out, but stopped and said, "Between me and the thief, remember which one of us left you with a fleeting bit of money and which one of us left you with your heads."

She went back toward the temple. As she passed the apostle, she shoved the jar of money into his hands. He tucked it into his chest and followed, looking back as if afraid the townsfolk might come after him later. The music at the saloon didn't start up again.

The persecutor rattled up in front of the regiment and shouted, "Go down to that saloon and recover every last coin. Burn the place down when you're done, but kill no one. The money goes to the temple. I'll see you in Prontis."

Her troops rode away in a cloud of red dust. The persecutor mounted her red spotted runner, an avian creature with black fur and red spots on its hairless, reptilian head. Before she rode away, a timid little akigo tugged on her foot.

"I can't tell you much," he said, "but I might have a name for you."

She looked back at the temple graffiti and thought about it a moment. She dug out a small pouch of coins from her saddle pack and tossed it down to him.

"They're saying the ixaquoi's name is Mal. Mal the Dissenter. I think he was on his way to Prontis."

The persecutor nodded and rode away.

When she arrived in Prontis, she went straight to the temple quarter in answer to the summons. Black smoke was in the air. The akigi were restless but subdued. Everyone looked tired. Something had happened. When she was just down the street from the temple, she noticed a message on the wall,

tHE tRootH CANt BE StoPPED

It was written in the same hand as the ones in Morlaj.

"Mal the Dissenter," she whispered.

She finally had a name. It wasn't much, but it was something. Things were about to change, a break was coming, she could feel it.

City constables and the purple armored, royal guards of King Jesus the Fifteenth surrounded the temple. They struggled to hold back throngs of akigi. When the guards saw the persecutor approach, they pushed the crowd apart to clear a path to the gates. Her runner was skittish because of the tension. Its head tilted sharply from side to side, fur fluttering in nervous waves.

After she passed through, she looked back at the chaotic horde. Very little scared her, but a peasant revolt wasn't something she was eager to experience again. She'd been through one in Sigate and remembered feeling like a big fish being eaten by thousands of smaller ones. She prevailed there, but it could go a different way in Prontis.

Inside, the cloister tree was slumped over, broken branches from top to bottom. Flowers littered the pavement, floating in pools of water from the rain the day before. The hall to the scriptorium was open, the pungent smell of fire, thick. The chief scribe came out of the hall, fanning himself with a banzo leaf. He stopped at the door when he saw her and lowered it. He didn't speak, only pointed.

Shirka went into Tim's chamber. Tim wasn't there. Time slowed.

King Jesus the Fifteenth and Hinnoben the Eighth were on the other side, standing side by side in the entrance to the Great Hall. They wore elaborate robes of silk and gold as if trying to outdo one another. A two-headed beast is what they were—wielding sheer physical power in one hand and unquestioned moral authority in the other. It was hard to tell which head was controlling what. Shirka longed for the day Selidin might become a pure theocracy, but the older she got, the more she feared she might never see it.

She fell prostrate before them, thinking only of Tim.

"Thank you for coming so quickly," Hinnoben said.

"Where is the Lord?" she said, rising. Her English was broken. She felt unworthy to speak it, especially there.

Jesus moved half a step forward and said, "We moved him

into the Great Ha—"

Hinnoben held out his hand.

"There's been a desecration," he said, voice breaking. "The ..."

He couldn't speak it. He stepped aside and nodded to Jesus.

"The heart stopped," the king said. "The body broke. We moved him into the Great Hall."

"Is it the prophecy of Zuzi coming to pass?"

"We don't know."

She walked around the empty altar. Plaster and chips of rust were scattered on the floor. She looked up at the dome. Someone had entered the chamber through it and climbed down the chain.

"We brought a scribe in from P'Aa, an extraordinary translator," Hinnoben said. "He came into possession of a letter. A partial might have been written by Judas the Betrayer. We can't verify that. This scribe, Nodi, translated the letter and then hid it from us. We think he intended to act on what he'd read. He went on leave to Kan Ludo and told his betrothed about it, but, according to Nodi, there was an eavesdropper. An ixaquoi. The ixaquoi came to Prontis and broke into the scriptorium to steal it. Nodi explained what happened when I confronted him about it. I don't think it a coincidence that he just happened to be back in town."

"So you think the ixaquoi and Nodi were in league?"

"I do. There's no denying the facts. The ixaquoi went straight to Nodi's desk. He knew exactly what he was looking for."

"And that's who entered through the ceiling?" the persecutor said. Her eyes directed Hinnoben's gaze up there. "And who desecrated the Lord?"

"The ixaquoi didn't desecrate the Lord," King Jesus said. "Nodi did. But he escaped. With the ixaquoi."

"Why would Nodi bother coming back if they were in league?" Shirka said. "Why didn't he just take the letter to begin with?"

"Who knows? Maybe the ixaquoi double-crossed him," Hinnoben said. "It doesn't matter. We can't think for the thoughtless. What matters is the state of things now."

Shirka scratched her row of missing tentacles, trying to make sense of it. "What did the letter say?"

"It challenges the reliability of scripture, attempts to undermine the identity of Tim, even challenges the authority of the temple," Hinnoben said. "Nodi said it mentioned Hijoon and that the rest of the letter is located there along with Judas' body, a map, and some priceless artifacts. If those two are looking to pursue this, that's where they'll go."

"Do you know of Hijoon?" King Jesus said.

"It's said to have been in northwest P'Aa, near Sigate, but no one knows for sure. It fell into legend hundreds of years ago."

"The letter came from Sigate."

Shirka smiled, not because she was happy, but because they were so sickeningly transparent.

"You're coming to *me* with this because of my connection to Sigate."

"You know it better than anyone. They fear you there. This needs a heavy hand," Hinnoben said. "We've dispatched the iperistis, but I'd like you to go personally. And send a regiment to Kan Ludo. That's where Nodi is from. His betrothed is called Aenna. He might go back for her."

"I'll stop in Kan Ludo on my way," she said.

Shirka understood the task, it wasn't complicated. What she really wanted was to see Tim. She craned her neck to look behind them. "Where is the Lord?"

Hinnoben hesitated then motioned her into the Great Hall. The persecutor went in. They shut the door behind her so she could have some privacy. Tim lay on a table with his head and jaw propped up so that he had some semblance of togetherness. The mystique of the transfiguration was gone, the mystery raped, the heart silent.

She reached out to touch a wisp of the Lord's hair but withdrew her hand as if the very idea of it was sacrilege. She whispered a passage from the book of Zuzi the Prophet, words written hundreds of years before Tim first appeared, "And when the heart stops, all hope stops with it."

Akigi had two hearts. Tim had one. How could Zuzi have known that apart from a revelation of God? Some said it was just a typographical error. Shirka knew better.

The ominous weight of an indefinable judgment bore down on her. God's path was elusive. Did she serve the righteous … or the wicked?

Persecutor Shirka fell on her knees and wept.

11

The suns were just coming up when Nodi awoke. Mal was already awake but tucked behind a bush, looking down a trail that ran along the cliff's edge. When he saw Nodi, he pointed. Three soldiers were coming toward them, but they were a long way off and hadn't seen them yet. Their armor reflected the pink of the morning light, their shadows long streaks of blue. Mal nodded toward the tree line and Nodi, with exaggerated caution, crawled down into the woods.

They descended through the forest, zigzagging between trees, remaining quiet. Rich sunbeams pierced the canopy and made stretched pools of light on the ground. The soldiers bantered somewhere above them, loose and relaxed.

Eventually, Nodi and Mal came out of the woods to a place where boulders peppered the rest of the way down. Mal had his shirt off because it was hot. His tattoos were barely visible in the light of day, just ghost shapes. His sinewy red back flexed and tightened as he jumped from boulder to boulder on his way down. Nodi was smaller, the jumps harsher, each one like a punch to his damaged shoulder. His body throbbed by the time they reached level ground.

They stopped in a dry riverbed. Mal looked to his left and right, then back again. He finally decided on right. They followed it to a heavily wooded area on their left.

Deep in a thicket of undergrowth, a home was built out of a semi-petrified tree that poked out of the ground like a half-cone lying on its side. Crude windows were on the sides, a half circle door on the far end. Mal tapped on the door.

"What are you doing? Whose house is this?" Nodi whispered.

Mal tapped again.

"Sull? You there?" he said. "It's Mal."

The door opened a crack and a reddish brown akiga peeked out. When she saw it was him, she threw the door open.

"Mal!"

"Hey, Sull."

"I wasn't sure you'd make it back. I was on the cliffs yesterday, saw the smoke at the temple. I *knew* it was you. The guards were looking for you last night. They've never come out this far before."

"I'm in more trouble than usual. We won't stay long. I don't want you caught up in this. This is Nodi. He's the scribe from Kan Ludo I told you about."

"Yeah, I recognize him from the description the guards gave me." She looked him up and down.

"Come in and eat before you go."

Nodi pulled Mal aside. "What if a patrol comes back?"

"Make peace with death and live a little." Mal jerked his arm away.

"What does that mean?"

Inside Sull's house, three steps led down to a wood-paneled floor built across the curved interior of the tree. It was a cozy fit for Nodi, but Mal had to lean over to keep from hitting his head. The furniture was nothing more than a few logs and a bed of golden hay in the back corner. An akiga was lying on the hay, staring at the ceiling, drooling. She mumbled incoherently. Sull dabbed some water on her forehead.

"Sull's sister," Mal whispered to Nodi.

"Is she okay?"

"She look okay? She was 'exorcised' by an apostle years ago. They drove three little spikes through the top of her head and that was that."

"What was she like before?"

"Oh, she was horrible. But at least she was alive. You can't call *that* livin'. Sull never forgave herself for allowin' it to happen. She's helped the Guild ever since."

Sull stayed next to her sister until she fell asleep and then dished out three bowls of soup and some ale. The soup looked good, smelled agreeable, but Nodi declined. Over lunch, Mal and Sull reminisced. For most of the time, Nodi stared out the window nervously, rubbing his injured shoulder. The dressing had come undone. He was trying to put it back when he saw some branches outside move.

"What is it?" Mal said.

"I thought I saw someone out there."

Mal went to the window and looked out. "I don't see anythin'."

Nodi relaxed and fumbled with his dressing again.

"Take your shirt off," Sull said. She reassured him it was alright, nothing salacious. She just wanted to see his wound.

He took it off gingerly. It was caked with dried blood that pulled at the cut. He winced as she cleaned it with some wet linen. It looked bad—the bone was probably fractured. Infection was a risk.

"Do you have any family? Anyone who can help you?" she

said. She held back his tentacles so they wouldn't be in the way as she dabbed the blood away from his deep purple bruises.

"I'm betrothed. Her name is Aenna. I'm going to Kan Ludo to get her."

"What about your parents? Your family? Are they there too?"

"Not much in the way of family. My parents are dead."

"I'm sorry. How did they die?"

Nodi was uncomfortable. "My mother died when I was a youngling. Shakes got her. Dad died in Lore a couple of years ago."

"*Lore?* What was he doing there?"

"He was a missionary."

He looked outside again and hoped she wouldn't press it.

"Weren't you raised by missionaries, Mal?" she said.

"No, no. I was raised by gologan spittin' dragons but I can see where you might confuse the two."

"Good luck getting a straight story out of him," Sull said to Nodi. She snickered. Mal had that look in his eyes, the one that said, "This has been fun, but I have to go now."

"Is J around back?"

"Right where you left her."

Nodi put his shirt back on and followed them outside. A dracol, the hefty cousin of the red-spotted runner, was tied to a tree. Nodi had never seen one. It was a two-legged beast, taller than Mal, with turquoise-streaked, deep purple fur, and a long, leathery head at the end of a long neck. Its movements were graceful, not herky-jerky like the runners. Mal rubbed its snout and kissed it on the head.

"This is J," he said. "Short for Judas. I named her after my favorite disciple."

"How long has she been here?" Nodi said. He touched her hindquarters. Her fur twitched around his hand.

"Couple of days. Sull looks after her when I'm in Prontis."

Before Mal mounted J, he kissed Sull. Nodi cringed. First J, now Sull? If Mal ever tried to kiss *him*, things would turn ugly. Mal, reeking of ale, pulled Nodi up.

Sull handed Nodi a batch of herbs in a small pouch. "What's this?" he said.

"Placa root. It's for your shoulder. Chew one piece at a time. It'll help ease the pain. Don't swallow it. Foul stuff."

"Thank you."

"See you 'round, Sull," Mal said.

He kicked J and she trotted, slow at first, and then broke into full stride. Nodi held Mal's waist tight, both of them leaning forward. The trees became streaks of color, the ground a bouncing cascade of motion.

"Were you having some kind of affair with her?" Nodi shouted, straining against the wind.

"I have needs," Mal shouted back. "What's it to you?"

"You're a different species! It's ... it's like bestiality. You might as well be having an affair with J here."

Mal gave it some thought and said, "Am I the beast, or is Sull?"

• ⊷═╍┇•⟫⊚⟪•┇╍═⊶ •

They rode for hours, heading northwest along a winding creek nestled in green hill country. A cloud of dust followed them, stirred by J's powerful feet. Nodi's tentacles whipped in the wind.

They came to a bend in the creek and then a fork where another tributary merged with theirs. After going past it, Nodi sensed someone to his right. He turned to see. An akigo in wheat colored armor on a spotted runner was trying to keep pace with them. His face was ghostly white that shone brightly in the evening suns—a frightening, skull-like visage. The runner fell behind, but others crested the hill ahead and cut them off.

"Mal!" Nodi yelled.

"I know! I know!" Mal broke left and charged.

Nodi squeezed him around the waist—if he was going to fly off J, Mal was going with him. The soldier in front of them tried to move, but it was too late. J jumped the smaller beast and rider and knocked them over. The rest of the soldiers turned and followed.

Mal veered right and over an embankment that led to a dry lakebed. A herd of yellow goliataurs knuckle-walked in the middle of it, twenty-five or thirty of them—simian creatures, two stories tall, with long tufts of hair at the wrists and ankles and bone stubs along their spines. Their hair gleamed in the evening suns like fine strands of copper.

J sensed danger and slowed, but stayed true. The soldiers were catching up. Mal aimed for the herd. The runners were next to them now, nipping at J, J nipping back. The disruption didn't go unnoticed by the goliataurs. They stirred, sidling sideways at first then standing up on their legs, arms raised, only to slam them down with thunderous force. It shook Nodi, blasts of wind swirled around him. He was lightheaded with fear. The very vengeance of God was in those creatures. Their guttural cries were close and loud, he could smell their putrid breath, feel it hot against his back.

The young goliataurs were not much bigger than J. They scattered outward, frightened, slamming into three of the soldiers. J wove in between thrashing limbs, giant toes, and fingers digging into the ground around them.

Nodi looked to his left. A yellow arm swept up four soldiers. They flew into the air, flipping end over end, and fell into a cloud of debris. Nodi tightened his grip on Mal and noticed another guard to his right, sword drawn. The soldier sliced at the air as J broke left. The soldier fell off his runner. Two others slowed and tried to snatch him up when one of the goliataurs fell over on top of them, rolled onto its back and wiggled as if it had an itch. Its stubs ground them into the stony ground like pestle and mortar. Another one barrel rolled toward Nodi and Mal, close enough that they could have run their fingers through its hair.

The goliataur herd ran east, Mal went northwest again, out of the midst of them. One last soldier gave chase. They rode to a place at the edge of the lakebed where the rock had eroded into a forest of natural monoliths. J moved between them, in and out, over and under. Nodi and Mal whipped around on top of her, out of control, holding on for their lives. J was spooked and unresponsive. The soldier was getting closer. Nodi saw a freestanding rock wall in front of them. J got around it with a narrow miss, but two tall monoliths were ahead, bending toward each other like the middle of an hourglass. There was no way to avoid it. Mal rolled off J, Nodi in tow, and they slid along the ground and smashed into the stone on the right. Mal cushioned Nodi's impact, taking the brunt of the force to his back. J ducked, passed under the wide bottom of the rocks, and ran out the other side.

Nodi heard a crunch, but couldn't see anything through the dust. There was growling and snapping. Mal struggled up and hobbled to the other side of the rocks to see if J was okay. Nodi's shoulder ached. He got to his knees and then his feet. He heard one final squawk and then silence. He went to the other side of the rocks to see what happened. J stood over the dying, red spotted runner, victorious and chewing.

"Where's the rider?" Nodi said. His eyes were wild, blue face pale from the chalky ground.

Mal nodded at the rocks. His face was bleeding. Nodi followed his eyes. The soldier was dangling there, wedged between the stones, leather armor ripped and folded, a few bones piercing through. His face and tentacles were painted white, the paint flaked unevenly to reveal green flesh beneath.

And the blood. All that blood. His legs wiggled. Nodi wasn't sure if it was postmortem twitching or if he was still alive.

"Wow," Nodi said. "That's just ... weird. Is he dead?"

"Don't know," Mal said. The suns were going down. They could still feel the ground quake from the goliataur herd. "He's an Ipiristis."

"A what?"

"Ipiristis. The king's elite. Don't see them every day. They're all male. They paint their faces white like that. Don't have tongues either, can't speak."

"Is he dead?"

In answer to the query, the Ipiristis groaned. Nodi went over to him as if to help. The soldier looked down, only one eye visible. Nodi tugged at his legs, but he wouldn't budge. The force of it hurt him.

"Help me get him down," Nodi said.

"He's not comin' down," Mal said. "Why would we *want* to get him down?"

"We can't leave him like this."

"Look at him. He's not comin' down alive. Those rocks are the only thing holdin' him together."

Nodi knew he was right.

"We either leave him like this," Mal said, "or put him out of his misery." He drew his dagger and held it out. "You decide."

Nodi looked at the dagger then back up at the soldier. "Tim forbade murder."

"Then there's your answer. Surrender this poor akigo's final, agonizin' hours to the mercy of the Lord. Let that be on Tim's conscience, not yours." Mal patted him on the back. "Let's go."

The shadows were getting long. The soldier groaned. It

was quiet except for J's sporadic shuffles in the sand ... and the groaning.

"Wait," Nodi said. The soldier's eyes spoke only of agony. Death would be a gift. "We can't leave him like this."

Mal held the hilt of his dagger out to Nodi. Nodi reached out to take it, but before he could, Mal pulled it back. Nodi was both relieved and ashamed. Mal went to the soldier and raised the knife toward his upper heart. Nodi turned away.

He heard gurgling, a pouring in the sand, and then silence.

The Akigi Bible

The Gospel According to Dumbass, 5:1-20

5 The next day, the akigi gathered together and the Lord taught them in the fields of Tumtuk saying:

2 "Blessed are the poor in spirit, for they are gullible.

3 "Blessed are they who mourn, for they understand their lot in life.

4 "Blessed are the meek, for society is built upon their backs.

5 "Blessed are those who hunger and thirst for righteousness, for they are easy to delude.

6 "Do not judge or you will be judged.

7 "Remember that there are no Gods, but me. Do not bicker about it endlessly. That is just the way it is.

8 "And do not take my name in vain.

9 "And honor your father and mother because you may need money from them some time.

10 "Do not murder unless you absolutely have to.

11 "Or steal. No one likes a thief.

12 "And do not bear false witness unless you are in a tight

spot.

[13] "And ask not what the Lord can do for you, but what you can do for the Lord."

[14] And he also said many other things, but it was not written down because he spoke too fast.

[15] When the Lord had finished saying these things, most of the crowd was amazed at his teaching, [16] but some grumbled that he did not seem to live by his own words. Others did not know what he was talking about. [17] He called fire down on those who questioned him and then spoke to those who were still alive saying, [18] "You shall do as I say and not as I do unless what I do is righteous. It is acceptable to do what I do when I do things that are righteous. The things I do that are not righteous are simply tests of your righteousness."

[19] Hinnoben spoke saying, "Lord, how can we tell when you are being righteous?"

[20] The Lord answered and said, "I just told you how."

12

For the next three days, they rode toward Kan Ludo. They didn't speak much, just simple, utilitarian phrases, things to get them by. On the evening of the third day, they cleared a tree line and rode into an expansive field of gentle hills carpeted with tall stalks of bluewheat. The sky was pink, aurora sparkling aqua-green above it.

The fields were called Tumtuk, where Tim delivered his most famous sermon. Every akigi knew it when they saw it. The crescent-shaped oasis had mystical significance, a well-known place of worship for fertility cults of old, before being re-appropriated by the Timians.

"Tumtuk," Nodi said. "It's not too much farther to Kan Ludo. Maybe a day?"

"More or less."

Not far off, a rock island sat in the sea of wheat. It stood at a forty-five-degree angle, a natural shelter below it.

"There," Mal said. "That looks good."

"There'll be pilgrims around, no?"

"The sermon monument is on the other end of the

crescent. They won't be out this far. We won't light a fire, to be safe."

The wheat was waist high on Mal, neck deep on Nodi. The stalks snapped and rustled beneath their feet.

"So how'd you meet Auhoinka?" Mal said

"Aenna."

"Oh yeah, right."

"Known her most of my life."

They arrived at the rock and looked beneath it. Nothing lived there—cool, soft ground for a bed. Mal took the saddle off J, hugged her, and let her wander the field to graze. She lay on her side instead, plopping her big head on the ground, black eyes staring at nothing in particular. Mal and Nodi crawled under the rock and sat down.

"Been here before?" Mal said.

"Passed through."

Mal considered him awhile, maybe assessing his mood. "Missionaries in Gologa used to read scripture," he said. "I used to go to a Timian school, before the war, before everythin' went to hell. I remember the sermon of Tumtuk and ... it makes me wonder ... Tim said don't lie unless you're in a tight spot. You were in a spot as tight as they come—"

"So why didn't I lie?"

"Yeah. You could've told him you didn't know nothin' about the letter, never seen it, ixaquoi must've heard about it from whoever turned it in. None of this had to happen for you, had you lied."

"You would have dragged me into this no matter what. Isn't that why you were there when I ran out of the temple? To take me with you? You needed someone to translate it for you."

"Well yeah, but the timin' was lucky. I didn't know they were chasin' you around like that. I was just goin' to wait 'til I saw you, but they started blowin' those horns. I knew something was wrong. But maybe this could have gone a different way for you."

Nodi thought about it. His shoulder throbbed so he tried a piece of the placa root Sull gave him. It was disgusting and he choked on it. Mal watched with restrained delight as Nodi fumbled the chunk from the left side of his mouth to the right and back again.

"Feel better?" he said.

"A little, yes." The words were garbled. He couldn't take the taste anymore so he spit it out and wiped the excess off his chin.

Mal chuckled.

"Yeah, yeah. Laugh it up," Nodi said. "In answer to your question, I *could* have lied. I don't know that it would have changed anything, might have made things worse, but I *could* have lied. But at the same time, I couldn't have. Like a loving father can walk out on his youngling, but can't. Like a true friend can betray you, but can't. You might find that hard to understand."

"Not that hard," Mal said. He lay down on his side, propped up on his elbow, and doodled in the dirt with his finger. "That sermon is nonsense to me. All scripture is."

"You don't understand it. Haven't given it a chance. And some meaning is lost in Gologan and Selidinese translations. Tim spoke in riddles. He was a humorist, in some sense." Nodi smiled, relishing the ingenuity of it. "He brought the truth to light by pushing it in unorthodox ways—to make us think. God writes the truth on our hearts. We know it innately, but suppress it because we're sinners. Tim used this kind of discourse to expose it, bring it to the forefront of our minds, make us aware of it, spur us to change. He was a genius, really. He leads us to the truth by leaving us mile markers along the journey. To make us think for ourselves."

Mal shook his head. "I don't accept that."

"What?"

"That little speech sounds rehearsed. I think you believe Tim was a fraud. You just can't allow yourself the freedom to speak it. You're scared of the implications. You've lived with it so long, you can't let go."

"Who do *you* think Tim was?"

Mal rolled onto his back. His tattoos glowed in the shadows. "Don't know. Deformed ixaquoi maybe. What do you think I'm doin' out here with you? Why do you think I stole the letter? I want to know the truth of it. You're a curious fellow—I see it in your eyes. We have that in common."

Nodi stared out at the field, taken in by the sway of the wheat, the bluster of the wind. Birds circled in the distance, shadows on the evening sky. "I've experienced God in ways you can't imagine."

"*Humph.* I experience God, too. When I'm drunk."

"What if you *truly* experienced him?"

"Well, that's up to *him*, no? There's nothing *you* can do to convince me by word or deed. I've seen it all before. You've got nothin' I haven't heard, got nothin' better to offer. I'm beyond your reach."

Nodi twisted a blade of grass between his fingers. He only half heard Mal. "I don't understand why He collapsed."

"What if there *is* a God," Mal said, "but Tim never had anythin' to do with him to begin with?"

"The thought has occurred to me. On occasion. But I can't explain away my own experience."

Mal closed his eyes on the brink of sleep. "Your experience?" he said. "*Bah.* Just a gross appropriation of misunderstandin' is all that is."

After Mal went to sleep, Nodi climbed to the top of the rock to pray and meditate. The wheat stalks glowed lavender, clusters of them pinching and contracting in the wind. They danced into the distance like a luminescent ballet. Black trees on either side swayed solemnly. The air was sweet, but not sickly sweet, just fleeting breaths. The majesty of it didn't fit Nodi's mood. It should have been raining fire from heaven, everything dead, sinking into pits of tar.

Heaven was so far away.

He wouldn't have admitted it to Mal, but scripture was just gibberish in his memory now, his experiences—his sanity—questionable. He desperately needed a sign, but pleading for one was hubris, a game for the weak-minded. As if God's integrity could be questioned. As if his promises were unreliable. Still, he desperately needed a sign.

He felt compelled to go to the sermon monument at the far end of the fields. Compelled by God, Tim, or his own hearts, he couldn't say. He jumped off the rock, careful not to wake Mal, and set off for it. The glowing wheat buds were just below eye level, so bright he had to look above the horizon else he was almost blind. The lavender blooms split around him like parting waters. He came to the northern edge of the fields where the wheat thinned and topped a hill. The fire lit monument encampment was at the bottom of it. Most of the pilgrims were asleep except for a few who prayed. Guards prowled the perimeter. On the other side, the main road lies north to south, a black trough in the purple glow that could take him to Aenna in half a day's ride. If he wasn't being hunted, that is.

He crept through the wheat to the edge of the encampment and observed the monument—a large, stone statue of Tim in a robe, features faintly akigi, arms outstretched in victory. Darkness shrouded most of it, leaving only the most prominent features visible in shades of moonlight and flickering fire. The hard cuts of light made it look sinister. Pilgrims rocked back and forth on their knees in silent worship. Nodi wished he could join them, to go back to the way things used to be, but something was broken inside him now, something missing.

Scripture said Tim first appeared in a field like Tumtuk. Nodi imagined the sky, swirling and chaotic, giving birth to the fire that brought the Messiah to Akigol. He imagined Tim standing in that very spot under the noon suns, declaring the word of God to the akigi. The crowds nodded and cheered from time to time while naysayers prowled the back like hungry beasts.

He imagined the naysayers waving him over, Judas among them, kindred spirits of some blasphemous cult. He remembered the nightmare of the gray threshing floor. Maybe that floor was reality itself—even, indifferent, cold.

He sat there in the field, bitter, desperate, wondering if he should turn himself in, but what would that accomplish? He needed Aenna. There was always Aenna. She was his constant. She kept him going even when God was unwilling.

He decided to return to the rock. The wheat at the edge of the encampment split behind him and flipped together. He worried that the movement might have given him up. He waited a moment, but all remained quiet and he went back.

The following morning, Nodi awoke to discover he was lying on his back fifty paces from where he went to sleep. All he could see was blue sky spotted with daystars, a faint orange aurora, and swaying grass on the periphery. Something sharp poked his neck. He batted it away, but it was persistent. He twisted his head to see what it was and discovered the end of a long, elegant sword.

He jumped up to find he was surrounded by five battered,

white-faced akigos. The surviving iperistis had caught up to them.

Mal was on his knees, hands tied behind his back. The look on his face said, "Well, we tried."

13

Aenna crossed a suspension bridge on her way to the market. The sky threatened rain but had yet to fulfill its promise. The bridge swayed in the blustering wind and the grass on the river banks below fluttered.

A guard stood on the other side of the bridge waiting for her to clear the way. Aenna quickened her pace. The guard led a group of ixaquoi across the bridge, bound to one another. She kept looking back at Aenna with suspicion.

Kan Ludo was on edge. Selidinian soldiers amassed there, streets aflutter with rumors of chaos in Prontis. All along the winding roads, onlookers stood in doorways and at windows, watching the captives march around the bend and out of view. A street prophet stood on a roof and proclaimed the return of Tim was imminent.

Aenna was on her way to the butcher shop. Out front of the shop, a gray awning rustled over stacks of caged creatures that croaked, hissed, and scurried. The stacks were arranged around a pen that held two longhaired oraks chewing cud—amphibian eyes expressionless, white fur dancing in the wind. Aenna caressed the soft, beardlike tentacles of one of them until it sneezed and galloped to the other side.

A clay counter was inside the shop, drenched in blood, fur, and scales. A hatchet and a prying hook were on it, lying next to a wood chopping block. A fire burned on the right. Several skinless things hung from wires at the back.

"The usual?" the butcher said. He stood by the window on the left wearing a stained burlap apron.

"Yes. Thank you." She looked back at the street.

A raised pool of water was on the other side of the window. The butcher held out a wicker basket on the end of a pole, scooped up a wriggling fish, and drew it in. He slapped it down and pried the green bone plate off its head like a fingernail. It had spikes along the length of its spine that puffed out reflexively. Its fins fanned in and out.

"Where's that akigo you run with? Haven't seen him around."

"He's a scribe in Prontis now."

"Prontis? Think he's okay? There's all these rumors."

"I don't know." She looked outside. More ixaquoi captives passed by. "I'm concerned. I think the rumors are true."

"Appears so. Wonder how long it'll be before they come for *me*."

"Why would they come for you?"

"I know you're a Timian, I mean no disrespect," the butcher said and waved his hatchet toward the street, "but this is about religious freedom. Timians won't stand for it, *can't* stand for it. They'll round up anyone who doesn't believe as they do. I've grown weary of it."

"Do you not believe at all?"

The butcher pulled up his left sleeve. Ancient tribal markings covered his arm, signs of the old Gods.

"You believe in the pantheon?"

"It's the true rel—"

A guard appeared at the door.

"Here we go," the butcher said. He put the hatchet down and took off his apron.

The guard looked at Aenna. "Come with me."

The butcher looked at her, puzzled. She walked toward the guard who grabbed her by the arm and jerked her away.

"What about the fish?" the butcher called after them.

<hr />

The military outpost at the edge of town was a series of clay buildings surrounded by a high wooden fence covered in poison raptor vines.

Soldiers shoved the ixaquoi into pits just inside the front gate. Hinged, wire mesh panels secured them inside. They took Aenna to the back of the compound to a blacksmith's shed that glowed orange beneath its canopy. As she drew close, the churning bellows and rushing steam drowned out the protests of the captives behind her.

It started to rain. The smell was crisp, mingled with the stark aroma of burning coal. The heat came in a wave as they pulled her inside.

Persecutor Shirka sat on a bench. Aenna knew who she was, everyone who served in Sigate did.

Shirka looked at the scar on Aenna's head. "Where did you serve?"

"Sigate."

"By your age, I'd guess that was, what, four, five years ago?"

"Four."

"You look familiar. Were you caught up in that business with Stilla?"

"Yes." Aenna looked down at her feet.

The persecutor displayed her own crisscrossing scars. "Stilla did this to me. Hit me across the face with a sewer grate. It cut me. I'm lucky I can still see out of this eye." She pointed at it. "I'd been stabbed, hit with a rock, disoriented. She took advantage of it but made the mistake of gloating to her co-conspirators. Gloated long enough for me to run her through with a fence post lying on the ground next to me. Do you think that was the providence of God?"

Aenna thought about it and gave her a single nod.

"I do, too." Shirka studied her face. "Did you get that scar there?"

Aenna nodded again. "My detail was assigned to public executions. I never saw battle until the day of the rebellion."

"Not a pleasant duty."

"No. Not at all. Stilla created an underground network to help the Dissenters Guild smuggle fugitives out of town. She became the primary focus toward the end of my duty."

"Do you know …," Shirka stood up and walked over to one of the glowing fire pits. She stared into it. "…that we never found any of those she helped escape? I often wonder where they went."

Aenna shook her head.

"And your scar?"

"When Stilla was arrested. I was behind her in the procession, just to her left. The execution platform was ahead, prefect standing on it. The crowd was thick, pushing and screaming. I prayed for deliverance. I knew what was about to happen. An akigo had a rock hidden under the cuff of his robe. I saw him lift it, throw it, felt a thud … I fell … there were arms and legs … under me, over me … Rocks and debris flying … I hit the ground again and could see Stilla's legs as she ran away. I felt another blow and that's all I remember."

"God heard your cry," the persecutor said. "Here you are. Alive."

"He rescued both of us."

"Yes." The persecutor looked as if she was trying to call something to memory. "I think maybe I saw you in the infirmary."

Aenna watched her poke the fire for a moment. "If you don't mind my asking, what's this about?"

Shirka turned back to her. "Are you familiar with the prophecy of Zuzi?"

"When the heart stops, all hope stops with it."

"Yes. Have you heard the rumor? The rumor that the heart stopped?"

"I hadn't heard that." Aenna felt weak and started to sit down on the bench closest to her—

"Don't sit," Shirka said. Aenna stopped and stood straight. Shirka stared at her for an uncomfortably long time. "I wept when I saw that it was true. I always thought the prophecy of Zuzi meant the end of all things. But then I remembered an old passage from the Apocalypse of Tim. Are you familiar with the Apocalypse?"

"No."

"It's not canon so I'm not surprised. I read it while I was on duty in Prontis. There's disagreement about its authenticity. Hinnoben the Eighth believes it's reliable, his predecessors did too, but they haven't convinced the scripture councils. Can you imagine? A group of old, stuffy akigos sitting around a table, pouring through sacred writings, deciding what's gospel for the rest of us? A day will come when akigi won't remember that. They'll think the holy canon just dropped out of heaven. Or maybe that day *won't* come, not now. I don't know." She drummed her fingers on the lip of the fire pit. "There's a passage in the apocalypse where Tim says, 'For in the days to come, the akigi shall face two enemies, one from without, one from within. The first will be a pagan culture from across the sea to the west and the second shall be from within your number. In both cases, I shall lead you to victory against them and establish my rule in your highest seats of power forevermore."

"What's it mean?"

"Can't know for sure. Sigate is in the west, a harbor town with a great unknown beyond the sea where akigi dare not venture." Shirka held her hand over the fire, testing its heat. "Maybe the third coming of the Lord is imminent. Maybe the prophecy is at hand. What do you think?"

"The return of Tim is *always* closer than ever before."

Shirka nodded. "I've always felt sorrow for the great betrayer. He had a role to play, ordained by God, yet received no mercy for it. Such is the plight of the wrongdoer. They do their evil only to see it thwarted by God, transformed for good, yet *still* they reap the punishment for their deeds." She faced Aenna. "We're looking for an akigo and an ixaquoi involved in what happened at the temple. You're betrothed to the akigo."

"*Nodi?*"

"When he was here on leave, did he tell you about his work in Prontis?"

"Some."

"Did he mention a letter? One written on a sleeve?"

She looked away, afraid to answer.

"Did he tell you what it said?"

"Yes." Aenna looked her in the eyes. "And I told him it was *nonsense.* He agreed."

"Agreed? If he agreed, why did he keep it to begin with?"

"He was upset, afraid of what it said. He just needed some perspective ... He turned it in ... didn't he?"

"No one is afraid of a falsehood, they fear *truth,*" Shirka said. "If he was afraid, it's because he suspected there was truth to be found in it. That makes him *faithless* and *weak.* But in answer to your question, no. He didn't turn it in. It was stolen before he had a chance."

The persecutor motioned to one of the guards. The guard brought a badly beaten ixaquoi over, hands bound behind his back. Aenna remembered him from the tavern.

"This is a friend of an ixaquoi named Mal the Dissenter," Shirka said, "a member of the 'Dissenters Guild.' I believe Mal is the one who broke into the temple. He was certainly one of the ones in the pub the night Nodi told you about the letter."

"You can't blame Nodi for the theft."

"Sure I can, in point of fact, but I know what you mean. Maybe he didn't *mean* for this to happen."

"Of course he didn't mean for it to happen."

"Except that when our leader, Hinnoben the Eighth, chosen by God, sent him into Tim's chamber to ask for forgiveness, Nodi desecrated the body of the Lord and fled. And do you know who helped him escape?"

Aenna could guess. "But *why?*"

"I don't know. You tell me."

"It's a misunderstanding!"

"You seem so sure." She walked behind the ixaquoi. She put him on his knees and held up one of the blacksmith's hammers. She twirled it in her hand. "Two enemies. One from without …," she waited until Aenna met her eyes, "and one from within." She cracked the ixaquoi over the head and he collapsed. He scratched his fingers in the dirt and muttered, "wait … wait." Shirka hit him again.

His body went limp, blood soaking into the dirt floor around his head. Aenna felt as if her soul had been raped.

"Let me ask you this," Shirka said. She tossed the hammer on the bench and placed a hand on Aenna's shoulder. "What would it take for you to stop believing in the Lord? Is there anything, just one thing, which would make you say 'I no longer believe'?"

Aenna shook her head.

"And can you say, *with confidence*, that Nodi would answer the same?" The persecutor sidled up behind her, put her mouth close to her ear, breathing in it.

Aenna shook her head again. "No."

14

The iperistis led Mal and Nodi, hands bound, through the pale blue fields. They'd captured J and one of them held her by a rope around her neck. She fought him all along the way. The leader was out front, another behind him, riffling through Mal's satchel to verify the letter was there. Two others limped behind, swords drawn.

The one digging through the satchel pulled the letter out and bumped the leader with the back of his hand. The leader looked, nodded, and the other one put it back and slung the bag over his shoulder. Soft orange sunlight streaked the sky— everything kissed with golden light. The soldiers looked like the walking dead with their white faces and uneven, pained footsteps. Sometimes they spoke in a sign language of their own making, peppered with grunts and moans.

"Why do they cut their tongues out?" Nodi asked Mal, voice trembling.

"So they can refuse no mission, tell no lies, and betray no confidence. It's their motto."

An iperistis knocked Nodi on the back with the hilt of his

sword to shut him up.

J bucked and stretched her neck to the right to pull free. One of the iperistis grabbed her hindquarters but she turned on him, bit his tentacles, and pulled him over. He howled and hit her on the snout to pull free.

Mal smiled.

They trudged through the fields until they could see the head of the statue just over the hill. It was humid, Nodi's shirt stuck to his chest, shoulder aching.

Birds of prey circled overhead.

When they crested the hill, J broke free, swerved left then right, rope swinging wildly from her neck. She feinted to avoid being grabbed, emitting a low, gurgling growl to warn them. She ran back the way they came, only one iperistis left to evade. He was steely-eyed, sword drawn, crouching low to the ground. As she passed him, he sliced her neck in one swift, precise motion. She stumbled to the ground.

Mal shook his head in disbelief. "No ... don't."

Nodi couldn't see her above the wheat but could hear her struggling to breathe, making an awful bleating noise. The iperistis ran toward her and the bleating stopped.

Mal fell to his knees, eyes unfocused, breath quick.

The commotion drew guards that were down at the statue encampment. Nodi heard their clanking footfalls as they charged up the hill. He saw no one over the brush.

"It's the iperistis," someone yelled. "Did you catch them?"

Nodi turned to his right. A blue akigo was there, face framed by the wheat stalks, close enough to touch. The akigo held out a dagger. Nodi fell on his back, afraid he was going to get cut, but the akigo rolled him over and severed his bindings. He handed Nodi a shiv made of sharpened stone and nodded. The guards were coming back now. Nodi lay on the ground holding the shiv. He'd never wielded a weapon in his life. He threw it down and got up. As he did, a host of akigi revealed themselves, standing in the wheat, holding knives, swords, hammers, and rocks.

They charged the iperistis.

Nodi stumbled and dodged left as one of them ran by. Someone shoved him out of the way when a guard tried to run him through. He spun and wobbled, confused, directionless, and then ran as if to escape some imminent explosion. He broke the line of wheat, tripped, and slid down the rocky hill. When he stopped sliding, he looked up and saw the wheat jittering in the turmoil. The battle spilled out onto the hillside, the combatants rolling end over end on top of one another. Nodi couldn't tell who was winning. He got up and scrambled aimlessly, unsure what to do. One iperistis came out on his knees, trying to hold his guts in, another spun and fell, the side of his head ruined. Nodi turned to run to the encampment, but they were fighting there too.

Mal backed out of the brush, engaged blade to blade with the lead iperistis. The iperistis kicked him, backhanded him to the ground, and stomped his hand to make him let go of the blade. Mal tried to spring up and charge, but was met with another blow to the face. He rolled to his back. The iperistis thundered at him, sword upraised in a stabbing position. Mal rolled to his right, but the iperistis wasn't fooled. Just before he stuck Mal, the akigo who'd cut Nodi loose ran up and lopped the iperistis' head off. Pieces of his tentacles followed the head down like weeds cut by a scythe. A fountain of crimson cascaded around the collapsing body.

Everything went quiet again.

It was as if some horrifying storm had blown through and left a path of destruction in its wake. Blood and viscera were all along the hillside. Pilgrims were on their knees in the encampment below, their hands on their heads. Mal was catching his breath, bent over, bleeding from cuts on his face. An iperistis came out of the wheat, the one who killed J, gushing from the throat. Mal took a rock and threw it at him, knocked him over, and killed him with repeated blows to the head. When it was done, he sat on the ground next to the body, wiped his eyes on his sleeve, and looked at Nodi as if to assert his karmic right to do such a thing.

Nodi was woozy. He sat down and watched an iridescent bug burrow into the dirt. Anything to keep his attention off what just happened.

The leader of the band of misfits surveyed the area and cleaned the blood off his sword. He wore nothing but brown pants and a belt—his tentacles pulled back in a disorderly ponytail. He looked at his companions down around the statue and yelled, "We knew there'd be resistance. Let's get on with it!"

Mal came up behind Nodi and helped him to his feet. They walked toward the encampment. The leader approached, smiling reverently, shaking a finger at them. "You're the ones that created all that havoc in Prontis. Aren't you?"

"You Guild?" Mal said.

"Us? No. Kindred spirits, though. We hate the Timians as much as the Guild. We're followers of the true Messiah, Kan Po Drudis."

"Who?"

"Kan Po Drudis. He's right over there."

Nodi and Mal followed his eyes down to the edge of the encampment to an akigo with milky blue eyes. He held his hands out in front of him as if trying to sense what happened.

"He can't see," the leader whispered, "but he's not blind."

"Were you here to rescue us?" Nodi said.

"No. We're here to tear down that damn statue. But we saw the iperistis before dawn and were tracking them. I suspected it was you when I saw them take you. You've really started something. A genuine revolution. Even Messiah

Drudis is impressed, and that's saying something. He was sent to Akigol to be expressly *unimpressed*."

"We weren't aimin' to start a revolution," Mal said, "But it'll do."

"What's happening in Prontis?" Nodi said.

"Some riots, but they've been quelled for now. Everything is right on the brink. We're trying to push it over. They're saying many of the outer regions are erupting. All the temples in Lopriya were burned down. They strung up the apostles down in Klipst."

"What about Kan Ludo?"

"It's on the verge, but so many soldiers have been stationed there, the citizens are frightened. A Persecutor passed through. They say she's on her way northwest now, dragging half a battalion with her."

Nodi watched the pilgrims. They were trembling. "What will you do with them?"

"They'll be given a chance to convert."

"If they don't?"

"They will. If you'll excuse me, we need to get to work. Keep up the good fight, brothers."

"Brothers?" Nodi said under his breath.

Five blechus, longhaired beasts of burden, were lined up with ropes tied to their saddles. The zealots strung the other ends around the statue's extremities while a few others placed pop pods around the base of it. The pop pods were tree seeds that exploded on impact. Though it wasn't a powerful blast, enough of them could weaken the base of the statue. Mal walked up the hill, picked up his satchel, and made sure the letter was still there. He went back to J's body. Nodi followed.

J was still warm, her head resting in a pool of blood.

"I'm sorry," Nodi said.

Mal shook his head and walked back over to one of the

iperistis' bodies. "Help me take his armor." He removed the wheat colored plating.

"What are we going to do with this?" Nodi said, pulling at a leg.

"You're goin' to wear it."

"I'm a P'Aanian, no one is going to believe the king would have a blue aki—"

Mal held up a white paint stick he'd taken from the body.

"Oh. Right. What are you planning? I'll never pass as a soldier. I think I lack that 'dead behind the eyes' look."

"Well *I* can't wear it, now can I?" Mal said, putting the undersized breastplate against his chest. "We might need it in Kan Ludo. You'll pass from a distance. Just keep the paint stick with you. Unless you want to carry the armor, you might as well wear it. And keep hold of your weapon for God's sake."

Nodi found a torn pant leg and used it to clean the blood off the chest piece. He gagged and tried not to look directly at the goopy mess. About the time he had one leg in the armor, there was a series of pops. The blechus ran out, snapping the ropes taut. The legs of the statue gave way and it toppled in a cloud of smoke and dust. The head rolled off and wobbled side-to-side then laid still. Everyone cheered.

Nodi sat down, the other leg still unsheathed, and stared at the broken statue, a symbol that had meant so much to so many. The false Messiah, Kan Po Drudis, was preparing to make a speech as his followers gathered around. *One Messiah for another,* Nodi thought. *A new tribe attempting to assert its dominance. How many have there been through the ages?*

"I don't think we should stay here," Mal said. "They're crazy."

"I agree."

"Hurry up and get dressed. We'll slip away before they demand a conversion out of us. We've lost a lot of time and we're on foot from here."

———— ·::═╡●D●C●╞═::· ·————

That night they made camp at the bottom of a hill. Mal made a small fire and they roasted a koboo he'd caught earlier. He wasn't wearing a shirt and his glowing tattoos cut across the black shadows. He looked like some spectral creature from the depths of hell and had a sorrow on his face to match. Red sparks floated up and became one with the starry night. Nodi doodled in the sand with a twig, chewing placa root for his shoulder.

He spit out the root, wiped his lips, and looked across the fire at Mal. "Does it bother you that so many are suffering and dying over this?"

Mal just stared at the cinders around the edges of the fire.

"I'm sorry about J. If I didn't say so earlier."

"You did." Mal laid down and looked up at the stars. The aurora was sea green that night, bands of deep purple and blue above it, peppered with sparkling pinpricks of light. The fire crackled. "Do you think anyone else could be out there in all that?" he said.

"I don't think so. I think we're alone here. The center of God's creation."

Mal put his arms behind his head. "What if Tim was from out there somewhere?"

Nodi looked up and scanned the night sky.

Mal sighed. "If someone *were* out there, could they be any more despicable than us here? Could they be any more unenlightened? What if the expanse of it is teamin' with things like us? What if Akigol is some tiny part of a greater whole, each piece just waitin' to crash into the others? They're out there killin' each other, arguin' about this God and that God, about politics and law and order. Claimin' they want peace. Waitin' to add us to the fray. What if Tim came here only to find exactly what he was tryin' to leave?"

Nodi scanned the sky. "That would be tragic. For all of us."

Mal said nothing more and soon fell asleep.

Nodi didn't rest much that night with Kan Ludo and Aenna so close. He laid there and looked at the heavens and, for the first time in his life, wasn't sure anything was looking back.

Then, as if by divine providence, a small point of light moved across the expanse, too dim and slow to be a shooting star. He watched it until it disappeared and wondered if it was a sign.

He hoped it was.

The Akigi Bible

The Gospel of Dumbass, 4:21-23

[21] And the Lord taught them many games of chance such as roulette, poker, and bingo. [22] He did this to demonstrate that apart from God, chance would favor ill fortune [23] for life is ruled by chance, and apart from God, the akigi have no chance at all.

15

When Nodi awoke, Mal was already up. They ate fruit he'd found along the banks of the Kimo river which bordered P'Aa and were at the perimeter of Kan Ludo by noon. It was a nice day, a little humid, no clouds.

They studied the military outpost at the edge of town awhile, perched on a hill, hiding behind some trees. Soldiers stood at its gates, inside its gates, marched up and down the street leading up to its gates.

Mal hung his head. "There's so many."

Nodi crept a few paces down and peeked around a tree. "This way."

He led Mal through a network of creek beds to an isolated patch of streamside undergrowth. They were just below Aenna's place, a small yellow igloo built atop an outcropped platform. Nodi wore the iperistis' armor and Mal helped paint his face white. They had no plan to speak of. Mal stepped back and had to admit that Nodi didn't have the battle-hardened look of an iperistis in his eyes. Instead, he had the puzzled look of someone whose legs had just torn loose and walked off without him.

"You're right," Mal said. "This'll never do. It might work from a distance, or if they're not really payin' attention, but if they get up close ... There were so many of them down at that outpost."

"What are we going to do?"

"Don't know yet ... There were so *many* of them."

"You said that already. If we're trying to stay inconspicuous, isn't this the wrong way to go? We're in my part of the kingdom now. I blend in here. *This* will call attention to us."

"Those who want to remain inconspicuous always make the mistake of tryin' to remain inconspicuous. You've gotta understand how the authoritarian mind works." Mal tapped his forehead. "They adhere to certain expectations of inconspicuosity. That's exactly what they'll *expect*. I always go with the *unexpected*, the flamboyant. They'll notice, but won't understand."

"Inconspicuosity isn't a word," Nodi said. "And this is so unexpected you seem to be surprised by it as we speak."

Mal examined Aenna's place. "Is there a back door?"

"Yes, on the balcony."

"You stay here."

He crept up the backside of the steep, bluegrass hill and got a finger hold on the platform. He dangled a moment, pulled himself onto her balcony, and disappeared. Nodi waited for a signal. He longed to see Aenna come out and look down at him, smiling, crying. Instead, Mal careened off the platform clutching a soldier. They twisted and rolled in the air and Mal landed on top of her. She hit her head and went limp. He got up, poked her to make sure she was unconscious, and then tied her up with her own belt. He dragged her into the brush. His nose was bleeding, he'd taken another beating. It occurred to Nodi that Mal wasn't very good in a fight. Luck seemed to favor him, though, if not God.

"Come on," Mal said, as if everything had gone according to plan.

The two of them made their way back up to Aenna's and went inside. The greater sun poured through torn drapes, ribbons flapping in the breeze. Clothes were strewn everywhere, empty water skins on the floor, a broken vase.

"They've taken her," Nodi said, crouching with one of her shirts in his hand.

"No blood," Mal said.

"Blood? Why would there be blood?"

"I'm just sayin' … if she was killed, it wasn't here."

Nodi sat down, overcome by the thought of it.

"I'm sure she's fine," Mal said. "If she's still in town, there's only one place they'd take her."

"The outpost. What if she's not even in Kan Ludo anymore?"

"We'll never know unless we have a look."

Nodi stood up and peeked out the window. Akigi walked up and down the streets with the considered steps of the oppressed. "The city is on edge, we'll never pull it off."

"Communities are like steam valves. This one's about to explode," Mal was throwing some of Aenna's things to the side, one by one. "We've just got to turn the heat up a bit and there'll be chaos. Chaos is the breakdown of order and order is exactly what we're up against." He held up a tattered green robe and pointy hat. "What's this?"

Nodi was embarrassed. He grabbed it and balled it up.

Mal snatched it back. "Is this what I think it is?"

"I don't know. Do you think it's a Hiller's robe and hat?"

"She's not a *Hiller* is she?"

"No, of course not … Her cousin was … He died in one

of their, you know … episodes."

They both stared at the garments—Mal as if he had an idea, Nodi as if he sensed what that idea was and wondered just how insane Mal really was.

The New Reformed Temple of the Holy Hill of Tim's Bloody Martyrdom or NRTHHTBM for short, or the Hillers for even shorter, were the most aggressive and fundamentalist denomination in the Selidinian kingdom. They were headquartered in Kan Ludo, right on the town square, much to the dismay of almost everyone. The Hillers believed that P'Aanians were the chosen race of akigi and insisted that if it hadn't been for Judas, Tim never would have died, nor been transfigured, nor saved the world. Therefore, in sharp contrast to Prontis, the Hillers exalted *Judas* as the most revered disciple and harbored a frightening sense of P'Aanian pride. The rest of Kan Ludo would never have stood for it, most P'Aanians enjoyed being victimized for reasons of self-important self-pity, but when the Hillers didn't get their way, they had a tendency to send their faithful hopping into crowded marketplaces in heaping sacks of poisonous lizards.

Mal was already squeezing into the outfit. He paused. "Her cousin didn't *die* in this, did he?"

"No. There wasn't much left of *that* robe. This one was a spare. Aenna kept it for sentime—what are you doing?"

"Look, there's no more volatile group in Kan Ludo than the Hillers. They are exactly what we need and they have a decent contingent of ixaquoi among their number. They count us as brothers in oppression. I shouldn't have any trouble getting' in, especially dressed as one of them."

Nodi shook his head. "They're crazy, Mal. You haven't lived a stone's throw from them your whole life. They've established themselves here through fear. Prontis only allows them to exist because they have a common enemy in the Dissenters Guild. They're useful tools in that regard. And if they realize your Gui—"

"Do you trust me?" Mal said.

"No. I don't. Not even a little."

Mal finished putting on the tight robe and hat and held his arms out as if in glorious presentation of a bride to her groom. He smiled and said, "Little tight, not bad. Wait for my signal and then go down to the outpost. See if you can get in with that getup."

He slipped out of the back door.

"What signal? ... Why ... What am I ..." Nodi realized it was no use so he just looked around for a place sit.

Mal crept along the banks of the tributaries, scaled the backside of a steep hill, and wormed his way through narrow alleys to the edge of the town square. The Hiller's temple was on the other side, blue, shaped like a blister, with smaller blisters on top of it. A few guards were in the crowded square, no other ixaquoi. He'd stick out like a tree among shrubs there. The city was tense, coiled, and ready to spring.

A leaflet advertising akigi bingo hung on a wall next to him, corners flapping in the breeze. Mal snatched it, tore away a few unimportant details, and ran. The guards saw him cut across the square, just another ixaquoi in their minds, not *the* ixaquoi, but he slipped through the front door of the Hillers' temple before they could catch him. There was only one way in or out and they wouldn't risk an arrest on the property of such a volatile group. They would wait outside.

The temple was packed with akigi deep in fevered prayers against Prontis. The walls were stark adobe, the floor cobblestone. Beams of light shined through a narrow row of windows, accented by gentle wafts of incense smoke. It smelled like berries and lizard dung. The apostle, a stout, dark blue akigo, stood on the stage behind the altar. Mal caught his eyes and scanned the room for anyone that *wasn't* looking at him yet. He grunted indignantly to draw their attention. Without a word spoken, he commanded his audience with unflappable confidence. They deferred to his authority, waiting to hear what he had to say.

"May I?" he said to the apostle, motioning to the stage.

"Please." The apostle was as intrigued as anyone was.

The believers formed an aisle and let him through. He took the stage and gave them an approving shake of the head. "You've probably noticed you have a terrible military infestation out there." The crowd nodded. "The soldiers of Prontis are like bugs that won't leave your picnic alone, are they not? What do we do when bugs interrupt our picnics?"

"Eat them!" someone shouted.

"*Eat* them?" Mal muttered, perplexed. *Damn country folk.* Still, "Eat" worked just as good as "swat" so he went with it. "We eat them!" He raised one hand in a fist and paced the stage. "I can't help but notice there aren't any ixaquoi around."

"They've arrested them all!" someone shouted and quietly added, "Except you."

"No doubt some of them were your brethren here at this very temple." The crowd agreed. "I'm from the western branch—"

"There is no west—"

Mal shot *that* akigo a hard look, narrow-eyed, teeth bared. The akigo cowered and Mal continued. "The good Lord sent me to warn you there's a plot afoot between the other temples in town and Prontis. Why, not but twenty minutes ago I overheard a group of them talkin'. They were in a shadowy mansion down on the east side of town—"

"The east side?" someone said. "That's where all those backstabbing town elders live!"

"Is it?" Mal said. "Well, I heard them talkin' to some soldiers. Talkin' about stealin' your land. They're goin' to eject you from Kan Ludo and they're goin' to use those Guild sell-out ixaquoi down at the outpost to do it! I swear it. Heard 'em myself. They caught me listenin' and chased me all the way up here. Waitin' outside right now. Have a look if you don't believe me."

Someone peeked out and yelled, "He's right! They're there."

"Those pagan ixaquoi can't be trusted," Mal said. "They have a price, and Prontis has money! What will you do when they storm your doors and drag you off into the night?"

There were gasps. A wildfire of chatter spread through the congregation.

"I knew this occupation had something to do with us!" another one said.

"What do they plan to do with this place?" the apostle asked.

Mal held up the flyer from outside. "It's all right here. They're gonna make it a bingo hall!"

At that point, things took a life of their own. The Hillers could take many things, but they'd be damned if their temple was going to be used for bingo. The emerging consensus regarding Mal was that no one would be so insane as to say something like that to the Hillers if it wasn't true.

Mal was surprised and horrified at how many poison lizards they had caged up in the back. In mere minutes, they were running for the door en masse, flooding the square, throwing lizards at the soldiers, screaming, "You can play bingo in hell!" and things like that. Mal ran outside, took off the disguise, and sprinted toward the outpost.

Nodi heard swift footfalls outside so he peeked through the

window and saw four soldiers running down the street. A commotion was at the town square, a cacophony of shouts and screams rang out across Kan Ludo. Someone ran the other direction with a swollen arm, saying something about lizards, Hillers, and bingo.

I suppose this is Mal's idea of a sign, Nodi thought.

He had no plan of attack, but the thought of seeing Aenna made him brave. He ran out of the back door, rolled down the hill, and stumbled toward the outpost. The armor was heavy and awkward, the white paint on his face streaked with sweat. He dropped his sword three times, each time running back to retrieve it. An abandoned stone quarry was just before the outpost. He stopped to peek around the corner of a rock. Most soldiers were running into town, but two were still at the gate craning their necks to see what was going on.

Nodi recalled Mal's bravado at the gates of the temple in Prontis and thought it might be worth a try. He breathed deep and walked up to the two gruff looking akigas with as much authority as he could muster.

"They need you to report to the Hiller's temple immediately," he said.

They looked down at him, steely-eyed. The one on the right smirked.

"And give me your keys," he added, wiggling his fingers at them.

One guard turned to the other and said, "Since when did the iperistis grow tongues?"

Nodi furrowed his brow, clucked his tongue, and ran back to the quarry. He cut around the corner of a large stone. The jangling of their armor was getting closer. He stopped and dropped to the ground, holding his legs up to trip them. The one he tripped took the other one down with her. He jumped up, grabbed one of their key rings, kicked them in their heads to knock them out, and ran away when it didn't.

He ran back to the gate and the third key on the ring got him in. The guards were almost to him, but he shut them out. He ran to the right and found the pits that held the prisoners. He fumbled with the keys, opened the hatch, and lowered his arm to help one of them escape. When the first ixaquoi was free, he helped the others up. The guards were through the gates and upon them in mere moments, but the freed ixaquoi threw them into the pit.

"Sorry. Sorry," Nodi called down at them. He held his hands out to demonstrate that he meant no harm. He was always apologizing for everything.

He looked for Aenna, but she wasn't down there.

Nodi grabbed one of the ixaquoi. "Have you seen an akiga?"

"There's one in the main house over there."

More soldiers rushed into the outpost, but the rebels were already overrunning it with weapons raided from the blacksmith's shed. Small clusters of fighting ensued. Nodi wove in between them until he reached the door of the building at the center of the compound.

"Stop right where you—" someone said, but they were interrupted by a thump.

Nodi turned around. Mal was there, standing over an unconscious soldier. Another soldier charged, kicked Mal in the shin, and gave him an uppercut. He fell back, dazed, but someone else jumped the soldier from behind and beat her like a wild beast.

Mal got up, rubbed his chin, and smiled. "I'm impressed!" he said, in recognition of Nodi's unintended prowess in the art of anarchy. Nodi used the keys to unlock the door and Mal followed him in. Several rooms with thick wood doors were along the main hall. Mal kicked each one open while Nodi stripped off the armor and tried to wipe the paint off his face. Aenna was behind the fourth door, standing in the far corner, confused. When she saw Nodi, a familiarity crossed her face.

"Nodi!"

He ran over and hugged her. He'd feared the worst. To see her, touch her, smell her was a sorely needed turn of good fortune, if not the very providence of God. Mal wedged them apart and pulled them toward the door.

"Wait," Aenna said. "I haven't done anything wrong. I can't just run. I'll look guilt—"

"We have to go," Nodi said.

She hesitated, afraid to make matters worse, but conceded.

They ran outside to the far side of the outpost. Bodies were everywhere. Smoke rose from the center of town, a mob of akigi was crossing the bridge up the street, coming toward them with clubs and rocks. Mal untied two red spotted runners from a pole. Aenna climbed onto one and pulled Nodi up behind her. Mal climbed on the other.

They raced out of town, away from the mayhem.

16

"Follow me," Aenna yelled. Nodi knew where she was going. They took the lead and Mal followed them down a dry creek bed that ran parallel to the main road. They veered right and hooked around to a narrow fissure that cut through the face of a small cliff. They dismounted. Nodi took the supply packs off the runner's saddles and chased them away.

"What are you doing?" Mal said.

"The runners can't fit in here."

"In where?"

Nodi plowed into a barricade of heavy brush on the left side of the fissure. It was so thick he had to push and hack his way through. Mal and Aenna followed. A patrol thundered down the creek bed and went around the bend. Nodi remained still until he could no longer hear them.

A cave was on the other side of the brush, void of light. They rubbed their hands along the walls to find the way.

"You two know where you're goin'?" Mal said.

"Yes."

"Somewhere safe?"

"Yes. Very."

A faint crack of daylight appeared at the other end. When they were near it, Aenna pulled back a stone to reveal an opening. They crawled through and emerged at the bottom of a crevice enclosed on two sides. An arch was on the far side, like a doorway to a vast complex of craters overgrown with bright green foliage and fruit vines. The air was crisp and sweet from the smell of honey flowers. Up above, thin trees swayed gently, the suns sparkling through their leaves.

The beauty of it entranced Mal. "What is this place?"

"It's a network of sinkholes," Nodi said. "They're like pockmarks in the foothills that lead to the Mobo Mountains. Miles of caves, craters, natural bridges. They call it Duvoi's Trap. We found that entrance when we were younglings."

"You sure they won't find us?"

"Not likely. It's too big, too many places to hide. We should push deeper in, though. I've spent a lot of time here. I always liked the solitude. I think I can get us to the other side."

"To the Mobo Mountains?"

"The foot of them, yes, but we can't go into the mountains. We'll have to go around."

Mal scoffed. "You're scared?"

"Aren't you?"

"Why should I be?"

"The Mobo Mountains are ... cursed. Haunted by a terrible history. No one goes up there."

"You believe in giants?" Mal said.

Nodi looked at Aenna. Her arms were crossed. She wasn't looking at him. He looked back at Mal and said, "You may not accept scripture as the whole truth, but you have to admit that at least some of it is rooted in history. The Giants of Mobo were not legend. They were real. I don't think we want to see what's up there."

Aenna remained quiet.

"They're all dead. You akigi exterminated them, remember?" Mal said. "The way things have been goin' for us, I'll take the dead over the livin'." He took a drink from a canteen they got off the runner. "You ever traveled northwest? If we don't go through the mountains, we'll go through one of four narrow passes, each with its own kingdom highway runnin' through it. We can't pass through any one of them without gettin' caught."

Nodi shook his head.

Mal pointed at Aenna. "You. You were in the military. P'Aanians get stationed in the *P'Aanian* region. I'll bet you've been through those passes on assignment, right?"

She nodded hesitantly.

"Tell him we can't get through."

She looked at Nodi and back at Mal. Her silence confirmed what he was saying. Nodi climbed up on a stone and looked at the tallest mountain peak. The tip was barely visible over the rim of the crater between two tree trunks. It was a great, snowcapped tombstone as far as he was concerned.

"We should go," he said. "We need to get as far in as we can before nightfall."

They pushed on in silence, going north along the western edge, jumping off rocks, climbing other rocks, finding ways around, over, and under. Nodi's shoulder throbbed. He chewed placa root as he walked. When the suns were almost down, they stopped for the night in a small, natural amphitheater. Mal built a fire and they ate nuts and berries they'd picked along the way. Nodi and Aenna sat next to the fire awhile, unsure where to begin. He rubbed the remaining paint off his face with a cloth. She stared at the ground, lost in thought. Nodi assumed she'd be happier to see him.

"I guess you want to know what's happening," he said.

"I heard."

"What did you hear?" Mal said. He was returning from filling the canteen with puddle water.

"That *you* stole that letter Nodi translated. What I *don't* understand, Nodi, is why you fled. And why you fled with *him.*"

"They were going to kill me, Aenna. And I didn't run away with Mal, he … he just happened to be there … he was going to … I don't know what he was going to do … kidnap me? Maybe."

Mal nodded. It was true. He was going to kidnap him.

"*Why* are you still with him, Nodi?"

"I … he …"

"I'm *very* charmin' once you get to know me," Mal said. He took his shirt off and smiled. "I've got glowin' tattoos."

Aenna shriveled her face, perplexed and angry. She stood up and put her back to them.

Mal pulled out the letter and handed it to Nodi. "You said you'd translate it if I helped you get her out of Kan Ludo. There she is. Can't do nothin' about her disposition. Let her hear it for herself."

Nodi took it and read it aloud. As he did, Mal leaned forward, transfixed. Aenna sat down again, listening, but looking off into darkness. The words fell across Nodi's lips like a curse whispered among the superstitious. The passion he'd felt when he first translated it was gone, replaced by the pain of its aftermath.

When he finished, Aenna looked into the fire. "Is it legitimate?"

"I'm as sure as one can be with these things."

"Just because it raises questions, doesn't mean those questions will lead you to the truth. They could just as easily lead you away from it. I'm *certain* they will, in fact."

"The only thing worse than getting' a false answer to a true question," Mal said, "is not to have asked at all."

Aenna was teary-eyed. She fought back a swell of emotion. "How many do you think died back home today?" Her voice cracked.

Nodi lowered his eyes. "I don't know. We never intended it to go that way ... *I* didn't, at least."

"So much suffering. Just so you could set me free. My life, *one* life, isn't worth that. We must always think of the greater good."

"You're worth it to me."

"There was a time you wouldn't have said that. Your priorities have changed."

"Yeah, well ... one says a lot of things when they're in the sterile confines of pure speculation. Real life is different."

Mal was picking his teeth with a thorn. He flicked it in the fire and said, "Everyone involved in what happened in Kan Ludo today is responsible for their own actions."

Aenna wiped her eyes. "This Persecutor Shirka who is after you ... us ... she mentioned a desecration."

Nodi picked at the calluses on the palm of his hand. "His heart stopped. It stopped and his body fell apart. It just happened. I suppose they think I caused it. I was the only one in there. But it just happened, it wasn't my fault." He met Aenna's eyes, black in the firelight. "I know in my hearts this happened for a reason. That God wants me to discover some hidden truth. Tim was in that chamber for two hundred and forty-three years. He just happened to fall apart with *me* in there? That can't be a coincidence."

"So what now?"

Mal lay down on his back and watched the sparks drift up and fade away.

"We're going to try to find the other part of the letter," Nodi said. "I promised Mal I'd go with him if he helped get you to safety."

"We can't go with *him*. We should turn ourselves in. We shouldn't have come *this* far. God will protect us. In the morning, let's go back."

"I can't do that, Aenna. I have to see this through. I have to know where this path leads."

"At best, this path will confirm what you already know, have *always* known. At worst, it will trap you in a web of lies only to lead you to Judas' fate. Is that what you want? Is that what you want to lead *me* into?"

"Of course not, but what if you're wrong? Aren't you curious?"

"I'm curious only in so far as knowing just how deluded Judas could have been at the time of his death." She turned to Mal. "What's *your* stake in this?"

He rolled over on his side to face them, propped up on an elbow. "Tim was a fraud. I want everyone to know it. This might lead to nothin' or it might lead to the greatest revolution of our time. No way of tellin' aside from seein' it through. We're committed to it now. What else are we goin' to do? Go hide somewhere for the rest of our lives?"

"Maybe hiding isn't such a bad plan," Nodi said.

Mal scoffed, sat up, and crossed his legs. "Either one of you ever been to Gologa?"

"No."

"They got these spittin' dragons along the eastern shores. Don't know why they're called spittin' dragons, they don't spit. Foul things. Hunt in packs, led by an alpha. They never forget a scent and they never quit on their prey once they have the scent, unless you kill the alpha. Kill the alpha and they quit comin'. They say if you kill an alpha, you could command the pack … if you spoke spittin' dragonese that is. Big bastards. Well, I knew a fella, we called him Flaccid for reasons I won't get into, that got tangled up with one.

Speared it by accident. Thought it was a woovie hidin' in the bushes. Spear went through the dragon's leg and pinned it to the ground. Old Flaccid got right up on the dragon, could have killed it, but he told me he had some kind of spiritual connection to it. Like its eyes cried out for mercy. He pulled the spear out of its leg and ran like hell. Told me about it an hour after it happened. I was drunk, but still remember the affected look he had on his face. We had a few rounds at the saloon, laughed it off. He left around midnight and that was the last time I ever saw him. Damn if those things didn't hunt him down that night. Rip him to pieces. Nothin' left, but a blast of blood in the sand like he'd just ... exploded. Had Flaccid saw it through, finished off the alpha, he'd still be alive. Fear, mercy, a desire to walk away, spiritual mumbo-jumbo. It cost him everythin'."

Aenna considered Mal a moment. "Nodi, why are you following him in this?"

Nodi closed his eyes and shook his head. "Because what if he's right?"

"How can you say that?"

"Look. I'm not saying he is, but I'm nothing if I don't pursue truth no matter where it leads me. I love you, Aenna, but this is who I am. It's just something I *have* to do."

"Nodi—"

He waved her off, got up, and walked into the dark.

He found a cold rock to lie on and thought he should pray but couldn't find the words. Lying there in a crater, the rim of it a black frame around a sky bursting with color, he felt as if he was looking through a porthole into heaven. He wished heaven would send him a sign, but it didn't. It just stared back, dead-eyed and indifferent. Heaven didn't seem so much a destination as an eternal nothingness.

The only two things that meant anything to Nodi were the truth and Aenna. As long as he'd known her, those two converged, they sought truth together.

He never imagined that one day the pursuit of one might come at the expense of the other.

Aenna and Mal stayed behind and watched Nodi fade into shadow. They sat in awkward silence until Mal said, "Look, the situation is what it is. We're at a crossroads here, neither road easy. I just want to know the truth. Nodi and I may not agree on much, but we have that in common. That's all that really matters. I know neither of you has any reason to trust me, but we have a common interest. I have no stake in betrayin' you. It's not like we're after money, where greed might be at play. Truth is a fount free to all, the more who know it, the better."

"*I* know the truth." Aenna laid back and watched the dancing shadows. "Shirka is a true believer. A patriot. She'll kill us without hesitation."

"Shirka?" Mal said.

"Heard of her?"

"No."

"She's heard of you."

"That's not good."

"Are we going to Sigate?"

"Yeah," Mal said. "I've heard Hijoon is somewhere near there. We need to find whoever found the letter, see if we can find the other half."

"They'll be looking for it too. You don't have a chance."

Mal shrugged. Maybe she was right, maybe not.

"You know," he said, "...Nodi loves you more than God himself."

Aenna squeezed her eyes closed. "That's why we're doomed."

17

Persecutor Shirka rode into Sigate with half a battalion behind her. The footfalls of the runners sounded like thunder, the rattle of armor, like a mechanical beast. It was the first time she'd been there since the rebellion. Everyone in Sigate knew who she was. They stopped and stared with hollow eyes.

The main street was hardpan, littered with potholes, the sidewalks cluttered, buildings collapsed like empty shells from years of disrepair. A thick smoke was in the sky, blown in from the sea, and flurries of ash drifted on the wind. It smelled like sulfur and sea salt. The harbor at the end of the road was sparse, a few akigi carried nets, and a drunken deckhand sat on the dock. The masts of ships, mostly military frigates, swayed with the tide beyond the boathouses.

Shirka went to the temple on the south side of town. A P'Aanian in a blue robe sat on a bench out front.

"Are you the apostle here?" she said, perched atop her runner.

"Yes." He stood up as if at attention.

The persecutor climbed down and observed the deplorable conditions of the temple—rotten wood, mold oozing beneath the windows, cracked bricks. It was an affront to God.

"I'm here on an urgent matter," she said. "I need to know about a letter written on a piece of orange cloth that was turned in a number of months ago. It was older than your normal acquisitions, written in an ancient form of P'Aanian. Do you remember it?"

The apostle scratched his belly. "Yes. It's the only one I've ever seen like it."

"Who turned it in?"

"Isu Kru. I've no idea where she found it." He made a sour face and added, "She's … troubled."

"Where is she?"

"Spends most of her time along the coast, scavenging, talking to herself. She's been hanging around the harbor the past week or so. Can't miss her. Her arms are longer than her legs. Purple. Runs on all fours like an animal."

• ⋯ ⸭•◗◖•⸭ ⋯ •

Shirka found Isu Kru scuttling around the hull of a ship, picking barnacles off it. The ship's hull was tar black all the way up, two stories tall, with three long rudders hanging off the back. The sails were tied on the booms, giant conch shell anchors planted in the silt floor of the harbor. The name on the back of it was *Eluding Distress*.

Odd name for a ship, Shirka thought.

"Get away from the boat, Isu, you freak!" an ixaquoi yelled down from the deck. "I swear you're the weirdest thing I've ever seen." He noticed Shirka seated on her runner up on the beach and withdrew out of sight. Isu turned to see. Shirka got down and waded, ankle deep, into the water. It was warm and oily on her feet. A fine layer of ash floated on the surface. She beckoned Isu over.

"Isu Kru?" she said.

"Aye," Isu said, as she paddled in. "No," she said to a question not asked. Shirka backed out of the water.

Shirka studied her as if she was some accursed creature—dripping tentacles, ash speckled body, powerfully long arms. Isu realized the tide was making her hands and feet sink in the sand. She giggled.

Shirka leaned to the right to catch her eyes. "A number of months ago, you found a letter. Do you remember that?"

"Papa," Isu said.

"Do you remember the *letter?*"

"Dinner."

The persecutor turned to one of her guards. "Give her something to eat."

The guard pulled a piece of bread from her waist pouch and gave it to her. Isu gnawed at it like a rodent.

"Can you take me to where you found the letter?"

"Stranger," she said and paused to listen. "Temple."

Shirka got the impression that she was hearing one side of an imaginary conversation.

"Do you remember where the letter came from?"

"Cave."

"Yes, a cave. Where is it?"

She put her arm around Isu to nudge her into leading them there.

"Defend!" Isu screamed and pushed her. Shirka fell down and tried to scuttle backward, but Isu jumped on top of her, pummeled her face, and locked her hands around her throat. It took four of Shirka's guards to restrain her.

Shirka stumbled to her feet, enraged. As the guards held Isu, she punched her in the stomach, screaming, "*Where is it?*"

Isu only mumbled.

Shirka backhanded her across the face. "Where is it?"

"North."

Shirka grabbed her tentacles and pulled her down. Isu whimpered. She didn't understand why this was happening.

"Where?"

"North," she said again. She cried out. "Caves."

Shirka let go of her and Isu collapsed. "Lock her up at the outpost." She dabbed at the wound on her cheek and inspected the blood on her fingers. "Send patrols north, search every cave, every possible location."

What Shirka didn't know was that to Isu, north was any direction her nose pointed. Presently, she faced south.

18

Do you remember the time we went wandering down Windy Mountain Road?" Nodi said. He was sitting next to Aenna by the remains of the fire, eating berries. The morning light was soft, the ground damp.

"Yes." She said and smiled.

"Apostle Cri and Apostle Fikijo ..." Nodi laughed. "Cri was wearing that thing ... with the thing ... and they were ... you know ... reenacting the battle of Molmo with the," he motioned with his hands, something round, something only the two of them would understand. "... Remember?"

Aenna laughed in spite of her efforts to restrain it. Her shoulders bobbed up and down and she held her hand over her mouth. "That was the weirdest thing I've ever seen."

After a moment, they stopped laughing. Nodi looked up at the sky, Aenna at the ground. The air was still and the charcoal smell from the campfire lingered.

Nodi ate a few more berries. "As younglings, we had such adventuresome spirits. Everything was filled with wonder. We were so innocent."

"We could afford to be that way. No stakes."

He nodded. "Do you hate me for this?"

"I could never hate you." She looked away.

"You've always had faith in me. I'm sorry I got you into this."

"I know you didn't mean to."

"The day before father died, we talked about you. He said you give me stability. That you temper my overly curious nature. Keep me honest. He was right. He loved you ... He'd be so disappointed in me right now."

Aenna rolled a berry between her fingers.

Mal was stirring.

"Whatever happened to those two apostles? Cri and Fukijo," Nodi said.

"They were executed for immorality while you were away in Pasica."

"Executed?"

"Of course. What did you expect?"

Nodi wasn't sure what bothered him more: the fact that the apostles were executed or that Aenna didn't seem to care one way or another about it.

They trudged north out of Duvoi's Trap. By evening, the northwest sky was blotted out by the mountainside. Nodi climbed onto an outcropping and looked back out over the trap. Lush greens carpeted the pockmarked land beneath them like an emerald moon, teeming with life. Creature calls, low-pitched grumbles, and high-pitched screeches echoed through the valley. Birds floated in circles, diving for things unseen. Kan Ludo was miles away. A column of black smoke on the horizon showed him where it was. A fresh wave of guilt washed over him.

They made camp again, slept little, and started out early in the morning. The awkward silence of festering emotions lingered. As they got higher, trees became sparse, gradually replaced by fire red shrubberies and tundra. They came to a treacherous incline blanketed with the remains of an ancient avalanche. Firm footing was scarce. The rest of the day was lost to traversing it. When Nodi crested the top and saw how far they had yet to go, he felt as if they'd made no progress at all. They spent a gloomy night up there, but it was too wet to build a fire. They were cold and hungry and huddled together to keep warm.

The next afternoon, they reached the foot of a jagged, amethyst cliff.

Nodi looked up. "Can we go around?"

"Not without goin' back down," Mal said. "Even then, there's no guarantee we won't end up in the same situation at another point along the pass. How's your shoulder?"

Nodi rubbed it. "Still hurts, but it's better than it was."

Mal began to climb, feeling for sure footing. Aenna followed with Nodi behind her. Nodi had the hardest time of the three, having the shortest reach. He found himself going sideways, working to grasp to ledges Mal and Aenna grasped with ease. The footholds weren't much, the finger holds even less. Rocks tumbled down around him as the other two picked at the cliff side. When he was high enough to die from the fall, he slipped and fell. He slid down a way, hit his head, but caught a ledge only a couple of inches wide. He brought his arm around awkwardly, the shoulder burning, and regained stability.

"You okay?" Aenna called down, panicked.

"I'm okay. Searing agony, but alive."

From that point on, he prayed that with each step God would give him firm footing. He thanked the Lord for every solid foothold and credited the shaky ones to lessons in humility. In the end, he made it to the top alive, proof that maybe God was with him after all.

Nodi slithered over the precipice behind Aenna and Mal. Everything was alien, a place few ventured. A field of tundra sprawled out before them spotted with yellow wildflowers and a patchwork of petrified tree roots. Strange blue appendages grew over the roots and intermittently spewed steam out of their tips. Nodi and Aenna gathered around to warm their frosted hands. Mal protested, saying they needed to keep moving. They crossed the hissing field to the foot of the last spire of the mountain. A path wound around it. The night was closing in, but they were eager to get to the other side.

Nodi heard something. "Wait."

Mal and Aenna turned back. "What?"

"The hum. Do you hear it?"

"Yeah."

"What is it?"

"Don't know."

It had gotten louder as they went. Gentle vibrations penetrated their bodies.

Mal got down on all fours and listened. He shook his head and got back up, rubbing his muddy hands on his pants. "Doesn't sound natural."

They kept going and soon, the moons were up. A blue-green aurora painted a delicate shimmer of color on the perilous mountainside. Snow glistened with sparkles of blue and white. The path wound gently to the left, a straight drop on their right. The higher they went, the more frigid it became. Nodi didn't think they could survive the night in that chill.

"Are we almost to the peak?" he said through chattering teeth. His tentacles were rigid, hanging like icicles. He'd fallen behind and couldn't see Mal or Aenna around the bend. When he followed the path up, their silhouettes came into view, both standing still. They stared up at the top of the last crest. He ran up beside them to see what they were looking at.

A cylindrical tower of white stone with long windows and a copper dome that glinted in the moonlight was up ahead. Pointed structures were on a downward slope beyond it, dark and abandoned. The quiet hum came from everywhere beneath them.

The lights in the tower turned on, glowing yellow.

They gazed at it, shivering. Condensation drifted out of their mouths in rhythmic wisps, their breathing labored. A shadow was in the windows, moving toward the door. They were too paralyzed to move. The door opened and a giant blot stood in a halo of light. A velvety voice came from the darkness, speaking a language even Nodi didn't understand.

They remained quiet, puzzled, frightened.

Mal stepped forward. "Uh … we're lookin' for God," he called out. "Seen him?"

The figure seemed to consider that a moment. "Define God," it said in Selidinese.

"I … I'm not sure I can."

"You had better come in. Get warm."

The Akigi Bible

The Sayings of TIM, 5:13-14

[13] "You shall not suffer the sorcerer who says he understands the things God has made. [14] These ones should be put to death. They corrode the fabric of the faith and seek to diminish my power."

The Chronicles of Selidin (Akigi Old Testament), 342:1-7

342 And the giants of the Mountains of Mobo were sorcerers who used magic to control the elements for their own evil purposes.

[2] In the fifth year of the reign of Queen BoKal III, the prophet Rubard came to her saying, [3] "Look, in the mountains the giants of Mobo practice evil and say there is no God. [4] We must strike them down and show them that there is a God and that he is the most high God of Selidin."

[5] The Queen answered saying, "Surely you are right! I shall crush them under my heel and they shall know the strength of our Lord."

[6] So the Queen sent an army into the Mountains and they slaughtered the giants.

[7] Fifty thousand were among their dead.

19

They approached the giant in the doorway with trepidation. Though Nodi was afraid they might be in mortal danger, he figured that as long as they were *cooked* before eaten, the warmth would be worth it.

"Come in. I will not hurt you," the giant said with a homely accent.

Mal went ahead. Nodi started to follow, but Aenna pulled him back. "He must be a giant of Mobo. If *one* is still alive, there may be many. They won't welcome akigi here. They'll kill us."

"I'm too cold to debate this. We'll die if we stay out here much longer, anyway."

Nodi kept a wary eye on their host as he stepped across the threshold into the enveloping warmth. The giant was thin, more than four times his size, most of it leg, fingers long and lean like the limbs of a tree. He was almost naked, except for a brown loincloth, with skin the color of ash and gray spots on his arms and cheeks. He had a skinny head with bulbous ears, and no eyes, just fleshy sockets. Nodi wondered why he bothered to have the lights on.

The lights.

They were like nothing he'd ever seen—lamps with no flame, connected to one another by thin strands of metal.

The giant shut the door, squatted down, and tilted his eyeless head as if observing them. Something was reassuring about him, in spite of his strange appearance.

A spiral walkway wound around the perimeter to the top of the tower like a corkscrew with bookshelves all along the way, more books than Nodi knew existed. On the top level, a ladder ran up to a hatch in the ceiling leading to the dome at the top. In the floor, another hatch was near the wall to their left. Nodi heard the distant rumbling of clanking metal and rushing water below it. The hum he'd heard on the mountain came from down there.

A fire in a cylindrical fireplace was in the middle of the room. They rushed over, permission be damned, and rubbed their hands together.

"Who are you?" the giant said.

"I'm Mal. This is Nodi and Aenna. Thank you for takin' us in, if only for a moment to warm up."

"I am Trej. What are you doing up here? There has not been an akigi here in over fifty years and a hundred before that." He faced Mal with his hollow eye sockets, somehow still able to see. "I do not even know what you are."

"He's an ixaquoi," Nodi said. "We're looking for safe passage to Sigate."

"Well, you picked an odd route to travel if safe passage was of interest to you." He stood up. "Are you in trouble?"

"Yes, we are, Trej," Mal said.

"Trouble from whom?"

"The temple ... and the crown. We don't mean you any harm. We're not interested in puttin' you out, but ...."

"Nonsense, you can stay. The temple and the crown have

no love for *any* of us up here, I suppose."

Mal hopped to the right and then to the left quietly. Trej followed his movement, brows raised. "You are wondering how I see?"

Mal smiled sheepishly.

"The hum. Do you hear it? The lights are for you, the hum is for me. We both see better. There are fewer mysteries that way. No?"

"Uh. Yeah. I guess. Why do you bother with the lights at all?"

"Why does the owner of an estate keep a room for a guest that might never come?"

"What is this place?" Aenna said.

"This is one of the last repositories of my once great civilization. It is …. was … our library and observatory. I watch the stars here. Make maps of them. Calculate the rotation of Akigol around the suns—"

"You mean the calculation of the suns around *Akigol*," Mal said.

"No. I meant what I said." He clapped his hands in remembrance of something. "It is almost time! There is one mystery I have been trying to solve for many years. Would you like to see?"

"Uh. Okay," Nodi said. He thought it might be rude not to.

"Me too," Aenna said, still distrustful of Trej.

"Got any ale?" Mal asked with desperate hope in his voice.

"In the cupboard on the left. Come on you two. Not much time. You do not want to miss it!"

"Miss what?"

"You will see. I was on my way up when I noticed you outside. I almost forgot about it."

Nodi eyed the huge books as they followed Trej. There were no titles, just patterns of bumps and gouges along the spines. When he was halfway to the top, he stopped to look at one of the lamps hanging over his head. It hummed with a steady, unbroken tone.

"I suppose that is unfamiliar technology to you," Trej said.

"How does it work?" Nodi climbed on one of the shelves for a closer look at the shining filament inside.

"There is not yet a Selidinese word for it. It is called 'electricity,' in English. A current runs through these things called 'wires'."

"I've never heard the word 'electricity'."

"Yes, well, I am sure there are many words in English you are not yet aware of. You lack the context."

"How can you know more about English than me? English came from Tim and Tim came to the akigi. I've dedicated my life to understanding it." He hopped down off the shelf.

"I met this Tim of yours once," Trej said. "He gave me English. I did not like him."

Nodi stopped to contemplate that a moment. He decided the isolation must have made Trej loopy.

Trej climbed the ladder, spindly legs pumping him up the rungs, and opened the hatch at the top to crawl through. Both Aenna and Nodi struggled because the rungs were so far apart from one another. They relied heavily on the vertical poles until Trej reached down and pulled them up, each in turn.

The only light poured up from the hatch. Star charts were carved into the floor and on the inside of the dome, wood puzzle boxes were half assembled on a long table to the right.

"I am missing pieces," Trej said of the puzzles.

He pulled a lever in the middle of the room setting large metal gears into motion. A sliver in the dome rumbled open and cold air swept in. Aenna pressed against Nodi, put her arm around him, and looked up. She was shivering. Nodi felt as if she was touching him for the first time, his hearts raced, and he thought maybe things were going to be okay between them. Millions of stars twinkled overhead, the aurora danced, and great swaths of deep purple and red streaked the heavens from east to west. Trej pulled the hatch in the floor closed and went to a crank in the middle of the room. He turned it until there was a steady pulse and then listened through a tube attached to the bottom of a bowl-shaped apparatus.

He put the tube down and tilted his head left to right as if tuning his ears.

"There! Look there!" he said, pointing. "It is clear enough to see, No? Look."

"It's clear, but what are we looking for?" Aenna said.

"The star. It is moving there, from southeast to northwest. I hear it, follow my finger."

Nodi squinted and saw a faint light moving in a straight path, the same light he'd seen the night before they rescued Aenna. She moved into him and saw it too. "What is it?"

"I saw it the other night," Nodi said. "Before we got you out of Kan Ludo. Maybe it's a sign! It's moving to the northwest, just like us."

"I have been tracking it for over two hundred years," Trej said. "It moves with impeccable precision. Fascinating, yes?"

"Over two hundred years? How can you have been watching it for over two hundred years?"

"That is when I first noticed it. I remember because it was my one hundred and third birthday. It is a piece of a puzzle I have not yet found."

Nodi didn't know which question, among potentially thousands, to ask first. He settled with, "Do you have anything to eat?"

"Of course!"

After waiting awhile for Trej to prepare soup made of mystery spices and cave fungi, they sat on books stacked on chairs around a lofty table. Mal finished one of Trej's bottles of ale, held it upside down, and shook it to extract every last drop.

"Do you like it?" Trej said.

"It's good. Not as good as back home, but good."

"Nothing is ever as good as it is back home. I make it myself." Trej turned to Aenna and Nodi. "Are you not having any?"

"They're not folk for the drink, kind Trej," Mal said. "They're devout Timians."

"I assumed as much. Not even one, in moderation, to warm your freezing bones?"

"No. Thank you."

"Suit yourselves." He opened a new bottle, poured himself extra, and served each of them a bowl of soup. It looked dreadful but smelled quite good.

Mal was sufficiently drunk, uninhibited to the point of having lost all social grace. That is, if he ever had any to begin with. He watched Trej, Nodi, and Aenna in turn. "Wait," he said as if something suddenly occurred to him. "You must *hate* these two, Trej, the akigi havin' wiped out your kind and all."

Aenna bristled. Nodi gulped and put his spoon down.

"Why would I hate them?" Trej said. "They have not done anything to me. I have but one life and as long a life as it is, it is too short to waste on bitterness and regret. No one should be judged by the sins of the many as long as they do not seek to repeat them. I trust neither of you plans to kill me in my sleep?"

Nodi looked at Aenna. "We're still waiting on a word from God on that."

Trej chuckled. "This is funny."

The brief tension slipped away.

"How long does one such as you live?" Aenna said.

"The average lifespan of a troogil is about four hundred years."

"Troogil?" Nodi said.

"Or Giant of Mobo, if you prefer. Or Sorcerer." Trej smirked. "I am indeed the last of your accursed ones."

"The last?" Nodi pushed the bowl away. "Words can't—"

Trej held up his hand to calm Nodi's apprehension. "We were a dying race before the akigi ever came. The akigi attacked the first time just before I was hatched. I think they did not understand us, did not trust us. We are a much older species, had been in the mountains long before the akigi could walk upright, had mastered technical things the akigi did not comprehend. We appeared as magicians to them, unnatural things. They feared us, struck out before we could do them harm. Their God demanded it. Who were the troogil compared to God?" Trej sighed and fell back in his chair, resting his hands on either side of his bowl. "Those who survived succumbed to thoughts of revenge. They prepared for war, but their numbers were too low. Troogils are patient, though, and were resigned to wait until our numbers could support the plan. I think your Tim realized what was on the horizon. Learned it from ...," he paused and nodded with a kind of sad resignation. "He sent the akigi up here to end us for good, fearing a war the akigi could not win. I suspect he was mad with power."

"You *really* met him?" Nodi said.

"Yes."

Aenna shook her head. "You're mad!"

"Oh, I have no doubts about that." Trej took the bottle of ale from Mal, poured half a glass, and took a sip. "I will tell you about it."

20

Trej," the clan leader called out. "We have an assignment for you."

Trej stood on the rim of a crater, mesmerized by the size of the blast radius. His senses exploded in waves of heat and sound.

"Trej!"

He turned in a daze. "What?"

The clan leader was coming toward him from the mouth of the cave.

"We have an assignment for you."

"An assignment?"

"Take these." The clan leader handed him a roll of thick hide, a knife, a dual shot pistol, and a sack of pellets for it. "We need you to map the region south of Mobo down to the Kimo River and west to the coast. We are looking for strategic locations—natural shelters, important landmarks, akigi strongholds. Could take you as long as six months."

"Just like that? I am being sent off?"

"You must do your part. You have no family ties, no

responsibilities here concerning the war effort. You are not the only one. Many are being sent out to chart Selidin."

Trej looked down at the crude gun. It was heavy, almost black in his spectral vision, and smelled like smoke. It was new technology, still experimental. He'd never held one before

"What am I supposed to do with this?"

"Protection. The akigi have never seen anything like it. It might as well be magic. One shot and they will scatter."

Trej spent his whole life living with the plans the remains of his once great society had for the akigi. Revenge was their lifeblood, a black stain, the fuel for their machinations. They couldn't win a war. Their numbers were too low, even the power of this new technology couldn't save them. The akigi were still winning. What began as an attempt at genocide would end in mass suicide.

He stood there facing the test site, a blown out quarry that shimmered in thermal patterns. He wanted to go back below the surface where he was comfortable, but their dreams of violence would only push him back out like a toxic geyser.

Trej left with no intention of going back.

He moved beyond the lower mountains and out to the plains then ventured up and down the coast, wary of cities and villages. The constant sounds of rustling trees, chirping insects, and rushing waters filled his mind with electrical topography. Everything was illuminated, sometimes confusing, and wholly alien compared to the drab reverberations of cave walls and dripping stalactites. He watched the akigi from afar, staying hidden, traveling at night. They were neither the demons troogils made them out to be, nor the saints they made themselves out to be. They just were. Like troogils just were.

One night, he was near the town of Gruno Ku, fishing in the moonlight with a rod he'd carved out of a tree limb. As he sat on the bank of the river, he sensed something behind him. He turned defensively, afraid it was an akigo, but saw a man just inside the tree line. He didn't know it was a man at the time, wouldn't know until a few moments later. All he saw was a creature, an alien whose temperature ran warm with a single white-hot heart beating in its chest. The man was small compared to Trej, but bigger than an akiga, and wore the traditional outfit of an akigi elder. He appeared to be inebriated and something was in his hand, something that produced a gentle hum.

The man stared at him, head tilting side to side, trying to comprehend what he was seeing. He took out a cigarette, put it in his mouth, cupped it with his left hand, and lit it with the device strapped to his palm. Trej smelled the pungent odor of it, could sense the warm wisps of smoke floating in the air. After a long moment of staring at one another, the man said something unintelligible.

Trej responded in his own language. The man approached him with caution and held up his hand. The device on his palm felt hot, hummed louder. Trej wanted to run but was too frightened to turn his back on the thing. His arms fell to his sides and he dropped the fishing pole. The sounds of the river got louder—the breeze blew through him as if adding itself to his substance—his mind merged with his surroundings.

The thing in the man's hand flashed. Blinding. Searing. Enlightening.

Every synapse in Trej's brain exploded. A flood of knowledge, distinctly human, rushed into his mind. He experienced the euphoria of a composer, waking in the middle of the night to realize his greatest symphony, or the breathless joy of a painter who steps back and realizes he's just completed his masterpiece. Trej's mind traveled to new heights and depths, but with every new epiphany, there were a thousand new questions, branching in unexpected ways, extending back into infinity. Just when he sensed he was on the verge of enlightenment, at the cusp of divinity itself—it was right there, he could grasp it as if it were a solid object—the man stumbled on a rock and fell down.

The lights went out. The epiphany was lost, swallowed in nothingness.

Trej was left with an inexplicable comprehension of the man's language.

The man stood up, dusted off his backside, and said, "You a troogil?"

"Uhhh. Yyyyyeassss," Trej said, surprised by his ability to speak this new language.

"You're tall, is what you are. Got a name?"

"Trej. It is ... Trej."

"Nah, I *hate* the names here. From now on, you're ... Daddy Long Legs."

"I do not like that name. My name is Trej."

"Oh come on, Daddy-O. It's nothing personal."

"How am I able to understand you?"

The man smirked. "Magic."

"I do not believe in magic."

"Maybe it's time you *start* believing."

"In magic?"

"In *me*." The man took another drag of his cigarette, held the smoke in a while, and then blew it out of the corner of his mouth.

"Who are you?" Trej said.

"I'm the savior of Akigol. Haven't you heard? The Messiah, with a capital 'M,' man. God's chosen."

"*My* people do not call this place Akigol, we call it Shemok—"

Leaves rustled behind the man. Trej looked over. Three akigos, one of them a P'Aanian, emerged from the woods.

They stopped and dropped the sticks they were carrying, wide eyed and slack-jawed.

The P'Aanian stepped forward. "Lord, that's a Giant of Mobo. Our people obliterated them many years ago for their sorcery."

"Shit, man. Doesn't look like you obliterated them to me."

"A few still live in the mountains, but they aren't long for this world. Be careful, Lord, their divinations are dangerous."

The man examined Trej. "That true? You *dangerous*?"

"They attacked us without provocation," Trej said defiantly, pointing at the akigos. "We would not worship their God. We developed power over elements like steam and electrici—"

"Whoa, what's that?" the man said. Trej's pistol was tucked in his belt. The man grabbed it. Trej tried to take it back, but the man jerked it away. "You're blind?"

"No. But I do not see as you do."

"You knew I was standing there in the dark with no trouble at all."

"Yes."

"That's wild, man." He held up the pistol. "Your people made this?"

Trej tried to grab it from him again, to no avail.

"Such precision." He examined it with an unsettling measure of familiarity. "Do you *all* have these?"

"Not yet."

"Are there bigger ones than this?"

"Much bigger."

The man glanced over at the akigos. Trej sensed a subdued alarm in the cadence of his speech as if he had a secret Trej was on the verge of exposing. The man stepped back, looked Trej up and down, and asked the akigos if all troogils were that defiant

"Yes, Lord. Most are worse, I'm sure. This one must be an

exile to be this far from the mountains. I've never seen one before."

"You shall not suffer a sorcerer to live," the man muttered with a dark smile and a slow nod. He flicked the cigarette into the river and held the pistol up. He pointed it at Trej and then tracked to the right looking down the barrel with one eye. He fired at a tree. The akigos dropped to the ground. The man laughed at them, doubled over, and dropped the pistol.

Trej ran.

They didn't bother to chase him. Trej supposed the man didn't care and the akigos were too confused. He climbed to the top of a tree to hide, spindly limbs blending into the branches. His thoughts were confused and full of knowledge that existed without context or applicability. He felt violated, but at the same time, couldn't escape the feeling that he was on the cusp of a grand revelation, like having a word on the tip of his tongue that he couldn't call to mind.

He would never outgrow it.

. ⫶⫶═╾•◦●▷◁●◦•╼═⫶⫶ .

After several years, Trej began to feel the call of home, as wanderers usually do, so he set off for the mountains of Mobo. It was about noon when he rounded the wintry top of the mountain that led to the observatory. As soon as he saw the observatory, he knew it was abandoned—snow covered the door, the windows were broken.

Down the hill, the rest of the village was in similar shape. He dropped his pack, crawled through a window in the tower, and slid down a snow embankment to the bottom. The library was damaged, but salvageable.

The skeletal remains of a troogil were splayed across a table, skull crushed by an akigi war hammer. The bones of a female were by the door, half buried in ice and mud. Some of the bookshelves were burned, nothing left of the books but scattered bits of ash and paper.

Trej fell to his knees and moaned, shaking his head. He fell asleep on the floor, clutching the tunic of the dead female.

He ran through the mountain stronghold, day after day, week after week. Everyone was dead. He fell into despair and fought back the madness.

As he collected the bodies of the dead, he discovered a pit that held the remnants of the guns. The akigi didn't carry them off, they destroyed them.

To what end? Trej wondered.

He remembered the man. Maybe he sent the akigi there to kill the troogils. Maybe he knew the weapons were a threat. Maybe he didn't want his followers equipped with such technological knowledge.

Every day, Trej tried to seize the elusive answers to the questions the man left him with. Every day, the grave called him to let it go.

But he couldn't let it go.

21

No one knew quite what to say to Trej's story. Nodi wanted to press him on his encounter with Tim—it was bizarre, almost anti-revelatory—but the horror of genocide left an awkward, untouchable spirit in the air.

Nodi, Aenna, and Mal sat in silence awhile, not looking at each other, least of all Trej.

Aenna bristled as she sipped her soup. Mal stared at the wall, swaying.

Nodi grabbed the bottle of ale and took a long drink. It burned his throat and tasted medicinal. He'd never drank before and wondered what all the fuss was about.

Aenna's face betrayed her outrage. Mal fell forward on the table, asleep.

"Would you like a cup?" Trej said.

Nodi considered Trej a moment and then Aenna. The room began to rock back and forth. He took another drink and then another until he grew so dizzy he fell out of the chair and onto the floor.

"That was strange," he heard Trej say before he passed

out.

Nodi dreamed his father was working in a clearing in the forests of Lore, helping a villager dig postholes for a hut. Nodol wore only a loincloth with sweat streaked tribal paint on his body. He didn't know Nodi was there. Aenna came out of the woods, dressed as a tribeswoman, and whispered in Nodol's ear. Nodol straightened his back and shook his head. Now he seemed to know Nodi was there, but wouldn't look at him. Aenna turned away, and as she did, she looked at Nodi, eyes full of spite, and ran down a path into the woods. At the end of the path was Tim—blue, shining, and out of focus. Tim watched her. Loved her. Received her. Together they put their backs to Nodi, looking at him only once to laugh like two lovers sharing a private joke.

Nodol continued digging, sweat dripping off his tentacles, back muscles flexing in the merciless suns.

"Dad?" Nodi said.

Nodol stopped, wedged his shovel in the ground, and leaned against the handle. He wiped the sweat from his brow, refusing to look back.

"No son of mine," he said and went back to work.

The ground shook and a fissure cut a rift between them. Nodol kept digging. Tim came out of the woods and rested a hand on his shoulder. Somehow, Nodi knew Tim and Aenna made love back there in the woods. The rift grew, the chasm filling with water. Time advanced—the hut completed, a village built, Aenna with child.

Nodi was on an island now. Nodol, Tim, and Aenna drifted away, growing smaller on the horizon until he could no longer see them across the gulf. The island dropped from beneath his feet. He plunged into dark waters and breathed in, felt the icy cold in his chest—

He sat up.

The room was dark except for the orange embers of the extinguished fire. Trej had made beds for them on the floor. Nodi's head swam. He plopped down and went back to sleep.

The next morning, Nodi's head hurt so bad he wasn't sure he could get up. His injured shoulder was tight but felt considerably better. Trej had fashioned a brace around it and treated it with some sort of herbal paste.

"I did not mean to wake you. You were groaning during the night. I made this brace for you. I think it will help."

"It does. Thank you." Nodi sat up slowly, blinking as if his eyes quit working in conjunction with one another. "I'm glad to have something other than placa root for it."

"Placa root? Foul stuff."

"I can't thank you enough for your help, Trej. You have no reason to help us. In fact, you have every reason to hate us. Your generosity humbles me."

"I am glad for the company. I made breakfast." He pointed at the table.

"I dreamed of an island," Nodi said.

"There are many of them beyond our shores." Trej stood up. "I have never been to any of them. Never cared for boats, much."

"Have you heard of a place called Hijoon?"

"Yes, but I do not know where it is. If you are going to Sigate, you are headed in the right direction, I think. Is that what you are looking for?"

"Yes, but we don't know where it is, either." Nodi tried to stand but decided that was a bad idea. He sat down with his back against the wall. The others were still asleep. He tried again and retrieved Mal's satchel, opened it, and gave Trej the letter. Trej took it to the head of the table and sat down. It was tiny in his hands. He laid it out and ran his long, thin fingers over it. "What is it?"

"Oh, right." Nodi sat down and read it to him.

"Where is the rest of it?"

"I can only assume it's still in the cave with Judas' body."

"Why are you so interested in this? Does it not pose a dilemma for you?"

"Maybe. But ... I *have* to know what it means. It's ..."

"Eating at you?"

"Yes."

"I know the feeling."

Nodi looked away. "My faith isn't what it used to be."

"Oh?"

"My father died. He was a missionary in Lore. I was visiting him on leave from my studies in Forwo. It was spring. I wandered off into the woods one afternoon and encountered a snarkliz. Do you know what that is?"

"No."

"Big. Bigger than *me*, at least, even on all fours. Leathery, purple exoskeleton with *huge* jowls. Freakishly huge. Teeth like daggers ... Dead eyes. Black, nothing eyes. It was the only one I'd ever seen—standing right there around the bend, growling. I think maybe I interrupted a hunt, maybe I was too close to its den, I don't know. I backed away, holding my hands out in front of me." He remembered something and nodded. "I smelled this flower, one the villagers prized for its curative properties. Very rare. Smelled like ... like honey and rotten fish, if you can imagine such a thing. It was just to my right and I remember wondering if I could snatch it. The snarkliz stepped toward me, though, and I forgot about the flower. I didn't know what to do. I tried to run back the way I came. It chased me, but I slid down an embankment and fell into a stream. Got carried off by the current a stone's throw until I planted my feet. I was so confused—flailing around. I just *knew* it was going to bite me at any moment, you know, like when someone is throwing rocks at you and you have that sense that at any second you're going to feel the crack against your skull. I turned and saw the monster jump the stream, heading toward the village."

Trej leaned back in his chair and rubbed his chin, considering Nodi's words.

"By the time I got back. The villagers were standing next to a shovel dad had been using. Its handle was broken, hellish tracks running up to it and beyond, swirls of dust drifting in the air, beams of sunlight cutting through them. They stared at me, shocked and horrified. One had blood on him, splashed across his chest. Dad was just … He was gone … I never saw him again. We found his bloody cloak down by the lake a day later and some …," Nodi turned away.

"Tragedy can be hard on faith."

"The thing is," Nodi said, turning back, "it wasn't so much the *tragedy* that caused me to question. Not directly, at least. I've always maintained that trials make us stronger, that they're a necessary part of spiritual growth, but he was killed by this thing, this horrible … thing … out of nowhere, and I can still see its uncaring, purposeless eyes and I just felt this overwhelming sense of—"

"Indifference?"

"Yes! That's it *exactly*. What happens, happens. No guiding hand. No plan. But that *can't* be right. If it is, all is for naught."

Trej leaned forward. "You fear that apart from God, his life had no meaning?"

"How *could* it? How can *any* of our lives have meaning? We'd be nothing but raindrops in an ocean. No … *No.*"

"The akigi faith was always a curiosity to us troogils. We never had a sense of the divine, I suppose, could never understand religious belief or why it was so important to your kind."

"Our beliefs make us better. Stronger. Gives us hope and inspiration."

"Maybe. Belief is a powerful thing to be certain. It can make one do things they would not normally do, for good or for bad. But that says nothing about the truth *behind* the belief."

"So what gives the life of a troogil meaning?"

"Ourselves. Our pursuits. Our communities. There is no need for meaning to come from outside ourselves. To want to mean something on the grandest of scales is vanity at its most profound." He held out his arm. "Is this not enough?"

Nodi looked at Aenna, then around at Trej's books, and back at Aenna. She was peaceful, tentacles splayed on the floor, breathing steadily. "I want to be with her forever. I want to see my dad again."

Trej raised his brows. "We are often caught between what we think *ought* to be and what is. The wider the gap between the two, the worse things are for us."

Trej went to a workbench and brought over a small stone cog. "Take this, Nodi. I want you to have it. Keep it as a symbol of our new-found friendship."

"What is it?"

"Just a cog. When I first returned here, the first body I found, an old friend of mine, in fact, held it in his hand. I do not know why. I kept it as a reminder. A memorial."

"I can't—"

"Please. You must. This cog has meant something to *me*, even if it has meant nothing to you. It is meaningful because I imbued it with meaning, but its meaning can be different for you. My symbol of tragedy is now your symbol of a meaningful interaction with a new friend. Is there anything anyone could do to make it any more or less significant? It is what it is."

Nodi smiled and ran his finger along the edge of it. "If this cog had fallen off God's throne and crashed to Akigol, it would be *much* more significant."

Trej laughed and patted Nodi on the back. "It would still just be a cog, Nodi."

Nodi nodded, paused, and nodded again with more conviction. "When I'm honest with myself. I have to admit I'm scared of what I might find if I continue looking. I don't doubt the existence of God, I'm just not sure Tim is his representative."

"What do you know of God, apart from Tim?"

Mal must have heard them talking because he got up and went to the table. He saw the letter lying there.

"Nodi was explaining your plight to me," Trej told him.

"Well, any help you can offer would be appreciated."

Trej nodded approvingly. "Wake Aenna. I made breakfast. We will eat and then I will help you get to Sigate. I will go with you. I miss the adventures of my youth. I am intrigued by your journey. Tim … *affected* me. I must know more."

───────── ⚹━◆⬤◆━⚹ ─────────

After breakfast, Nodi went outside to see their surroundings in the light of day. His breath was vapor in the fierce cold. He pulled one of Trej's giant blankets tight around his chest, walked around to the other side of the tower, and looked down the hill.

Round, gray buildings, precisely crafted, poked up through the snow. He thought about what it must have been like—troogils forging their machinations, chiseling stone, laughing, drinking. Now, other than the sound of the wind and crunching snow beneath his feet, the mountain was quiet. Cemetery quiet.

Down to the right, on a gentle slope between the two rock spires, the snow gave way to rows of graves that lie in the flower spotted tundra. Aenna came out and stood by Nodi as he surveyed it.

"It's awful," he said.

"It is."

They stared at it awhile. Akigi did this. Nodi felt an unspeakable shame.

Trej called them inside. Aenna went first, and Nodi followed a few moments later. When they went back into the observatory, the hatch in the bottom of the floor was open. Trej was climbing down as Mal stuffed one of the huge bottles of ale into his satchel. The sight of the ale made Nodi nauseous.

"Thirsty?" Aenna said with narrowed eyes.

"Not in the least."

"Get your things and come on," Trej said from the cavity beneath the floor. "Last one, close the hatch behind you."

22

Nodi closed the hatch and proceeded down a winding staircase that seemed as if it would never end, hopping from stair to stair because his legs were too short. A sharp echo announced each landing. It was dimly lit, but he could see the silhouettes of the others circling the bends in front of him.

Finally, level ground.

A passageway extended before him. The sounds of rushing water, clanking machinery, and bellowing steam got louder as he approached, the source of the surface humming, he surmised.

The passageway ended at a walkway that spiraled down around the perimeter of a spacious cavity. High above them, a fissure exposed greenish-blue sky. The edges of it dripped with snow melting in the mid-morning suns. A waterfall cascaded out of an orifice and crashed onto a water wheel that turned metal gears and pulleys below. Everything moved, creaked, and clanked, steam spurting out of pipes that jutted out at sharp angles. Wires corkscrewed from the machines and spilled out in every direction along the walls, purr of electricity surging through them.

"It's magnificent!" Mal said, raising his voice above the waterfall.

"It *was*." Trej said. "I have kept this small part of our home running all these years."

"*Small* part?" Aenna said.

"Oh, yes. There is a labyrinth of places like this throughout the mountain range. Far too much for me to maintain alone. Many parts are inaccessible now, fallen into ruin."

"Why did you bring us down here?" Nodi said.

"We can travel the network of caves all the way to the Whistling Forest just outside of Sigate."

"And you're sure *that* route hasn't fallen into ruin?"

"No."

"And if it has?"

"That will be inconvenient."

It didn't matter. Nodi wasn't in a hurry. Aenna was safe. That was what was important.

The rock face had dwellings hewn into it all the way down. Nodi felt like a youngling in this giant's underground abode. Each living space looked inhabited though they'd been deserted for over two hundred years. Tables had place settings, old bones upon the plates, unmade beds sat dusty and broken, Braille books lie open on floors, pages desecrated by the erosion of time.

The water spilled into the bottom of the cavity, a cool mist rolling off it and leaving beads of water everywhere. They hopped a muddy puddle at the foot of an elevated generator and Trej slid a door open on the other side. They went through the adjoining tunnel. It led to even more cavities and pathways that wove through every part of the hive. Trej started the machinery and turned on the lights as they went, tinkering with machines that were stuck or otherwise incapacitated. If the machinery wouldn't start, they held hands as he led them through the dark, making guttural clicking noises in areas where the humming was too faint. Eventually, none of the machines worked and then, further ahead, there were no machines at all, just velvety darkness. Many of the tunnels had collapsed and left little space for Trej to stand upright, but he was adept at contorting his arms and legs in ways that allowed him to traverse low ceilings and tight spaces with ease. He was made for this environment and guided them through it, reassuring them with his voice and pulling them along by the hands. They ate small portions of dried vegetables Trej brought with them, a tiresome but nutritious diet.

Nodi didn't know day from night, but it seemed they had been down there for about three days. At one point, they found a cache of old wood and Trej used it to build a fire in a cavity with a through draft. The light hurt their eyes at first but was a welcome sight when they adjusted. He made a small, unappetizing meal out of cave shrooms and fetched them some water. A steady breeze passed over them and Nodi thought he smelled rain, though no daylight was visible anywhere.

"We're lost, aren't we?" Aenna said, chewing a shroom.

"No," Trej said.

They finished the meal in silence, slept, and then continued.

Everything was dead, the caves unstable. Many pathways were impassable, obstructed by rock and debris. Mal made torches out of wood they had left over from the fire. Eventually, they reached a place where everything had caved in leaving nothing but a steep drop into the inky black below. They lowered their torches down as far as they could, but it was no help.

"What now?" Mal said.

"I do not know. It has collapsed since I was last here." Trej made his clicking sounds and inspected the drop. "Perfectly smooth, no climbing possible. There is a pool of water and an adjacent cave down there."

They heard a *swoosh* of water, but Trej wasn't sure where it came from. An updraft blew out of the darkness. It smelled like wet clay.

"What was that?" Mal said.

"Probably a steam pocket. They spurt out from the hot core beneath us from time to time. I have seen them in the deeper regions. It is nothing to worry about."

Aenna craned her neck out and looked down. "How deep is the water?"

Trej made a series of clicking sounds and noted how long they took to echo back up. "Deep enough. There is dry ground down there, too."

Mal tossed his torch. It landed next to a stream and painted a murky view of what was down there. Firelight rippled on the water to one side of the torch. To the other, the mouth of another cave sat black and hungry.

"Isn't there another way, Trej?" Aenna said.

"That would mean a *lot* of backtracking. We are already quite close to getting out of the mountains."

As they stood looking down, Mal tossed his satchel to Nodi and jumped. He sank below the surface and the splash of water put the torch out. The red glow of his tattoos faded into the murk and disappeared. They waited. And waited. After a long, breathless moment, his red glow reappeared just under the surface, getting brighter.

"Woooo, it's cold down here!" Mal yelled when he surfaced.

Nodi sighed in relief.

"I suppose it is okay," Trej said. "Who is next?"

"Be our guest." Nodi invited him over the precipice by sweeping his torch toward it.

Trej hopped off. His slender body fell like a spear.

"Will your shoulder be okay?" Aenna said to Nodi. "Can you swim?"

"I'll be fine. Do you want me to go first?"

"No—"

They heard another loud *whoosh* of water. This time, they realized what it was. A horizontal geyser.

"Mal? Trej!"

Silence was the only response. Nodi tossed the last torch down to see if they could tell what happened. All they could see was the violent ripples on the water that receded into darkness.

"What happened?"

Nodi dropped to his knees and peered down. "I don't know."

"What do we do?"

"I say we jump and get out of the water as fast as we can. We can't go back without Trej. The terrain is too rough and it's too dark."

"Do you think they're … you know …"

"I hope not."

Neither of them was anxious to take the leap. As they procrastinated, the geyser fired off again and subsided.

"This is our chance," Nodi said.

Aenna jumped.

"Aenna!"

He was relieved when he saw her silhouette crawl out of the water in the dim orange below and pick up the torch.

"There's no sign of them," she called up. "I think they were swept downstream. It's too dark, I can't see. *Mal? Trej?*" Her voice echoed, but there was no reply.

"You should have waited for me!"

"You're going to need my help to get out, there's a current and you won't be able to swim very well."

"I'll jump as soon as the geyser goes off again."

When it was clear, he jumped, eyes closed, yelping. The water was piercingly cold and he thought he might pass out. Aenna pulled him over with one hand and struggled to fish him out just before the geyser triggered again. They stood shivering in the fading torchlight, water dripping from their tentacles, feet sinking in the wet sand. Still no sign of Mal or Trej.

"The satchel!" Nodi said. "I forgot Mal's satchel. I left it up there. It had the letter in it."

"Then it's gone." Aenna placed her hands on the sides of his face, orange light flickering. His eyes were pools of glinting black. "This is a sign," she said. "We've lost the pagans *and* that stupid letter. It's time to turn ourselves in. End this nightmare. A genuine effort to make it right might be credited to us. They might be lenient. Everything is possible with God, Nodi."

The torch faded in the damp mud. Aenna tried to keep it burning to no avail and everything went dark. They grasped shaky hands. Nodi led, feeling for the cave wall until he made contact and followed it through.

They fumbled in the dark as if wearing velvet blindfolds, shuffling their feet forward to find rocks, obstructions, drop-offs. They followed the cave around several bends and fell many times before they saw a sickly green glow ahead.

The glow emanated from phosphorescent moss that grew on the walls and ceilings of the tunnel. They followed the dim light until stumbling into the biggest cavity they'd yet encountered.

The gleaming moss-covered ruins of an ancient temple stood in the middle, foundation broken, walls crumbling, left side buried under rubble. Old stone pews sat in rows, some overturned, others cracked in half. Great swooping columns curved in and out like horns and kissed the vaulted ceiling.

"Have you ever seen anything like this?" Aenna said.

"No."

They walked up a set of stairs that led to the middle of the structure where there stood a statue of an akigo on his knees, arms raised. It was smooth like marble with one hand broken off and half its face worn away. An inscription in an ancient form of Selidinese was at the base of it.

"What's it say?"

Nodi analyzed it. "All to Bula, Goddess of Akigol."

"This is a temple to Bula?"

"From before the time of Tim."

Nodi spotted the altar on the other side and went over to it. The creation account was inscribed on its surface, a well-known passage, but as he read it, he found it absurd in a way he'd never noticed. Though Timians rejected the pagan Goddess Bula, remnants of that old religion seeped into their theology, creation included. Tim never explained the existence of life, its diversity, or by what means God created it.

Nodi imagined worshippers, every bit as devoted as he'd always been, praising Bula there. He wondered what scribe had carved the lettering into the altar, what ancient prophecies they preached in that hall, what desperate prayers were offered in its benches. He imagined its dwindling numbers as the years passed until the elements reclaimed what was rightfully theirs to begin with.

He drew his finger through the dust on the altar. "How many Gods have there been? How many lie dead in ruined temples like this?"

"Only the ones that never existed in the first place," Aenna said.

Mal struggled to breathe, taking quick gasps of air every time his face emerged from the rapids. Trej was near and thrashing.

Mal wouldn't admit it later, but he prayed for a miracle. He felt like he'd been caught in the current for an eternity, but he didn't *really* know how long it took. Eventually, he slowed down enough to hold his head above water so he could see where he was going. A hole was ahead, daylight beyond it. He was about to go over a waterfall. He drifted faster and faster until swallowed by warm sunlight. In a dizzying twist and tumble, he fell back first into the river.

He paddled madly toward the shore until he could climb up on the muddy bank. Trej was indeed alive and followed behind. They convulsed and heaved water out of their lungs and then took great, panicked breaths. Trej got up first and pulled Mal to his feet. Mal looked up at him as if they'd just witnessed a real live miracle.

They turned to walk up the embankment and just before Mal gave thanks to God for rescuing them, he realized they were standing at the edge of an encampment.

None of the akigi standing there looked happy to see them.

The Akigi Bible

The Creation of Akigol (Akigi Old Testament), 1:1-18

1 In the beginning, Bula created Akigol and the heavens above it. ² The waters were not created by Bula, but spilled from the great beast, Duvoi, who was smote by Bula. ³ Duvoi was smote by Bula when he attempted to hit her with a rock and steal her tunic.

⁴ After cutting Duvoi in half and spilling the waters from inside him into the seas, Bula took the lower half of Duvoi and formed the great islands by sprinkling the pieces over the waters.

⁵ Then Bula took the upper half of Duvoi, stretched him from expanse to expanse beneath the light of heaven and punched holes through his flesh so the light of heaven would shine through. ⁶ This is how Bula made the stars.

⁷ Then Bula used the right eye of Duvoi to make the suns and the left eye to make the great moon. ⁸ The smaller moons were formed from the seeds of Duvoi's loins as a reminder that Duvoi still had a presence in the world.

⁹ Then Bula took the two inner testicles of Duvoi and created beasts of the field, and flying things, and swimming things ¹⁰ and from the two outer testicles, she caused all growing things to spring forth.

¹¹ Bula saw that it was good.

[12] But Bula was sad that none of the creatures she made were able to speak to her, going about their lives without acknowledging her at all. [13] So Bula decided to make the first akigo from what remained of Duvoi's genitalia.

[14] Now, Bula saw that it was good and liked the akigo, but saw that he was small and needed a protector, [15] so Bula put the akigo to sleep and fashioned an akiga from a piece of the genitalia of the akigo. [16] Then Bula said, "She is truly worthy to protect the akigo," and thus were they created, female and male to rule over Akigol.

[17] To this very day, the genitalia of the akigo is half its original size as a sign that the akiga was created from the genitalia of the akigo. [18] And the akiga saw that the genitalia was small and the akigo was not ashamed.

The Gospel According to Hinnoben the First, Chapter 5:6-16

[6] Tim held out the fire talisman in His right hand and burned them until they were dead. [7] When the akigi of Mo saw this, they marveled at His power and knew that He was the Messiah [8] because He had the very power of death in His hands.

[9] And speaking to those who were still alive, He said to them, "If you doubt that I have been sent by God, you shall surely know His wrath."

[10] And then He told them a parable saying, "A Shepard was working in the fields one day and called out to his tamed furry beasts. [11] All but one of the beasts knew his voice and followed him. [12] But for the one beast that did not follow, the Sheppard killed him and ate him.

[13] And so it is with God. Those who know God will recognize His voice through Me and follow My word, but those who do not shall be consumed by fire."

[14] Those who heard these things trusted Tim from then on, but a small group of them ate the akigi that Tim had burned.

[15] But the Most Holy Lord didn't say to eat the dead akigi, but was telling the parable of the tamed furry beast. [16] Even today, the heresy of cannibalism occurs because they didn't understand Tim when he spoke to them.

23

Nodi woke up from what he hoped was a nightmare, only to see the glowing moss-covered ceiling above him. Aenna was asleep on the floor to his right.

He climbed up a broken column to see if he could spot a way out. As he scanned the ghostly ruins, he noticed an archway that framed a black hole on the far side of the chamber. He hopped down and ran over. The ceiling had collapsed beyond the archway, but in the midst of the dark, a small sliver of daylight shone like an oasis in the desert. Nodi tried to peer out of it, but couldn't see anything but pale light. He placed his fingers over the crack and felt a draft. Sweet, fresh air.

He felt for the seams between the rocks and pushed forward until one of the stones tumbled forward. A bolt of light burned his eyes.

"Aenna!" he called out. "Aenna, come quick!"

"Nodi?" She said, groggily.

"Here." He ran back to signal her over.

"What is it?"

"I found a way out!"

She ran over to see for herself. "Praise God!"

They shoved out enough stones to squeeze through the opening and tumble into a patch of weeds on the other side.

They looked up at the sky and breathed it in, basking in the light. Their eyes were still adjusting. It was overcast, but they might as well have been staring directly into the suns.

Nodi brushed the dust off his clothes and turned back to see where they'd come from. There weren't any distinguishing marks on the entrance except for a couple of half-buried stones with illegible engravings on them. It stood at the bottom of a flat wall of rock that stretched as far as they could see in both directions. At their feet, a grassy hill met the red, billowing trees of the Whistling Forest below. A spec of civilization was beyond it—Sigate sitting before the Gray Sea that reached out to a storm that never came.

"I'd hoped to never go back," Aenna said looking at Sigate.

"I know. I'm sorry."

"We should turn ourselves in. I might know some people there."

"I can't do that, Aenna. I'm sorry. I've come too far."

She looked away. "So what are you going to do now?"

"I don't know. I assumed Mal had some sort of plan. Without him—"

"That's what misplaced trust leads to," she said with an arrogance that irked him.

"I have to find out who discovered the letter. The temple apostle in Sigate should know who found it since he's the one that sent it to Prontis."

Nodi scanned the distant beach. *Where would Judas have fallen? Swam ashore? Somewhere out there, an island might hold the key, but where is it, and how will I get there?* He'd heard legends about the sea to the northwest—rumors that the very edge of

Akigol was out there. It filled him with curious terror. That sea didn't just hold the end of the world, but the very fringes of akigi knowledge.

Aenna sighed, grabbed his arm, and nudged him down the hill. Her eyes were downcast and unfocused. Nodi sensed that she was tempted to tell him something she knew she shouldn't.

"Listen," she said, deeply conflicted. "I never told you this, but … I *may* know the general location of Hijoon."

Nodi stopped. "What? *How?*"

She held up her hand to calm him. "When I was stationed in Sigate … there was a group, the group involved in the riots—"

"Stilla's revolutionaries?"

"Yes. They used tunnels south of Sigate to smuggle dissenters out of the city. The rumor was that Stilla found a way into Hijoon and when she explored it, discovered there had once been *many* ways in. She kept the entrances a secret. No one knows why she was so protective of it. Obviously, I never went there myself, but I know where it is … generally."

"Why are you just now telling me this? I never heard anything about akigi being smuggled out of Sigate."

"That's why Stilla was arrested. She helped the Dissenters Guild by providing safe passage for the underground. She was something of a folk hero. The riots broke out when they arrested her and condemned her to death."

"Why isn't the location of Hijoon common knowledge? How do *you* know what no one else does?"

Aenna hung her head. "I was helping her."

"*What?* You took part in that rebellion? You went against the temple? Against the crown? What I did was *nothing* compared to that—"

"You weren't there! They were killing indiscriminately in the name of justice—in the name of the *Lord*—execution

after execution, day after day. I thought Stilla was saving lives
… but …"

"*What?*"

She sat down on a rock. "She approached me one evening
on the beach outside of town. I was upset over a particularly
unjust execution. The prefect over Sigate was insane,
bloodthirsty. Next to him, Stilla seemed like a saint. I wasn't
going to help her, I told her no, but she asked me to think it
over and meet her back there the next night if I'd
reconsidered. That night, I had a dream. I was standing guard
over a condemned akigo who was bent over, waiting for the
ax. The prefect was there, leering like a pervert, and just
before the ax fell, time stopped. Tim appeared to me, Nodi.
There was such stern power in his eyes. He said, '*Do
something.*' So I did. For over a year, I gave Stilla information
about our raids, our movements, our warrant lists. I was
terrified the morning she was arrested because I thought
she'd turn me in, but she never had a chance. The riots broke
out … she was killed … and that was that."

Nodi knew there was more. "*And?*"

"And no one heard or saw from anyone she helped again.
I know in my hearts that something bad happened to them.
That Stilla was responsible for it. And *I* helped her."

"You thought you were doing what was right. What you
believed God *wanted* you to do. That's what I'm doing. That's
all any of us can do."

"I was wrong, Nodi! I was *wrong*. Just as you are now." She
stood up. "I don't want to fight."

"Neither do I."

The sky grew darker, the wind picked up.

"We should head for the tree line." She put her hand in
the small of his back to lead him down.

They went into the Whistling Forest as a gentle rain began
to fall. The trees had knotholes along the higher segments of

their ivory trunks that emitted flute-like tones in the wind. The harder the wind blew the louder and more varied the notes were. The shake and jitter of the red leaves in the canopy rustled like paper tambourines. Pokreys, small creatures with fire orange fur, jumped from tree to tree, digging nectar out of the holes as they went. Aenna watched them compete for it in exaggerated displays of aggression.

Nodi found a dirt pathway that led to Sigate, or at least in its general direction. "Should we follow it?"

The rain picked up, the trees shook harder and whistled louder. Drops of water fell through the canopy and tapped on the dead leaves below.

"We might as well. All paths lead somewhere, right?"

"But is it somewhere good or somewhere bad?" He looked back and forth several times. "Let's follow it."

They stayed on the winding, narrow path and it took them to a small commune of shoddy tents and wood shacks. They decided to avoid it and cut through the woods, but when they turned to leave the path, they saw an old P'Aanian standing in a clearing, watching them. He was hunched over in a tattered beige robe, clutching a walking stick.

"Who are you?" he said.

"Ehhh, we seem to be a bit lost," Nodi replied.

"Well, we're all *found* out here," the akigo said. The tips of his tentacles were graying, his blue flesh paper-thin. "What is it you're looking for?"

"Hijoon. But we'll settle for Sigate."

"Hijoon? No one knows where Hijoon is and Sigate is a den of immorality. Even the temple can be bought there. What is it you want with either of those places?"

"We should go," Aenna said, pulling Nodi's arm. "We'll find it ourselves, thanks."

"Would you like something to eat?"

Aenna's eyes begged Nodi to walk away. "No," he said.

"Thank you, though."

The akigo lowered his shoulders and hung his head as if this rejection took a severe emotional toll on him.

Nodi turned back. "Are you alright?"

"Oh, I suppose I'm a bit lonely, is all. Everyone went hunting three days ago."

Nodi looked at Aenna again. She gave him a reserved nod. "Well, maybe just a bite. We'd hate to be an imposition."

The akigo perked up. "No imposition. I'd be remiss in my duties to the Lord if I didn't offer you help. Name's Fyzel."

They followed Fyzel into camp. The tents were full of multi-colored patches, sewn together from old garments. They billowed and shook in the wind. The shacks behind them were so feeble, they looked like they could fall at the slightest touch. It certainly wasn't a permanent settlement.

The rain was subsiding.

Nodi and Aenna sat around a fire as Fyzel cut meat from a spit and dished boiled regaaba root out of a pot. He handed them wood plates, meat still steaming.

"Thank you," Nodi said. "I wish I could offer you payment, but we have nothing."

"I wouldn't accept it if you did."

Nodi smiled at Fyzel and gave him a half nod. He took an exploratory nibble at the meat.

"It's good!" he said to Aenna.

She picked a little off and ate as well.

"Are you Timians?" Fyzel asked.

"Yes," Aenna said. Nodi pretended not to hear the question.

Fyzel considered them carefully, rubbing his chin. His odd disposition made them uncomfortable. "What're your thoughts on the Gospel of Hinnoben, Chapter five, verses fifteen and sixteen?"

Nodi and Aenna stopped chewing.

Fyzel referred to a controversial passage about cannibalism. Chapter 5 verses 15 and 16 explicitly condemned the practice, but small, fierce factions of Timians insisted those verses were forgeries added by scribes trying to make the text more palatable. The evidence they cited was that the passage used an unusual title for Tim, referring to him as "Most Holy Lord," and that it was the only place in the English text where conjunctions were used. As a result, they concluded that *all* sinners should be field dressed and eaten. Usually, these communities erupted into squabbles over the definition of sin and then devolved into a grotesque buffet that only left one or two standing.

Nodi stared at Fyzel, mouth full, scared to swallow.

"Oh, don't worry, it's not akigo," Fyzel said, chuckling.

Aenna relaxed. "Thank God."

Fyzel smirked. "It's ixaquoi."

Nodi grabbed Aenna by the arm, pulled her up, and they ran like hell, spitting the meat out along the way.

Some of Fyzel's friends appeared down the path. Fyzel called out to them and they broke into a sprint. Nodi and Aenna turned right and wove in and out of the trees. The smacks of mud under their feet gave them up wherever they went. They tried to double back, but the pursuers were too fast. As they cut around a dead tree trunk, the cannibals tackled them and held them down. Nodi fought, bowing his back, but they were too strong. Aenna kicked one in the face, but that only earned her a punch in the gut. Soon, they were tied up and unable to move.

The cannibals dragged them by their feet back to camp, leaving their tentacles caked with mud and wet leaves. Nodi watched the treetops sway in the breeze as his body cut a shallow groove in the forest floor. Water dripped in his eyes, his head pounded. Once they were back at the encampment, Fyzel tied them to stakes and took some exploratory pokes in search of prime chunks of meat.

"What sin have we committed that you think you're justified in this?" Nodi's voice betrayed his terror.

"An akigo alone in the woods with an akiga?" Fyzel said. "Something immoral had to 'ev been going on out there. And you're headed for Sigate. There are *none* righteous in Sigate. Why go to such a place?"

Nodi struggled to break free of his binds, but it was futile.

Fyzel sharpened his blade.

All Aenna could do was whisper, "please don't do this," over and over.

The Gospel According to Hinnoben the First, 3:21-40

[21] And then the apostles said, "Please tell us, Lord, what is it like in heaven?"

[22] Tim answered and said to them, "Heaven is the place where you get to do all the things you are forbidden to do here. [23] You will have a stable of akigas for your pleasure and you may be greedy and materialistic [24] and walk naked through your great and majestic mansions on streets paved with jewels under skies that never go dark and are always pretty. [25] All those things that your hearts want, but God forbids in this world, will be given unto you in the next."

[26] The apostles said to him, "But Teacher, if this is so, why does God forbid these things here? Could He not allow us all of these things in this world?"

[27] Tim replied saying, "But then you would have nothing to look forward to. [28] And besides, do you not want evil doers weeded out before you get there? [29] That is what this life is about—separating the righteous from the wicked.

[30] "And know that a great and eternal torment awaits those who disobey Me. [31] The homosexual akigi shall be imprisoned with the heterosexual akigi, [32] masochist with masochist, sadist with sadist, murderer with murderer, cannibal with wild furry beast, [33] and their desires shall never be quenched and their prisons shall be very hot, boiling the flesh, but the flesh shall never peel off, [34] and twice a day they

shall be stabbed in the eyes with hot pokers, and their genitals will be mutilated and grow back every day only to be mutilated again, [35] and the hungry shall be fed, but they shall never get full, and their entrails will burst from their bodies and crawl back in over and over for eternity. [36] For as long as the faithful shall be in heaven, the faithless shall be in hell."

[37] But the apostles said to Him, "But Lord, why must the penalty be so severe?"

[38] And He responded saying, "How else will you be motivated to do My will?"

[39] When the apostles heard this they began praising Him and went out to tell the akigi of the pleasures of heaven, but mostly they told them of the horrors of hell. [40] All the akigi were frightened and did all that Tim asked of them.

24

It was evening and the bindings had rubbed Mal's wrists raw by the time the soldiers marched him and Trej into Sigate's military compound. It was a filthy place with a stone wall around the perimeter that was a few heads taller than Trej. Six wire holding pens were in the middle, filled with destitute prisoners, and heavier duty cells were at the back, as tall as the outside wall and made of concrete.

Persecutor Shirka was waiting at the entrance when they got there. She followed them to the back of the compound and stopped them in front of the farthest cell back. Everyone who saw Trej stared, gape-mouthed. They'd never actually seen a troogil before. Ropes were tied around his neck and the soldiers kept it taut, close to strangling him. Shirka measured Mal with her eyes, holding his dagger. She looked at it, saw it was military issue, and slipped it in her belt.

She looked up at Trej. "How many of you are still in the mountains?"

"Thousands," Trej said. "If you count the dead among the living."

She circled him and kicked him on the back of his knees so that they buckled. It brought him down, but he was still taller. "Where's the letter? The scribe? His companion?"

"We do not know. We were separated."

She turned to Mal and surveyed him feet to face. "You're all spectacle. No substance. You wreak havoc without regard for the destruction you leave in your wake."

"Without regard for it? Hell, the destruction is the whole point!"

She punched him in the stomach and when he doubled over, kneed him in the nose. Blood spooled onto the ground.

He laughed.

"You find it *funny?*" She pulled out his dagger but stayed her hand. "This trouble your friends are in is because of *you*. The scribe had his hand in it, I know, but he didn't mean any harm. His actions weren't premeditated or malicious. Not at first, at least. But *you* ... you knew *exactly* what you were doing. You deserve every bit of torment you've got coming. In this world ... and the *next*."

She turned to the guards standing by. "Hold him." They each grabbed an arm while a third put him in a chokehold.

She cut him across the side of his abdomen four times in fast succession and then cut across them in a checker pattern. They weren't deep cuts, but it burned fiercely. As he grimaced, she flipped the knife and hit him between the eyes with the hilt. His vision blurred, all color washed out for a moment.

"The Dissenters Guild will be irrelevant soon, Mal ... *the Dissenter*. Its influence is dwindling, buoyed only by the silly antics of you and others like you."

Mal spat at her. She backhanded him across the face. The guards had trouble keeping him upright.

"Where's the letter?"

"Trej already told you. We don't know. Doesn't matter, anyway. It's the *content* of it that's important."

"That's true. That's why we must not only destroy the letter but the *minds* that carry its content—"

A panic-stricken guard rode into the compound on a runner, a cloud of dust billowing in front of her when she stopped. She looked down at Shirka, breathing heavy.

"*Well?*" Shirka said.

"Cannibals attacked an ixaquoi caravan this morning. We tracked them to the Whistling Forest, not far from where these two were found."

"We can't risk letting them capture that scribe," Shirka said. She turned to the guards. "Lock these two in a cell."

As Shirka mounted her runner, the guards opened the only cell that wasn't already full. They dragged Trej down to fit him through the door and shoved Mal in behind him.

The door slammed shut and the locking rod slipped into place with a resounding echo. The floor was cobblestone, the walls made of thick timber, roof reinforced thatch. The thatch was frayed in the back corner, water dripping through it from the storm earlier that day. It was too high for Mal to reach, but Trej could reach it on his tiptoes if he weren't tied up. The bindings around their hands were twisted around their fingers, clenching them together so that they couldn't untie each other. The rope around Trej's throat was still firmly in place.

They were alone, except for a small, purple akiga sitting on the floor in the back, muttering. Mal tried to hear what she was saying, but couldn't.

"If we could get our hands free, you could pull the roofin' down a bit and pop out over the top," Mal said.

Trej chirped, faced that direction, and nodded. "So it would seem."

Mal waddled over to the akiga. She stopped muttering and locked wary eyes on him. She was badly beaten, dried blood caked around her nose. She was pitiable.

"I won't hurt you," Mal said. "What's your name?"

"Isu." She looked at Trej, nodded, and said, "Big."

"Oh, yes. He is. His name's Trej and I'm Mal. We're prisoners here like you. I noticed your hands aren't bound. Could you free us?"

She shook her head. "Beatings."

"No, I won't beat you."

She shook her head again.

"I think she is trying to say that she is afraid of the guards," Trej said.

"Papa," she said.

Mal leaned against the wall. "She's mad."

"I am surprised they have not exorcised her yet," Trej said with disdain.

"Skeleton," she said and then a string of words, seemingly disassociated from context, peppered with nods and head shakes. "Cave ... no ... beatings ... death ... missing ... dinner ... letter."

Mal perked up when he heard her mention a letter. It suddenly occurred to them why Shirka might keep one such as her in solitary confinement. "Letter? Did you say something about a letter?"

Isu nodded.

"Did you give it to an apostle?"

She nodded again.

"Isu, if we can get you out of here, could you take us to the skeleton?"

"Aye."

"We can help you, but you have to untie us. Can you do that?"

"Beatings," Isu said, shaking her head and recoiling her arms and legs.

Mal sighed and slid to the floor, back against the wall. "She's stubborn."

"What do you think happened to the others?" Trej said.

"Don't know."

"The geyser was new, brought on by a quake, I suppose. I had not been down that far in probably a hundred years. If they made the jump and got out of the water fast enough, there was only one place for them to come out at ... I think."

"I can't get over the fact that we survived that waterfall," Mal said. "It's somethin' of a *miracle*." The scope of it seemed to dawn on him. "What are the chances that letter would end up in *Nodi's* hands, or that I would overhear his conversation in Relovo's that night, or that I would be able to retrieve the letter, or that Tim would collapse in front of Nodi, the very scribe I'd need to help translate it ... and ... and what are the chances we'd get put in the cell with the very akiga that found the letter to begin with? ... I don't know ... Maybe Nodi's right. Maybe it's all bein' orchestrated from on high."

"Nonsense," Trej said. "Everyone is so quick to use the word 'miracle' in place of anything that is *'improbable'* or merely *'unexamined.'* Do not be lulled into sleep, Mal. There are no miracles as far as I can tell. The very nature of a miracle has within its exclusive purview that which has no explanation and *cannot* have an explanation beyond what defies the natural order of things. Let us not label such a lowly thing as 'ignorance' with so high a word as 'miracle.' We survived the waterfall by chance. *All* these other events are interrelated matters of cause and effect."

"Ehh. You're probably right." He wiggled up and down to try and get comfortable, but couldn't. "Speakin' of cause and effect, the night I stole the letter, I beat the hell out of Tim's sarcophagus. I think that's why he collapsed. Nodi doesn't know that ..." He rested his head against the wall.

"Why are you telling me this?"

"I don't know. I feel bad about it. Not that I care about Tim, but his collapse *affected* Nodi, I think. He read too much into it." Mal sat in silence awhile. "Why did you come with us, Trej?"

"Tim left me with questions. Questions I would like answers to. And Nodi is a kindred spirit. I sense a difficult road ahead of him, a road I myself have traversed. Maybe I can help him, maybe not." He took a deep breath. "Also, I do not trust *you*."

"Few do," Mal said. "What is it about me that *you*, in particular, don't trust?"

"You do what you do *for* you and you do it under the guise of a 'greater good.' It is like you are blind, swinging wildly at an enemy you do not even understand."

Mal sat there with his head against the wall, yellow eyes trained on the ceiling. "When I was a younglin' back on Gologa, I'd go to the Timian mission down the street 'cause they'd give out free snacks if you sat through their spiel about the lord and such. I didn't have anythin' better to do, so I'd endure it—the snacks were pretty good. But the missionaries got to where they wanted to put us to work, makin' tracts out of berry juice and banso leaves to hand out around the village. Now listenin' to a bunch of religious nonsense was one thing, but I'd be damned if I was goin' to help them spread their crazy. They wanted us to write 'Tim saves' on the leaves with a little stick figure of his holiness takin' a lowly ixaquoi sinner by the hand. Wanted us to pass them out door to door. Well, it's an amusin' fact that in Gologan, the only difference between the word for 'saves' and 'fondles' is just a small jot above the last letter. I talked everyone into leavin' that jot off—we did a few correctly for the tops of the stacks so the missionaries wouldn't notice, y'know—then we adjusted the drawin' so that Tim's hand was shootin' a bit low if you know what I mean. Up to that point, no one in Gologa took the Timians too serious … but they took them serious after that! Took weeks for them to convince the rest of the town they weren't there on a mission of mass molestation."

Trej's ears twitched, one brow raised. "I do not understand your point."

"Yeah," Mal said. "There isn't one."

Trej dismissed it and stood up.

"Isu," he said.

She turned her body sideways against the wall as if she might be able to melt into it.

He towered over her, focused on her fragile frame with his unseeing eyes. She looked up at him in awe.

"Isu, be a dear and untie me, please."

She stood up and complied without protest.

"Ah," Trej said to Mal, extending his arms. "You just have to ask nicely."

"Doesn't hurt, she's crazy," Mal mumbled.

Trej tried to free Mal, but his hands were too big to achieve a solid grip on the tiny rope. Isu helped him. Mal stood up and rubbed his tender wrists.

"Shiny," Isu said of his tattoos.

"Yes," Trej said. "He is very shiny."

Trej quietly punched through the damaged thatch, pulling debris down on top of himself. When he'd made a hole big enough, he grabbed the edge of the wall, pulled himself up to have a look, and dropped back down.

"It is clear. It is dark," he said. "We must be quiet."

In a show of reverent comprehension, Isu remained silent, nodding like a scared youngling.

With Trej's help, they climbed out of the cell and over the equally high perimeter fence.

When they were free, they ran into the woods until a safe distance away. The air smelled like the sea and they could hear the faint sound of crashing waves. It was night and the moons shone brightly above the aurora. Down the hill, the torches of patrolling soldiers flickered through the trees without haste.

Trej considered Mal. "Shall we go without Nodi and Aenna?"

"What else *can* we do? We're all lookin' for the same place. Maybe they've found their own way."

Trej was hesitant but looked down at Isu. "Will you help us find the cave where you found the letter?"

"Aye," she said.

25

N odi spent the night tied to a post, Aenna to the right of him. They stayed deathly quiet under the watchful eye of the cannibals who rotated guard duties every few hours. The horror was surreal—a pit of the stomach, raw ache at the thought of what would happen at dawn.

The cannibals were late sleepers, but little by little, they emerged from their tents, stretching and yawning. Fyzel sat on a stool, sharpening his knives while another stoked the fire. Some of them sang hymns, off key and off beat.

Nodi couldn't take his eyes off those knives. "Who are you to judge us?"

Fyzel stopped and pointed a blade at him. "You all say the same thing. Who are *we*? We are God's chosen, that's who *we* are."

"Aren't we all," Nodi muttered bitterly.

When the fire was hot and bright, Fyzel approached with the knife at his side. He stopped before them to offer a prayer of thanksgiving.

"Bless us, oh Lord," he said, "and these your gifts which we are about to receive from your bounty through Tim, our Savior. We consume these sinners, ingesting their darkness so that it might be extinguished by the light that burns within us. Amen."

Nodi had blessed many dinners, but he never imagined being the entrée over which such a prayer would be offered. He recoiled and clenched his eyes shut, waiting for the first cut.

Aenna writhed and shouted, "Leave him alone!"

Fyzel turned on her and ran the knife through the right side of her chest. Her stomach muscles convulsed, she would have doubled over if it weren't for the bindings keeping her up straight. Nodi flinched in horror, eyes still clenched shut.

"No," he cried. "God, I'll do anything. Please."

He heard shouts and clanking footfalls ring out through the forest in all directions. "Go, go, go!" someone yelled just beyond the tree line behind them. The military had tracked them down.

Amidst the distraction, Nodi tried to twist to his right to see if Aenna was still alive. He couldn't tell.

Fyzel, in an effort to cover up what he was doing, cut Nodi free, but before he got to Aenna, he was struck by a blow to the head from Persecutor Shirka herself. Nodi looked up at her and could tell she recognized him. She tried to restrain him, but the cannibals attacked. The soldiers were better equipped and better trained, but outnumbered. Bodies crashed together, metal clanking. One akiga fell through the fire in a tornado of sparks and smoke. A tent caught fire, then two, then three.

Nodi crawled over to Fyzel's body to get the knife and he cut Aenna free. She was bleeding badly. He pulled her into the brush behind them. Shirka yelled, pointing at them, but the fighting was too fierce for anyone to do anything about it.

Aenna gasped for air as Nodi put his arm around her, lifted her to her feet, and dragged her away. He found one of the soldier's red spotted runners just off the path ahead. He mounted it and pulled Aenna up behind him.

"Go south," She muttered. His back was already sticky-wet with her blood.

They rode a jagged line between the trees, jumping dead logs and full bushes. The battle noise got fainter and fainter until they could no longer hear it above the clopping of the runner's feet. Eventually, they broke free of the forest and crossed the main highway. Sigate was close, but they bypassed it, going straight to the jagged plateaus and deep fissures of the Obsidian Hills to the south.

"This way?" Nodi said.

"Yes." Aenna was growing weaker.

Nodi could see the sparkle of the hills ahead. The area was vaster than he'd imagined. Finding Judas' corpse would be nearly impossible, but he couldn't think about that now. Aenna's grip grew weaker around his waist as they rode.

"Hold on, Aenna. Please."

When they reached the Obsidian Hills, he found a wide crevice and rode in as far as possible. He stopped the runner, climbed down, and pulled Aenna to the ground. The runner had soldier's provisions strapped to it. He wrapped her in a blanket and gave her a drink from a canteen. He thought it was water, but it was actually an ale. As soon as he poured it into her mouth, she choked and spit it out.

"It'll take a lot more than a knifing to turn me to drinking," she said.

Nodi let out a nervous laugh. "I thought it was water. I'm going to pour some on your wound. It'll hurt."

She groaned as he poured it over the cut. When the burning ceased, she propped herself up to look at it. "If anything vital had been hit, I'd already be dead."

Nodi sighed and sat on the ground next to her as she lay back down. Her breathing was irregular and she stared at the sky, lips moving as if summoning the strength to say something.

"I'm done with this," she said.

"What?"

"This is a warning. It's a warning. This madness has to stop."

"We were delivered! It's not a warning, it's ..." He almost said 'blessing,' but didn't want to be insensitive.

"I'm turning myself in. It's the right thing to do, Nodi, a show of good faith. I would have stayed back at that camp if the pain hadn't clouded my judgment." She reached out and squeezed his hand. "I don't want to go alone. Please go with me. Please."

He looked away.

The wind blew heavy across the hills. The crevice they were in was deep enough to keep them completely in shadow. The cliffs on either side of them were black, shiny, and jagged. Nodi's reflection was nothing more than fractured images on angular shards of obsidian.

Around the corner, an incline led to higher ground. He decided to go up and see if he could find his bearings. "I'll be back in a minute."

She didn't respond.

Once he reached the top, he could see the sea in the distance to the west and could just barely make out the ships in the port at Sigate. To the south and the east was nothing but the Obsidian Hills. They sparkled under the afternoon suns like a black chandelier.

From the description in the letter, he figured their best chance was to stay closer to the coast and look for any distinguishing landmarks. If they traveled in the crevices as much as possible, he thought they might have a chance at avoiding detection. There were a few provisions in the runner's pack, but they wouldn't last long.

His hearts held out hope, but his mind said it was hopeless. *I can't wander here indefinitely. I'll never find the rest of that letter.*

He spotted movement some distance away. He lay flat on the ground, watching and waiting. The figures jittered in the heat coming off the rocks. As they came clear around a rock, he saw the unmistakable outline of Trej's tall, spindly body.

"Trej! Aenna, it's Trej and Mal!" He jumped to his feet and waved to get their attention.

The fierce cannibal resistance caught Shirka by surprise. She won, but at a heavy price. She entered the cannibal's camp with twenty soldiers and left with only six. All of the cannibals were dead, dying, or captured. She ordered her subordinates to kill the dying and bind the captured and then she searched the camp for the letter. It wasn't there.

She returned to Sigate late the next afternoon intent on picking up where she left off with Mal and Trej. The guards who'd been watching their cell stood aloof, resisting eye contact with her.

The cell was empty.

She inspected the hole in the roof and the bloody ropes on the ground and then went back out and placed a reassuring hand on one of their shoulders.

These fugitives are on a charmed path, she thought. *Is the Lord for them or against them?*

She'd ordered the area north of Sigate scoured after she first met Isu Kru. That proved fruitless. Something on the wind, something in her spirit, told her to try the other direction. She turned to her commanders who stood nearby.

"Move the search south. To the Obsidian Hills."

26

"Trej!" Nodi yelled without regard for the fact that they were being hunted.

Trej lumbered toward him, followed by Mal and a purple akiga that knuckle-walked like a goliataur.

"We thought you were dead," Nodi said once he was close.

"We almost were."

"You look terrible."

"Yes, we were caught. Briefly. Where is Aenna?"

"She's over there. She was stabbed ... I think she'll be okay."

"*Stabbed?*" Mal said.

"Yes. Don't ask." Nodi didn't want to tell Mal about the cannibals, eating ixaquoi in particular. Too awkward.

"Lunch?" The strange akiga said to Nodi, holding out her palm.

"Uh ... we might have a bit of ... something ..." He looked at Trej as if to inquire.

"This is Isu Kru. We met her in Sigate." Trej put his hand on Nodi's shoulder. "She is the one who found the letter."

"I can't believe you found her! This *is* God's path."

Mal pulled Nodi over. "You and Isu have a lot in common. She has an imaginary friend, too."

Nodi pushed him away and led them to Aenna. They thought it best to rest, so they decided to stay until early evening. Trej and Mal kept watch on the cliffs above.

Isu sat near Aenna, munching on a morsel of bread. She seemed to enjoy the breeze, eyes fluttering, crumbs swirling around her head. She didn't pay Aenna any mind at first, but when she did, she couldn't stop staring at her. When Aenna noticed her gaze, Isu tapped her temple. "Remember."

"What?"

Isu pointed at her. "Traitor."

"*Traitor?*"

Nodi looked at Aenna, concerned.

"Papa," Isu said and turned to someone who wasn't there. She shook her head and looked back at Aenna. "Gone."

She said nothing more to them but said plenty to her imaginary friend. For some reason, it made Nodi think of his conversion in Pasica so long ago.

When the suns cast a deep evening gold on the Obsidian Hills, Isu left to be alone on the cliff top, squatting on the precipice above them, arms hanging over the side. Aenna had gained some strength and Nodi helped her up.

"Can you take us to the skeleton now?" Trej asked Isu.

Isu scanned the area. Her purple tentacles flapped wildly in the wind.

"There." She pointed to a place closer to the sea.

After Nodi chased the stolen runner away, they followed Isu. He helped Aenna negotiate the rough terrain. She would have left if she'd had the strength to carry on alone. It was only a matter of time. The suns were deep orange by then, their lower halves obscured by clouds. When they surfaced on the plateaus, the sparkle of sea and obsidian made it hard to tell one from the other.

"Here," Isu said, pointing at a small opening.

Nodi ran forward, scarcely able to believe they'd found it. When he saw the tiny hole in the rock face, he thought it was a joke. It was barely big enough to squeeze through. He couldn't see inside to tell if it went anywhere. He'd envisioned a cave big enough to live in, not some little nook like this.

"This *can't* be it," he said. "Who knows what terrible thing lives in there, just waiting to eat us."

"Here," Isu insisted.

Nodi stuck his head in, but it was too dark. Mal pushed him aside and wiggled through. Nodi shrugged and followed him until they squeezed into a chamber that *was* big enough to live in. Rose-colored light shined down from a hole above them and formed a circle on the floor. Judas' ashen-gray skeleton protruded from the dirt at the circle's edge. His arms were pulled out in an unnatural pose. Isu must have caused the disturbance when she found the body. The finger marks of her excavation were still visible.

"Come in! It's here!" Nodi called out to the others.

Trej was too big to crawl in that way, but he heard Nodi's call echo through the hole above the cavity. Aenna went in, maintaining balance by holding onto the walls. Isu popped in behind her and Trej's head appeared in the opening above them, just a silhouette against the dying light.

"He must have jumped from up here," he called down.

"Head first." Mal squatted and rubbed Judas' cracked skull. "From his position, I doubt he died instantly. He moved over here against the wall after the impact. Bled out from the head wound. Painful way to go."

A hole was on the far side of the cave that looked like it once led somewhere deeper, probably the network of caves that made up Hijoon. It was sealed off. Weathered etchings were on the walls, but Nodi couldn't read them. Stone tools were half buried in the dirt and a fire pit was in the middle.

The pouch that had contained the letter was still sitting on the ground where Isu dropped it. Nodi picked it up and looked inside. The rest of the letter was there, in good condition, but he didn't take it out, not yet. He set the pouch aside, hands shaking, frightened of what he might read.

Trej dropped some driftwood through the hole and shimmied down the shaft behind it. He had to sit with his head cocked to one side because the ceiling was too low. Mal built a small fire with some flintstones he found. The firewood gave off a salty sea smell, smoke billowing out of the hole above them like a chimney.

Nodi noticed a rock in the corner with markings on it. "Look."

Upon closer examination, he saw that the markings were a crude representation of Tim using the talisman. Mal pulled it up and cast it aside. A stone hewn box with a lid was under it. He pulled it out and glanced at Nodi. Nodi nodded. *Open it.* Tim's legendary talisman was inside, placed on top of an old book wrapped in a swath of burlap. The talisman was like a thin, black glass stone, contoured to fit the palm of a hand with five finger loops coming out of its sides. Mal tried it on. A brief surge of energy flowed from his palm to his arms and then it went dead.

"I remember that thing," Trej said as he nursed the fire.

Nodi looked up at him with raised brows and then turned his attention back to the box. He took out the book and removed the burlap. It had gold trim around it with worn, brownish gold letters on the cover that said *Holy Bible.* Its pages were torn and fragile, almost falling apart in his hands. He wrapped it back up, put everything back in the box, and closed the lid.

When the fire was going strong, he settled in to translate the rest of the letter:

I, JUDAS THE UNLOVED, WRITE FEARING THESE WORDS WILL NEVER BE READ. I WAS A FOLLOWER OF THE ONE WE AKIGI BELIEVED TO BE THE MESSIAH, THE LORD OF AKIGOL. THERE ARE MANY THINGS HIDDEN FROM US, THINGS I DO NOT KNOW, BUT WHAT I DO KNOW, THOSE THINGS THAT I ALONE SAW THAT NIGHT ON THE MOUNT OF SUFFERING, I SHALL SHARE.

I HAVE NOTHING LEFT.

I HATE HIM.

I AM SO CONFUSED.

GOD ABANDONED ME, IF THERE EVER WAS A GOD.

ON THAT CURSED NIGHT, WHEN I WAS LEFT ALONE WITH OUR UNDYING LORD, AFTER I TRIED TO KILL HIM WITH A ROCK, A VESSEL APPEARED FROM THE WEST AND LANDED NEAR US. ANOTHER ONE LIKE THE LORD—THE LORD CALLED HIM JACKASS—CAME OUT OF THE VESSEL TO HELP HIM ESCAPE HIS BINDINGS. WHILE HE DID THIS, I SNUCK ONTO THE VESSEL. IT WAS LIKE NOTHING I COULD HAVE EVER DREAMED.

I HID WHEN JACKASS DRAGGED THE LORD ABOARD. THE DOOR CLOSED, THE WALLS BECAME INVISIBLE, AND THE VESSEL BEGAN TO MOVE. I WAS FRIGHTENED AND TRIED TO STAY HIDDEN, BUT THEY FOUND ME. JACKASS QUESTIONED THE LORD, BUT

DID NOT SEEM TO TRUST HIM SO HE ASKED *ME*
WHAT HAD HAPPENED. I SAID THAT THE AKIGI
BELIEVED HIM TO BE OUR MESSIAH AND THAT HE
HAD CLAIMED AS MUCH. JACKASS POINTED AT THE
LORD AND SAID, "*THAT* IS NO MESSIAH."

HE YELLED AT THE LORD SAYING THEY WERE SENT
TO AKIGOL TO PREPARE THE WAY FOR JESUS, WHO IS
DESCRIBED IN *HOLY BIBLE,* BUT THE LORD
PRESENTED *HIMSELF* AS THE MESSIAH, INSTEAD.

JACKASS SUMMONED A MAP OF A PLACE BEYOND THE
SEA, MAYBE BEYOND THE EDGE OF AKIGOL, AND
TOUCHED A SPOT ON IT. THIS IS A DRAWING, TO THE
BEST OF MY RECOLLECTION, OF WHAT I SAW:

Nodi flipped it over and checked to make sure there was
nothing else and then he held the map up so everyone could
see it.

"Now read the bottom half, again," Mal said.

"I lost your bag in the cave, Mal. I'm sorry."

"That's too bad. I could go for some ale right now."

Aenna was lying on the ground, staring out in cold silence.

They sat awhile, processing what they'd heard before the quiet was broken by Isu snoring.

Mal looked uncomfortable. "Who's Jesus?" he said. "Or Jackass? Do you have any spooky stories that might fill in *that* gap?"

"We know from scripture that Jesus was a character in *Holy Bible*," Nodi said. "It's a silly story—walks on water, raises the dead, that sort of thing—but, like Tim, he was betrayed by one named Judas. *Holy Bible* was a book of myths that Tim carried with him from heaven ... or wherever ... to show us how scripture should be written. The letter seems to suggest that this other ... being ... Jackass ... anticipated this Jesus coming *here*."

Mal puckered his lips and furrowed his brow in intense reflection.

"You're going to try to go to that island aren't you?" Aenna said. She rolled onto her back, defeated.

"Well, *I* am, that's for sure," Mal said.

Nodi noticed Aenna didn't use inclusive language. "I've come too far to stop now. What do I have to lose, anyway? But how will we get there?"

"By boat," Mal said.

"How will you hire a boat?"

"The ixaquoi in Sigate are friendly to the Dissenters Guild. We can find passage."

"I am not so sure," Trej said. "If this map points beyond the eternal cyclone, seafaring folk will not be inclined to go that way."

Mal grabbed the map and took a closer look. "That's the edge of Akigol, beyond the cyclone! Judas must have been mad!" He threw it down in disgust.

"The world is round. There is no edge ...," Trej said. They balked at him. "Stop that! It is *round*, I tell you! ... But the fear of the cyclone is merited."

The contagious fire of reckless abandon was in Mal's eyes. "It's really round?"

"Absolutely."

"No way to fall off?"

"No way."

"The Dissenters Guild will stop at nothin' to bring the truth to light. Judas hasn't led us astray yet and we got nothing to lose. We'll get passage."

"I'm done with this," Aenna said. Her voice was weak. "I can't go with you any further. My soul, all our souls are in danger for this course we've taken. I love you Nodi, but I can't. You're asking me to choose between you and the Lord and … I just *can't*."

"Aenna, God has *blessed* our journey!"

"We're being guided by the evil one," she said in a pained whisper, "not God. God allows you to continue in your folly to expose the futility of it. You can seek destruction. I seek *redemption*. I've been arrested, hunted, stabbed. I can't go on like this. This madness has to stop."

"You go on and on about God's will," Mal said, "but you never stop and think that it's all random. There's no guidin' hand. We're not special. Nothin' in the great beyond is lookin' out for us. We make our *own* way. And that's a good thing. It's within our power to make a difference … to *change* things."

"Change is good," Aenna said, "but only if it is a change that brings us closer to the Lord. What you're proposing is precisely the opposite. Your whole purpose is to prove the Lord a fraud. He is already your enemy. You've deemed him the villain and in your wickedness, have lost sight of what is *truly* wicked."

Nodi held Aenna's hand.

"Stay with me," he whispered.

"*You* stay with *me*," she whispered back.

"I'm sorry. I have to know. I'll regret it if I don't go."

"And you will have no regrets with regards to *me*?" She withdrew her hand and turned to go to sleep.

Nodi reached out to touch her shoulder but withdrew. There was nothing he could do.

The Akigi Bible

Selidinian Victories, vol. 4, Chapter 27: 1-13

27 This is how Fezra the Great, Queen of the Selidinian Empire, defeated the nation of P'Aa with only a youngling and two small fish.

[2] When the P'Aanians were defeated at the battle of Sigate Beach, their king retreated to the caves of Hijoon where they had made a place of great fortification, impenetrable to the Queen's army.

[3] The Queen built an encampment on Sigate Beach and laid siege to Hijoon for seventeen months. [4] When her soldiers began to catch P'Aanians sneaking about, searching for food, she surmised the enemy was starving.

[5] Now, a minor king from the far east had given the Queen a tribute in the form of two rare fish, one male, one female. They were deadlier than any fish the Queen had ever seen and could live on land as easy as in water. [6] The king instructed her to keep them separate and contained, lest great misfortune befall her should they breed.

[7] Believing the fish to be a tantalizing meal for starving P'Aanians, she painted one of her youngling servants blue, gave him the fish in two separate containers, and sent him to Hijoon at nightfall. [8] The guards, seeing fish they might eat and believing the youngling to be P'Aanian, let him in. [9] The youngling set the fish loose upon the floor and fought the guards unto death and the fish escaped into the bowels of

Hijoon. [10] In four day's time, they had multiplied thirty-fold and run amok in the P'Aanian stronghold, devouring everyone in their wake.

[11] When the P'Aanian threat was no more, the Queen ordered all entrances to Hijoon sealed and from that day forward, the place was cursed. [12] Hijoon fell into ruin, destined to be swallowed by time and forgotten, [13] and to this day, P'Aa bows at the feet of Selidin.

27

The next morning, just before dawn, Trej stuck his head down the hole to wake up the others. "We must go." Mal was already outside. Nodi rolled over, tapped Isu on the shoulder, and went over to help Aenna. Before leaving, he put the letter back in its pouch and put it in the box with the talisman and *Holy Bible*.

Mal and Trej were waiting at the cave's entrance for them.

"What's going on?" Nodi said.

"During the night small fires started to burn along the edge of the hills," Trej said. "They are probably soldier camps."

"Persecutor Shirka knows we're gone by now and this is the most likely place for us to have come. They'll be everywhere soon." Mal shot a thumb in Trej's direction. "Havin' this behemoth with us doesn't exactly make us inconspicuous."

Trej's ears were twitching; he could hear something. "Get back inside," he said with haste, keeping his voice down.

Aenna stepped forward as if she was about to walk away,

but Mal pulled her inside the cave and Nodi followed. Trej pressed himself against the rock face on the opposite side. Pink sunlight crested the horizon and the shadows of two soldiers appeared on the floor of the crevice just outside the tunnel. They stood right above Trej. Mal held his hand over Aenna's mouth, sensing she had the urge to call out. The shadow moved to the North and the clanking sounds of their armor faded away.

"There are a lot of them now," Trej whispered. "I can hear them."

"Let's go back inside. Trej, can you get in through the top?" Nodi said.

Trej listened for a minute and nodded.

Mal's hand was still over Aenna's mouth. She elbowed him in the ribs to make him let go. Nodi was still blocking her path so she pushed him to squeeze by. He backed out of the cave.

"I can't go any further with you. I have to do what's right. I'm going to turn myself in."

"The hell you are," Mal said, "at least not until *we're* safely on our way."

"I don't take orders from you."

Mal shoved her against the wall and put his hands around her throat. Nodi grabbed his arms, but Mal kicked him away.

"You don't intimidate me," she said, struggling to breathe. "Kill me if you must, but I won't go another step with you."

Nodi pushed Mal and tried to strike him, but Mal knocked him to his knees. Trej reached out with his huge hand and pinned Mal in a show of strength almost unfathomable for one so skinny.

"I'm sorry," Mal said, "but she will go straight to the authorities. We can't risk it."

"You *will* risk it, Mal," Trej said. "We are not ones to oppress, are we? What are you going to do, kill her? Leave her here to die in the elements? Tie her up and drag her behind us?"

"The third option sounds okay."

"We do not have time for this."

Mal stopped fighting against Trej's spindly hands and calmed down. Trej loosened his grip and sat down with his back against the wall. Nodi turned to Aenna. She wouldn't look him in the eyes. She took a few steps back and stopped. Nodi studied everything about her in that moment—the way her tentacles hung down, her sad eyes, her scar, her beige clothes so soft and breezy with dried blood on them. "Aenna."

"I love you, Nodi. Have since we were younglings, but you know that without the Lord as the foundation of our relationship, our relationship doesn't have a prayer. We are nothing if we don't follow Him."

"Aenna," he said again. "Aenna."

She walked away and he watched her until he couldn't see her anymore.

She's in God's hands now, he thought, and it was no comfort. No comfort at all.

"Your relationship could never be so deep as to rival her love for the lord, could it?" Mal said. "Tim is the omniscient, omnipresent, omni-illicit-lover."

Nodi punched him in the stomach. Bowed over on one knee, Mal held his hand out as a sign of submission. Nodi unclenched his fist and slumped against the cliff. "I hate to say it, but Mal's right," he said to Trej. "She has every intention of exposing us."

"I know," Trej said. "Where is Isu?"

"Here," Isu said from inside the cave.

Mal went inside, but Nodi waited a moment. He hoped to catch one more glimpse of Aenna, but she was gone.

Inside Judas' chamber, Isu had already dug out a portion

of the opening that was sealed shut. Mal came back in and helped her clear it. There was a way through. The four of them stood staring down into the dark shaft.

Trej held his hand out. "There is a breeze coming from inside."

Nodi gazed into the dark opening. "Are you aware of the Legend of Hijoon?"

"Even if that story's true, it's been hundreds of years. The fish thingies are long dead," Mal said.

Trej took the lead, crawling on all fours, thin body adept at navigating the tunnels. His feet were faintly visible in Mal's red luminescence.

Deeper in the depths, it smelled like mud and sulfur and the wet packing sound of slimy things resonated through the chambers. The ground was soft. Trej stopped from time to time and made some of his strange auditory mapping noises.

Nodi heard the sounds of scraping metal behind them. "Do you hear that?"

"Yes," Trej said.

"What is it?"

"Soldiers. I do not know what the sound in *front* of us is."

"Stickyfish," Isu said.

"Stickyfish?"

"Hungry. Eat."

Trej stopped and leaned on one elbow with his back to the wall. He looked back and forth, clicking and sniffing. The sound of metal was louder, more consistent. "The soldiers are scraping their swords along the walls to find their way in the dark. We must keep going forward."

They followed the tunnel until a dim blue glow appeared ahead, growing brighter as they approached. The tunnel became shiny like glass and opened into a naturally formed tube crystal that extended out along the floor of the sea. Bright colored coral swayed in the current outside between wildly painted fish that swam back and forth, pecking at the other side of the walls. The dizzying motion of sun squiggles beamed in the depths.

"It's magnificent," Nodi said.

Mal rubbed his hand along the surface. "I've never seen anything like it."

"I sense nothing but another cave," Trej said. "Odd sounds. Gurgling base waves, high-pitched squeals, thin cracking noises. It is almost disorienting."

"If only you could see as we see, Trej."

They continued down the tube and came to a dark chamber where the path broke in two directions. Cave crabs scavenged in the soft peat of the floor inside, snatching worms and insects between their powerful claws, crawling in and out through a myriad of rubbery membranes on the tips of spouts that led back to the sea.

A flutter of wet slapping sounds emanated from the tunnel on the right, getting closer.

Mal picked up a rock, poised for attack. "Let's go left."

Isu lunged for the rock and the two of them fell over.

"Let go!" he said, but she grabbed it and smashed several of the cave crabs.

"She's surprisin'ly strong!" Mal said, getting up and watching her. "She hungry?"

The slapping sounds were getting louder.

Isu rubbed crab blood on herself and slung some on the others. Nodi stood in shock, blood dripping down his face. It was warm and smelled of rotting flesh. He felt ill.

"Well that was unexpected," Trej said, a bit of blood dribbling down his nose.

Isu handed the rock to Mal and ran down the corridor to the right.

"No! Isu!"

The clanking of the soldier's armor was coming at full

speed now, alerted by Isu's episode.

"Follow Isu," Trej said.

"But—"

"Follow her!"

The slapping sounds reached a fever pitch like the applause of an oozing crowd. A swarm of black creatures appeared ahead, swirling around the walls of the tube like a sideways tornado. Nodi turned to run, but saw four soldiers in the crystal tunnel across the way, looking at them through the expanse of water between them. Mal's tattoos were a beacon.

The stickyfish blotted out the light of the sea as they coalesced.

Darkness consumed Nodi as the fish flowed past, clinging to the surface with suction cup finger-fins. Their mouths were full of green, needle-like teeth that protruded up from their bottom jaws. Bony spines stuck out of their backs and their eyes were like pink pearls with little dead pupils. They wriggled, slapped, and hissed, but didn't touch Nodi or the others. The fish also kept a wide berth of the crabs, flowing up to the top of the cave to avoid them. The crabs snatched a few stragglers between their fierce claws and devoured them.

The swarm passed with a breeze and flowed out of sight. Nodi looked at the soldiers across the way. The fish flooded their tunnel and ingested them in a swirling mass of darkness. The fish paused there awhile and then moved down and out of view.

Everything fell quiet again except for their distant echoes.

A blue glint of armor lay on the tunnel floor where the soldiers were, blood dripping down the walls.

Nodi stood in stunned silence, afraid something else might happen.

"The crab blood saved us," Trej said. "The fish caught the scent of a predator and kept clear."

"Well that was the single most terrifyin' moment of my life," Mal said. "I'll never eat fish again."

Once they collected themselves, they continued down the main tunnel, wondering if they were getting any closer to Sigate. From time to time, they stumbled into large bubbles of crystal that showed decaying signs of civilization within them—broken mosaics on the floor, clay pots, cutting stones, bones. Any riches those places might have held were long since plundered. Everything was dark blue and smelled like seawater and dirt. Trej, exhausted from being on all fours, found those bubbles an oasis where he could stretch his legs before the next section of tube. Mal would look up through the ceiling at the surface of the water from time to time, trying to determine their heading by the light of the suns. He believed they were going the right way—toward Sigate.

After several hours, they found a haphazard door that separated the crystal labyrinth from a grandiose rock chamber, bigger than any other they'd seen. The radiant blue light of the tunnels spilled in enough for them to see unused torches in sconces along the walls. Mal still had the flintstones they'd found in Judas' cave so they each lit one and shut the door to keep the stickyfish out.

The chamber was a natural habitat with high, vaulted ceilings and several smaller adjoining recesses. The shadows were alive in the firelight, but nothing else was. Hundreds of akigi skeletons smiled at them, empty-handed and hollow-eyed.

As they wandered through the communal tomb, Isu ran to a body that wore tattered red pants and a leather necklace.

"Papa," she said.

28

Aenna crested a plateau where she was plainly visible to the soldiers. She stumbled in pain from the stab wound, dropping to her knees a few times.

Nodi, she thought. *I'm so sorry.*

A patrolling soldier saw her from an adjacent hill and waved the rest of the search party over.

"My name is Aenna," she said as they approached.

One of them examined her injury. "What happened?"

"I was stabbed … in the forest. Yesterday."

"Where are the others?"

She said nothing, a conscious act of defiance. God surely disapproved of such half-measures, but she would find a way to justify it later.

"She came from down there," one of the others said, pointing back the way she'd come. Her footprints betrayed her.

"You go investigate. I'll take her into town."

Aenna looked back and clenched her eyes shut to keep from crying.

"What is this place?" Nodi said.

Mal was squatting, examining a cup he'd picked up off the ground. He tossed it aside and dusted his hands. He examined a couple of the bodies, turning them over, pulling their clothes taut looking for signs of violence. "They were murdered and I know who did it. Stilla."

Nodi stepped toward him. "*This was Stilla?*"

"Look at all the cups."

"Poison?"

"She was known for it. And there's nothin' of value left either."

"She was a common thief," Trej said. "She killed them and kept their possessions."

"Appears so."

"I ... All this death," Nodi sat down. *Aenna helped Stilla draw these akigi into this. It's better she didn't see this. God is merciful.*

"This was Stilla's underground movement," Mal said. "She promised to get them to safety. She had them gather up their possessions so that she could—"

"So she could kill and rob them," Trej said.

"It's unconscionable. We would never have accepted her contributions if—"

"What contributions?"

"She helped fund the Dissenters Guild with ... this. We didn't know. We *couldn't* have known."

Trej went to Isu, who held her papa's skeletal hand. "We should go."

He tried to pull her away, but she resisted.

"Stay," she said.

"No, Isu. We must—"

"Stay!" she screamed and caused a furious echo.

He knew it was no use trying to take her out of there. She'd been looking for her father for a long time.

"We can't just leave her," Nodi said.

"She needs this. She will be okay."

Nodi put his hand on her shoulder. She flinched. "I ... I just wanted to thank you."

She looked back at him and then at Trej. "Thank you," she said.

They left her on her knees, holding her father's dead hand and stroking his skull. After seeing what happened to the troogil's, Nodi was convinced of the ongoing cruelty of his own religion, but now, as his current exodus took him farther away from it, he wondered what new horrors might await him. Was there *any* civility to be found anywhere?

There were no more crystal caves after that, just dank tubes of solid rock. They took the torches and walked for over an hour until the path ended at a sharp drop off. They shimmied over the edge, dropped down, and crawled through a tight little hole on the backside of a crumbling wall. A foul smell overtook them. They were in the ancient stone sewer system that ran below Sigate.

"Akigi filth," Mal said. "I'm gonna be sick."

"There are as many ixaquoi in Sigate as akigi," Nodi said, covering his nose.

Mal and Nodi ran through the unpalatable stench, leaving Trej to crawl the long length of the wet, dripping shaft lit only by small grates on the sides of the streets above them. The sewer shaft opened to the span of beach underneath a wide pier. The bottoms of ships rose and fell gently with the waves. The harbor to their right was devoted to a fleet of Selidinian Naval ships, but the civilian docks were in front of them. A well-worn boat was at the end, "Eluding Distress" painted on the stern.

Mal nudged Nodi. *"Eludin' Distress.* It's an anagram for

Dissenters Guild. It's our headquarters sittin' right under the nose of the Naval Fleet. Wait here."

"Mal …"

Mal darted up a ramp to their left and disappeared.

Nodi turned to Trej for some sort of elaboration, but Trej didn't know any more than he did. They waited awhile, immersed in shadow and stench. Minutes turned into a quarter of an hour, half an hour, a whole hour.

"You think he got arrested?"

"I hope not. I did not hear a commotion."

"Do you think Isu is okay?"

"As okay as can be expected."

Nodi picked at the calluses on the palm of his blue hand and looked vacantly at the harbor. "I hope Aenna is okay."

Trej had nothing to say to that.

The red sails of the *Eluding Distress* began to unfurl.

Nodi watched with puzzled interest. "Mal will come back for us … won't he?"

"I do not know. He does not need us anymore, does he?"

"I still have the map. I don't know if he needs it to get to the island."

"He does not inspire trust."

"No. He doesn't."

The *Eluding Distress* began to move.

"That bastard! He's leaving us!" Nodi said, standing up straight.

The ship turned out to sea as its anchors rumbled into their perches. As it pulled away, a small dinghy was revealed on the other side.

"There he is!"

Mal was rowing toward them, waving them over. They ran into the surf. Trej climbed aboard the dinghy—it looked like a toy with him in it—and pulled Nodi up behind him. Nodi rolled down to the floor and held his tender shoulder.

The guards amassed along the docks, watching, pointing, yelling.

"Sorry for the hasty departure," Mal said. "Captain thought it best. Help me row back to the ship, Trej." Trej took the oars and, with his long arms, propelled them faster than Mal could ever hope to go. They reached the bottom of the ship and the deckhands lifted them out of the water.

Before the *Eluding Distress* set sail, Persecutor Shirka stood near the beach looking out at the Obsidian Hills. The civilian docks were behind her, the *Distress* not too far away. She was oblivious to the fact that Nodi and Trej were hidden from sight just a stone's throw away. Aenna sat at a table nearby where she'd been most of the day, shackled and surrounded by guards. Shirka was just getting around to her, being more concerned about the ones she *hadn't* captured yet.

The persecutor was dirty, tired, and bad-tempered. She looked over at Aenna as if she might devour her if the mood should strike. "Why turn yourself in?"

"I just want to do the right thing and be done with this," Aenna said. "I've done nothing wrong."

"Did they *force* you to leave Kan Ludo or did you go with them willingly?"

Aenna looked down at her shackles. They were hot from the day's merciless suns.

Shirka grabbed her face and forced her to look up. "Will you refuse to tell me where they are?"

"The last time I saw them was near where your akigas arrested me … Nodi found the rest of the letter and a map. They're pursuing it, that's all I know."

Shirka let go of her face. "Pursuing it *where*?"

Aenna looked out at the water, at the darkness on the horizon. "An island. Across the sea. There, to the northwest."

"Beyond the storm?"

"I think."

"They're daft!"

Aenna stared at the ebb and flow of the water in the distance, at the sparkle of it under the rose-colored sky to the south. Its beauty struck her. She was surprised to find that, in spite of her predicament, she was at peace. She knew she'd done the right thing, no matter what ill fortune might befall her. Nothing in this world could compare with what awaited her in the next. The vista before her was a just a shadow of things to come.

She smiled sadly and looked back at the dark horizon. "Judas' letter made it sound like Tim went there sometime before his body was discovered. It's a fool's errand, you know that. Show them mercy. They're only doing what they think is right."

Shirka scowled, grabbed her upper arm, and pulled her to her feet. "You've come to make things right, yet still you plead their case? I have no further use for you."

"Persecutor, look!" one of the guards said, pointing.

Nodi and Trej were climbing into a dinghy steered by Mal the Dissenter. Trej's lanky form was unmistakable even from there. The *Eluding Distress* was setting sail.

Shirka hurried to the dock, dragging Aenna by the arm.

She caught Nodi's eye after he stumbled onto the deck of the ship and looked back. He saw Aenna and tried to jump overboard, but the deckhands held him back. Aenna was useless even as a bargaining chip, they'd already gone their separate ways. Shirka saw Nodi squirm in terror, trying to break free of those who held him. Sometimes akigi knew death before it arrived.

He knew.

Nodi knew.

Shirka took the battle hammer from the sling on her back

and struck Aenna over the head. Aenna fell to her knees, eyes swirled back, tentacles curling in the throes of death. Shirka hit her again, a vicious, shattering blow. Aenna's body tumbled off the dock, splashed in the water, and began a slow drift out to sea.

Shirka heard Nodi cry even from there.

She turned toward one of the naval frigates nearby and told the captain to prepare the ships.

29

Mal had no illusions about the fact that Aenna might be executed, but not then and not like that. Although he didn't particularly like her, her collapsing body was more than he could watch. His vision narrowed to nothing but Nodi falling on the hardwood, hands on the sides of his head, screaming in futile desperation. If Nodi wasn't done with that cruel religion before, he was now.

The boat plowed away from Sigate, water splitting across the front end and sending a cold mist up and across the deck. They swayed gently left and right, sails billowing in the wind while seabirds sang. The natural world didn't bother to take notice of what happened. The deck hands, mostly ixaquoi, worked with their heads down, silent. They didn't understand, but they knew suffering when they saw it. Trej sat defeated on a crate.

Mal walked back to the captain, Jonroc Io, an akigo friend

of his from Gologa. When Mal fled Gologa, Jonroc was the one who took him to the mainland. He was tall for an akigo and deep red. The tentacles on the left side of his head were sheared off, a sign of disownment in some akigi clans. He wore a leather half-cap to cover the stubs. Thick scars covered his chest and his black pants hung low on his waist.

"They'll be coming after us, Mal," he said in Gologan. "Do they know where we're going?"

"I can only assume they do. That akiga they just … she almost certainly told them."

"Then that means *you* know where we're going? You left that part out, remember?"

"Yeah, sorry. We were in a bit of a hurry as you saw."

Jonroc looked at Nodi. "We don't *have* to go wherever it is they think we're going."

"Yes, we do. And we have to get there before them. Can we outrun the squadron?"

"No. But they weren't ready to sail. We have a good head start. I'm afraid to know what you're getting me into."

"The end game, Jonroc."

"*Endgame*, you say?"

Jonroc went to the back of the ship and took the wheel from his first mate, a chubby green akigo with a limp. Mal went over to Nodi who sat with his back against the side rail, head down. Judas' box sat next to him. Mal took the letter and paused as if to say something, but what *could* he say?

Nodi didn't seem to notice or care.

Mal took the letter to Jonroc, unfolded it, and pointed at the map. "Here's where we need to go."

"Are you *mad?*" He snatched the letter from Mal and flicked his fingers at the first mate to take the wheel again. He took a second look to make sure he understood what he was seeing. "You know I'd do anything for the Guild, Mal, even at my own expense, but that's a death sentence."

"Jonroc, this is it. We might finally be able to reveal the truth. This letter was written by Judas—*the* Judas—and it says that Tim might have gone to that island. It was certainly of some importance. Hell, the very fabric you hold in your hands is one of Tim's sleeves. I saw Tim's body in Prontis and I can verify it myself. We've always believed that Tim was a fraud, that there is more to the story. This might finally be our chance to prove it."

"No, Mal," Jonroc said.

"Jonroc, imagine the strength, the fortitude, the sheer iron will it would take to be the *only* captain in akigi history to brave the cyclone and live to tell about it. To prove the world doesn't end *there* ... but a little farther to the west."

"Appeals to my ego?" Jonroc grinned and shook his head. He measured Mal with some degree of respect then looked out at the storm. "I've always had this fantasy of sailing into it. Of glimpsing that magnificent destruction as my body turns to ash and blows away in the gusts of oblivion," he breathed it in. "Fine. But what do you think we're going to find there *if* we make it through?"

Mal shrugged and shook his head.

The captain chuckled with resignation. "The fleet stands a good chance of catching us before we even get there."

"I'm willin' to die tryin'."

"It's *your* willingness to die that gets everyone *else* into trouble."

Jonroc looked at Nodi again and studied his stillness awhile. "That one just lost all motivation to carry on."

"No," Mal said. "As cruel as it sounds, I think he just lost the only thing holdin' him back."

Jonroc looked at Mal as if he wondered how someone could be so deaf to matters of the hearts.

He handed the map to his first mate. "Set the course."

Nodi slept in a bunk in the underbelly of the ship that night while Mal and Trej stayed up top, keeping watch between naps. It was dark and humid and the boat creaked as it swayed.

He had two dreams. In the first, he was alone on a dinghy in the middle of a sparkling sea and Aenna was on a pier that went nowhere. She looked out at him when a battle hammer hit her from behind. Blood and bone flicked and sputtered in all directions like a gory crown, and she tumbled into the water. Tim, wearing Persecutor Shirka's armor, wielded the dripping weapon.

"Why Lord?" Nodi asked.

"Why not?" The Lord of Akigol responded.

In the second dream, Nodi playfully wrestled with Aenna in the soft, grassy fields near Kan Ludo as they did when they were young. The breeze was gentle, younglings giggling in the distance. Aenna smiled and stood up, eyes giddy with joy. She backed into the high grass at the edge of the field and disappeared behind a veil he knew he could never penetrate.

The second dream left him with such a profound longing that he wished he'd only had the first.

He opened his eyes. Gray daylight pierced the slats of the wood ceiling. The sea was choppy against the hull. A net hung from a hook to his right and it swung left and right, back and forth.

"I did not mean to wake you," Trej said as he crawled into the small cabin.

"I was dreaming." Nodi sat up and hung his legs over the side of the bunk.

"Of her?"

"I'll relive that moment for the rest of my life."

"You have had your share of horrible moments to relive."

Nodi smiled, but it was a smile as tragic as a single flower growing atop a mountain of dead bodies. "One time, when we were younglings, I got Aenna and my best friend, Ruwisci, into some trouble with this schoolmate of ours named Looyo."

"Oh?"

"I overheard Looyo claim that his mother had a vestigial tail that she kept hidden underneath her cloak—"

Trej chuckled. "Well, that is not normal."

"Oh no, not at all. Not even for a P'Aanian." Nodi laughed a sad little laugh. "He said it was really long, too ... One night I snuck over to peek through a window to see if I could see it. I was curious, y'know. I snuck over there and caught her putting a tunic on and there it was. This long, thin tail, I swear. Just like Looyo said. It even wiggled under its own power, a little."

Trej laughed and Nodi continued, "I was so stunned, I let out an 'oh my God' or something like that and Looyo must have heard me from the other room because he ran in and spotted me through the window as I ran away."

"He caught you?"

"No. Not then, at least. The thing was, he thought it was Ru because I was wearing Ru's tunic. I'd borrowed it. Ru was so confused when Looyo confronted him about it, accusing him of being a pervert. The more Ru denied it, the madder Looyo got until he just started hitting him."

"That is awful ...," Trej said. "And funny."

"I was too terrified to say anything. Looyo was huge! Aenna saw what was happening and pulled Looyo off Ru and pinned him on the ground until he promised to stop."

Trej raised his brows, impressed.

"Ru just kept looking around, at a loss. I still remember his eyes wide and swirling in puzzlement." He grew solemn again. "Aenna was *always* trying to make peace. It was her way."

"What did they say when you told them the truth?"

"I never did. Guess I never will now."

Trej put his hand on Nodi's back with the gentleness of a father to a child. "Do not let regret consume you. We are never in control of our lives as much as we imagine."

"That's what bothers me. *Mal's* been in control of my life since the moment I first saw him. I can't stop thinking that she'd still be alive if it weren't for him."

Trej nodded. "Perhaps. Perhaps not. One of the deckhands left you a change of clothes and some food. Come up when you are ready."

———— • ::——:•◗●◗●:•——:: • ————

Nodi changed and left the cramped cabin to go up the steep, well-worn steps to the upper deck. The sky was cloudy and ominous—blood-red storm on the horizon in front of them, nothing but sea behind them.

Mal grabbed Nodi's shoulder and squeezed as a show of support. It rang false and like a wounded animal, Nodi shoved Mal away and stuck an accusatory finger in his face. "I've tried to tell myself there's a reason for all of this, Mal. That maybe God led you to steal the letter, even if you refused to acknowledge it. I even thought, somewhere in this misguided, addled head of mine, that Tim might be orchestrating these events, using *us* as a vehicle to bring his plan to fruition. But now I think maybe you were right all along, that this is all meaninglessness. There's no God. No Messiah. It's all a joke and you're just a selfish *ass* who cost me *everything*."

"Have I cost you the *truth*?" Mal walked away grumbling.

Nodi called after him. "I'd rather live a thousand years in ignorance *with* her than a single day in the truth *without* her, you bastard."

Nodi regretted what he said almost immediately, but it couldn't be helped. His hearts were raw, his mind numb, his mouth unfiltered.

He noticed Captain Io standing by the forward mast, watching him. He made Nodi uncomfortable. "I'm sorry."

"Don't apologize. My name is Jonroc Io, Nodi. I'm the captain of this ship."

"You lead the Guild?"

"We don't really have a leader. It's all very ... informal. We foster the illusion of organization while resisting its burdens." He walked Nodi to the back of the ship. "While you have my sympathies, I won't offer empty consolation. Many of us aboard this ship have suffered tremendous loss at the hands of the temple. Take what little comfort in that you can."

Nodi looked back at Mal who stared at the black sky ahead of them. "Is that why *he's* so determined to destroy the faith of my people? Some great injustice done to him?"

"Mal? No. I've known him most of my life. You'd think there's some great trauma, some tragic story that fuels his hatred, but there isn't. Mal's not really that complicated. He just doesn't like being told what to do. Especially, if those doing the telling have no rightful claim to do so."

"That doesn't make me feel better."

"No ... I suppose it doesn't. We're headed for troubled waters, Nodi. Perhaps tonight we'll meet this God of yours. Perhaps you'll be reunited with your beloved. After that, no more questions. Just peace."

Trej stood on the bow as they penetrated the storm, senses exploding with the smell of rain and smoke and dead things on the wind. The waves were aggressive so he braced himself by the boom. The gusts picked up, pushing them ever faster.

"This will be bad," Jonroc said, coming up behind him, straining to raise his voice above the wind. "I've never sailed through anything like it."

"We're just going to go right over the edge of the world," a deckhand called out.

"Shut up, and get back to work!" Jonroc yelled. He leaned in close to Trej. "We won't go over the edge, will we?"

"The world is round, captain. There is no edge."

"Well, at least you're keeping your sense of humor." Jonroc turned to address everyone on deck. "Secure yourselves!"

The boat took a steep dive and crashed into a wall of water that sent waves over the top. The scorching crimson water stewed with giant bubbles that rose to the surface and billowed steam into the air. Trej felt the tumultuous volcanic activity in the deep. The rain fell sideways, sometimes cold, sometimes hot.

He called out for Nodi, but remembered he was already down below, the best place for him. He was too unfocused to face the trials of the cyclone.

Tossed side to side across the deck, Trej held onto anything he could for stability. He was almost blind from his inflamed senses, auditory sight returning nothing but deafening static. A barrel rolled across the deck and knocked him over. He slid over the side but grabbed the railing to keep from falling into the sea. His long legs plunged in and out of the oily surf. The slick surface of the rail was causing his hands to slip. Mal appeared over the edge with a rope and ran it under his arms to form a harness. He kept the other end of the rope wrapped securely around his body and pulled Trej up. Trej swung his leg over the railing and was able to climb aboard. The deckhands made them go downstairs. Once they were below, Mal inspected the rope burns he received during the rescue. He grimaced as he caressed the raw cuts. Trej nodded a *thank you*. Mal nodded a *don't mention it*.

The motion of the boat was sickening—Mal threw up in one of the back rooms, stumbling around as if drunk. Trej was enveloped by the sound of waves and creaking, cracking wood. He visualized drowning—his mental sonar projecting images of the mountainous sea floor below as he faded into black.

Two terrified deckhands crawled into a hammock and held one another, rocking back and forth until they passed out.

"No way in hell I'm huggin' *you* to sleep," Mal said.

All Trej could do was laugh.

After two days of gradually subsiding terror, the movement of the ship calmed and eventually stopped. Nodi's body was bruised and aching from being thrown around. He left the cabin and waded through rising water on his way to the stairs. Pieces of wood and spoiled food floated past him. The deck above had gaping holes. He climbed up top to see if maybe they sailed through the very gates of hell. When he emerged, he wasn't sure.

The reddish sky was speckled with maroon clouds, the sea calm, wind hot. The ship's masts were broken like twigs, sails torn to shreds with strips waving lazily. Segments of railing along the sides were torn away in splintered chunks and the back of the boat was sheared off. They were lodged in a sandbar.

Strange lizard-like birds, needle-beaked and the color of ash, were perched along the edges, squawking and nipping at each other. The ship's crew was gone. Nodi walked to the back looking for anyone left alive. Trej and Mal were okay, but Jonroc was dead, draped over the helm. He'd chained himself to it, but the storm proved too much. The birds congregated, anticipating a meal.

Mal tried to shoo the creatures away, but there were too many of them. He hit one with a stick and several of the others hissed, spread their wings wide, and faced him. Their iridescent, beady eyes were hungry. He relented and watched helplessly as they picked at his friend.

"Sorry, Jonroc." He turned away.

"Our cabins proved to be the most secure place," Trej said. "We made it, Nodi. Look."

Nodi went to the side of the ship and looked out. A black island steamed off the starboard side, extending to the North as far as he could see. Volcanoes, violent and imposing, oozed lava in the distance. The cooler colors of the palette, those in abundance back home, were absent here.

The colors here were those of violence, death, and destruction.

30

Nodi gathered his things and some provisions and put them in a leather backpack he'd found below. They rowed a dinghy with a slow leak to shore, just barely making it before it sank in the shallow surf. As Nodi crawled out of the boat, he thought he saw a snail-like creature down the beach. He took a second look, but it was gone.

The sky had changed from red to deep pink as morning ebbed into afternoon. The sand on the shore was ashen gray, peppered by leathery beige vegetation that crunched when they walked. Sharp spikes of rock rose along the edges of the beach like a stone forest. In the distance, dwarfing everything, volcanoes leaked rust colored plumes of smoke into the air.

"Which direction should we go?" Trej said.

Mal looked both ways. "No idea. I think we're close to the southern tip of the island. Let's follow the coast north." He walked along the beach with his head down. He'd lost a great friend in Jonroc and Nodi caught a glimpse of Mal the victim rather than the instigator.

Nodi held him back while Trej lumbered ahead. "I'm sorry for what I said on the ship. We all made our own choices, Aenna included. Had we forced her to come with us like you wanted, she'd still be alive."

Mal looked relieved, but also troubled. "I kicked Tim's sarcophagus."

"What?"

"I beat the hell out of it the night I stole the letter. It's probably why he fell apart in front of you."

Nodi smiled.

"You're not mad? It seems like you should be mad. I didn't tell you because I thought it might be useful if you believed there was some divine reason for it."

"I'm not mad ... I'm relieved."

With that one confession, Mal took the heavy mantle of divine will off Nodi's shoulders and replaced it with a yoke of indifference. Nodi wasn't sure which was heavier, but the difference was refreshing.

After half a day's walk, they crossed a hill and followed the beach around to a cove surrounded by steep, foliage-covered dunes. Midway up the inland-most dune, a tall black obelisk protruded from the vegetation.

"What is that?" Nodi said.

"I don't know."

They wrapped around to the back of the cove and plodded over the thick, stubby plants to the obelisk. Nodi thought he saw a large snail again, peeking over the dune behind them, but when he looked back, it was gone.

"Did you see something?" he asked Trej.

"I have sensed them. We are being watched."

"Do they mean us harm?"

"I do not know. We must wait and see."

"At least they don't look terribly threatening." *Small comfort.*

The obelisk had no discernible entry point. Nodi stepped onto the stone perimeter and walked the outside edge, rubbing his hands along the smooth, black surface. When he got to the surface opposite the sea, an etching depicted a vessel crashing into the side of the mountain. Six Tim-like beings stood with their backs to it. An inscription said,

DEPART FROM EVIL AND DO GOOD

"Look at this!" Nodi said.

Mal came over. "The inscription's in English. Could akigi have put this here?"

"Don't know. Is it a tomb?"

"Perhaps," Trej said, squatting down to run his hand over the engraving. He put his ear to the surface and chirped. "Almost certainly. This *could* be the vessel from the letter that is depicted in this etching."

"Could this have been where it came down?"

"Let's find a way in," Mal said.

Nodi noticed a well-worn path that led up the steep incline of the dune behind the obelisk.

Mal took an interest. "Where do you think it goes?"

They walked up the path. It led over the hill to a valley that was home to a sprawling city of ornate cave entrances, hewn in rock, and laid out in spirals. Huge, multi-level cones were at the center of each. The city was walled in, but the wall on the far side, closest to the line of volcanoes, dwarfed everything in the valley. It held back a millennia's worth of dried volcanic flow, fused to the outside of it.

Three snail-like creatures were down the dune a bit, pointing crossbows up at them. They were no taller than he was, with two stubby arms and jelly-pad hands. Their shells were iridescent red and purple with blue stripes across them.

The one on the right moved forward. "Don't any of you move," he said in English. He had a tiny mouth and eyes perched on translucent stalks that swiveled side to side.

"We mean you no harm," Trej said, holding out his hands.

"You speak English?" The one on the left said. They both spoke with a lisp, presumably for physiological reasons. "What manner of creatures are you? How do you know the language of the Lord?"

"The Lord?" Nodi said. "I've been a follower of the Lord, too! I'm Nodi, an akigo from the region of P'Aa in Selidin across the sea. This is Mal. He's an ixaquoi from Gologa—he doesn't speak English. And that's Trej. He's a troogil."

"Well, we're Vespalids. This is Vespala, you'll do wise to mind your surroundings," the one on the right said. "How do you know the Lord?"

"He came to us many years ago."

"Came to *you*? He hasn't come to *us* yet and you say he's come to *you*? Sounds like heresy to me."

"Yes, well ... there seems to be some confusion," Trej said, "about where he came from, went to, and ended up."

"There's no confusion on our part. The Lord Jesus went to Earth first and is prophesied to come to *everyone* in the universe in the last days. But he hasn't come here, yet. Not to my knowledge, at least."

Nodi was perplexed. "Jesus? The one from *Holy Bible*?"

"Of course Jesus," the one on the right said. "What lord are you talking about?"

"Tim."

"Who's Tim?"

"The Lord."

"*Jesus* is Lord."

Mal could understand English well enough to glean the nature of the conversation. In Gologan, he said, "Maybe, we could have the lords wrestle. The lord that wins reserves the right to be the one and only."

The Vespalids didn't understand him but noted the

sarcasm in his voice. "Keep that vile tongue in your mouth, creature," the one in the middle said. "You'd better come with us."

"Where are we going?" Trej said.

"We're taking you to King Solomon."

In the midst of this curious exchange, none of them noticed that far off on the horizon four surviving ships of Persecutor Shirka's squadron were sailing toward Vespala, tattered and wind-torn.

They moved dreadfully slow through the city, the Vespalids were every bit as sluggish as Nodi would have imagined. He wondered if he was being held by force or just escorted to the king for an inquiry—a crucial bit of information to be certain about. He thought that if he was in any real danger, he could just walk away without even breaking into a jog. What could the Vespalids do about it? *Chase* him? Of course, the crossbows complicated matters.

Thousands of Vespalids collected along the streets, staring at them, whispering. They had all sorts of adornments on their shells, but other than that, Nodi couldn't tell one from another.

The cave entrances were simple, some bigger than others, sometimes with windows cut into either side of them. The buildings at the centers of the spirals looked like lofty turds with cross-adorned spires on them. He concluded they were temples. They had names like "First Vespalid Church of Jesus," "St. Matthew's Church of Vespala," and "St. Mada and the six Holy Martyrs Church of Christ." They had grotesque statues of their Messiah on his cross, the violence done to him exaggerated and gory—far beyond what probably happened, assuming this Jesus person was real to begin with. It all seemed so pagan to Nodi, so strange, wicked even. It had all the power of a myth, a literary oddity, a bizarre cultural allowance of delusion, signed, sealed, and certified as a perfectly acceptable alternative reality.

They finally entered the gates of the palace, a series of interconnected domes of different sizes with plain beige walls and diamond-shaped windows along the circumference. King Solomon, who bore no markings or clothes to indicate he was a king, waited in the courtyard for them. It would have all been rather boring if it weren't for the mountains of death looming large over them.

The guards presented them to the king and explained the situation. The king's black slit eyes analyzed them with trepidation. His tiny hole of a mouth hung open. It occurred to Nodi what an odd sight they must be—blue Nodi with his tentacles, red Mal with his tattoos, gray Trej with his ... tallness.

"Why are you here?" Solomon said.

He spoke exactly like the guards that brought them there, lisp and all.

"A little over two hundred and forty years ago," Nodi said, "one called 'Tim' came to Selidin. My people worshiped him as our Lord and savior—"

"There's only *one* Lord and Savior."

"Yes ... eh ... Jesus ...," Nodi said, "but be that as it may, this one, Tim, came and presented himself as the Lord and savior to *us*, the akigi. But we ... well, I ... have reason to think that what we've always believed may not be accurate—"

"Of course it's not accurate, there's only one Lord and Savior and his name is definitely not Tim, it's—"

"Jesus, yes, but—"

"Is this Tim the one who taught you English?"

"Yes. Yes, he did. Look, we found this letter. It's only the top half, I lost the bottom half, but it's what brought us to your shores."

Nodi pulled the letter out of his bag and handed it to the king. Solomon perused it dismissively. "I can't read this."

"Oh yes, of course. Sorry." Nodi took the letter from him and read it aloud.

"*Judas?* What an unfortunate name," the king said.

"We're wondering about the obelisk by the cove," Nodi said. "Could that be where the vessel came down or crashed?"

"The black obelisk of the evil one? That *would* make sense. The obelisk has been there for over two hundred years."

"Is there anything inside of it?"

Solomon was apprehensive. "Yes, but no one's been inside since it was built."

"Was it built by Vespalids, sire?" Trej asked, making every effort to interrogate the king with the utmost delicacy.

"Yes. But the internal structure was built by humans. *That* structure contains the evil one."

"Tim was a human, too," Trej said. "Any light you could shed on this would be deeply appreciated, sire. We seek nothing but information. We do not wish to interfere with the affairs of Vespala."

After a long silence filled with eye swivels and chin rubs, the king beckoned them to follow. He scooted toward the main door of the palace. One of his advisors voiced concern, but the King silenced him with a wave of his hand.

The throne room was understated with few furnishings or ornamental decorations. The throne was a raised wood platform with a ramp up the back for the legless snail king. Trej had to crouch in order to fit through the door, but once he was inside, he could stand upright under the tall, domed ceiling. The king continued into an adjacent chamber, his long, slimy tract inching him forward in waves.

The chamber was as tall as the throne room with clay walls and diamond patterned marble floors. Troughs filled with burning coals lit the room and six tombs sat, three per side, with names engraved on the ends of each:

DAVID ANDERSON CALLMAN
JULIA TREVINO-STEIN
JOHN WILLIAMS BRUCE
PAOLO ILEANA
ANDERSON SMITH III
HALEY RUIZ MADA

Along the outside perimeter were clothes, papers, and other personal effects that presumably belonged to them. Nodi noticed that some of these objects were similar to Tim's belongings that sat in the Great Hall in Prontis. In the middle of the room was an altar with a small, metallic device that sat on top of it.

King Solomon moved to the center near the altar. "These tombs are for a group of humans that visited us many years ago."

He pointed to a painting of a planet on the ceiling overhead. Mal nudged Nodi as if to point out the fact that it was round just as Trej had said.

"That is Earth, where they came from," Solomon continued, "to deliver the good news of the gospel of Jesus Christ to us. But they were betrayed by the evil one. This 'Tim' I suppose, who was buried inside the obelisk in the cove."

"Sire, Tim's body is back in Prontis. In *our* temple. He *can't* be in that obelisk."

"He *is* in that obelisk, I tell you. Of the humans that came here, only one of their bodies is missing. The great one. The one who led them here. Perhaps he is the one you speak of."

Nodi looked at the floor as if trying to do complicated math in his head. "I don't understand any of this."

"You don't have to take *my* word for it." Solomon approached the central altar. "One of them, the daughter of the great saint Mada, left us with this device and a message that explains what happened. Would you like to see it?"

Nodi very much wanted to see it, but he couldn't take his eyes off the monument that stood alone on the other side of the room. It wasn't a tomb, but a statue of a man on his knees in prayer. The great saint.

TERISE INEZ MADA

T.I.M.

TIM.

The Letter of Pat Robberbaum to the New Century Baptist Association of the Former United States, 1:1-15

1 To all the brothers and sisters of the New Century Baptist Association,

[2] Many of you have become disheartened by the fact that Jesus' promised return has not happened yet. [3] Some of those among you have left the faith and renounced the Lord. [4] Is this the faith of the apostle Paul or of all the great martyrs that have died since the Lord's resurrection? [5] A faith that crumbles when human reason interferes with what we know in our hearts to be true? [6] Is it the faith of Peter or John? Of Augustine? Of Calvin or Luther? Of Spurgeon? Of Lewis or Graham? Of Ogle Orlock of Gamma VI? Or Rufie Q'Kaklaktikoo, the one and only convert of Planet 298.6B? Of course not! [7] So why should you have a weak form of the faith that is Christian in name only, but lacking the power of the Holy Spirit?

[8] Since we know that there are many intelligent civilizations throughout the universe and sin abounds among them all, some say the salvation Jesus offers is meaningless. [9] That it was only for mankind to the exclusion of all other intelligent life. [10] But we know that Jesus is the *only* path to salvation, so if there are other sinful beings among the stars, the salvation the Lord offered to Israel first, then to the rest of the Earth, is also for them.

[11] Jesus said in Matthew,

> [12] *"THEREFORE GO AND MAKE DISCIPLES OF ALL NATIONS,*
> *BAPTIZING THEM IN THE NAME OF THE FATHER AND OF*
> *THE SON AND OF THE HOLY SPIRIT, [13] AND TEACHING THEM*
> *TO OBEY EVERYTHING I HAVE COMMANDED YOU. AND*
> *SURELY I AM WITH YOU ALWAYS, TO THE VERY END OF*
> *THE AGE."*

[14] Jesus made no distinction about whether these nations exist on earth or on any other planet and so our job is to *GO*, brothers and sisters. [15] We must spread the word to every corner of space until all have heard the gospel of Jesus Christ.

[16] It is then, and only then, that the Lord will appear to all, and all will stand before Him and be judged, be they righteous or wicked.

Amen.

31

King Solomon went over to the small metallic device in the middle of the room and touched it. Nodi was startled when a blue light flashed toward the ceiling. The translucent face of a human woman appeared, three-dimensional, staring off into space. She was fair skinned with brown hair and eyes, head turned to the right, with a bright orange jacket barely visible at the bottom of the image.

"She's not bad," Mal said.

Nodi narrowed his eyes at him, disgusted by his penchant for bestiality. "I'm not so sure she would have thought the same of you."

"Be patient," King Solomon said, "it takes a moment to begin."

The blue light faded then appeared again, stronger. The woman's face became animated. She turned her head to the left revealing that the side of her face was pockmarked with bright red sores. She looked defeated, glancing side to side to collect her thoughts before beginning.

"My name is Haley Mada," she said. "It's been four years

since we came here. We were only supposed to be on this mission trip for three, but the mechanic we picked up at UniPort VII betrayed us.

"We sent two teams down. One to the island of Vespala and one to the other island across the sea—I don't remember what they call it. Some of those in our group were jealous of the others. Vespala is a cruel pocket in an otherwise perfectly lovely planet. Jealousy gave way to sorrow, however.

"As soon as we landed, we realized that the other ship didn't make it. All we know for sure is that it burned up on entry. As far as we could tell, it was a total loss, no survivors. We were devastated. We lost friends and family in the crash. Dad flew over the area after dark, but there was nothing but a crater left. He decided we should stay here with the Vespalids and continue the mission. It's what the others would have wanted.

"At first we failed with the Vespalids of the northern kingdom, they weren't ready to hear the word of the Lord, but God, through us, had great success among the Vespalids of the southern kingdom. The kingdoms are engaged in a bitter cold war. We aren't here for political concerns, so we stayed where we were welcome. This island is fairly inhospitable to humans—digestible food is hard to come by, water must be purified, we have to have regular oxygen treatments—but we grew to love them and their culture, in spite of it all. After about two and a half years some of us developed symptoms of a disease," she touched her face and grimaced. "We prayed for healing, but none came and dad started to feel like the Holy Spirit was moving us to bid farewell to Vespala. Most of us concurred. While he was preparing the ship to take us back to Seraph, dad received a weak signal from the other island. It was an automated distress signal triggered by some kind of trauma to the mechanic. We thought he was dead the whole time. There was no way to know exactly what triggered it after all that time, but one thing was certain, he was alive and in trouble.

"Dad told us to continue preparations while he went to investigate …" Tears welled up in her eyes. "That was the last time I saw my father." She broke down, the video cut, and then came back on. She'd regained her composure. "We received a final message from him. He was … he was bloody, apologizing, saying the mechanic was coming to kill us. Not long after, the ship crashed into the mountainside by the cove on the outskirts of the city. The mechanic was alive, but horribly injured and pinned in the wreckage. I don't know for sure, but I think dad had Seraph change the course of the ship. He crashed it on purpose. To protect us from *him*."

She seemed to have difficulty admitting the next part.

"Dad saved us *and* doomed us. Both away ships were destroyed. He changed the access codes for Seraph … to keep the mechanic from gaining control … I guess. Our second-in-command, Klaus Fontenot, was the only other one who had access, and he was killed in the *first* crash. I don't know what dad was thinking. He must have panicked, acted rashly, but we were doomed. He was always a better missionary than space jockey." She laughed in spite of the tears. "No way to leave. No medicine. And because of 'no contact' laws for unreached planets, we came here without notifying anyone of our destination. Violating no contact law carries a hefty penalty. Usually death, but we make no apologies. We answer to a higher authority. Someone will find Seraph eventually …, but not in my lifetime."

The transmission paused, her face frozen.

"What happened?" Trej said.

"There's another part. Wait for it," Solomon said.

"Do you think they have any ale?" Mal asked Nodi.

King Solomon didn't seem to like hearing conversations he couldn't understand. He narrowed his eyes at Mal.

The hologram resumed. "The others were livid," Haley said. "Hate got the better of them. They built a brick and mortar enclosure and entombed the mechanic in it. He was still alive, cursing them when they put the last brick in place. Scripture forbids murder ... what they did ... I guess sometimes technicalities can be a Christian's best friend. Their forgiveness only extended so far. I didn't exactly stop them. The thought of him buried in the darkness still haunts me. It's too late now."

She paused awhile and then, with a pained smile, said, "The others are dead. I don't have long. The water purification unit broke down. The disease is spreading through my body faster than ever. In spite of it all, I still count this experience a blessing. A privilege. We did well here among the Vespalids for they received the word of the Lord with enthusiasm. Now ... I willingly lay down my life for the advancement of the word of Christ. I'm proud to die in the service of Him. Haley Mada, out."

The transmission faded and died. Solomon was teary-eyed.

"So 'T.I.M.' were the initials of this one called Mada?" Trej said. "But the akigi scriptu—"

Nodi had sorted it out. "Tim was his exalted name. His heavenly name. Revealed *after* his soul ascended to heaven. The earliest book, the Gospel of ... Dumbass—such a stupid, mocking name for a gospel, now that the context is clear—never referred to him as 'Tim.' The later books, like the Gospel of Hinnoben, were written *after* Mada's body was found in the canyon. They saw the name on the uniform and made that connection. You said yourself that they never called him Tim when you met him."

"They could not tell it was a different man?"

"They called it *transfiguration*, but it was really just *decomposition*. I would imagine he was unrecognizable."

Nodi felt like he was on the topside of a downward spiral.

Tim had been the central figure of his life. His commitment to the gospel was the reason he learned all those languages, became a scribe, endured abuse in Prontis. His father died in dedicated service to Tim—Aenna died in a misguided attempt to *stay* committed to him, just as Haley Mada had. Their commitment was the same but to two different Messiahs. He had held out some small bit of hope that everything he believed about Tim was true. He *wanted* it to be true, but Terise Inez Mada was just another victim of the one Nodi had called Lord all his life—one who was nothing but a villainous parasite on akigi culture. All those temples built, tithes demanded, lives dominated, moral mandates delivered, foreign societies converted, wars fought, dissenters executed, exorcisms, condemnations, disownments ...

All for "Tim" in their own ways. All for a fraud, perpetrated upon the innocent.

The word "indifference" kept swimming in his head.

"Ask him if we can have a look inside that obelisk," Mal said.

Trej asked, but Solomon balked. "Of course not! Stay away from it. I've given you as much information as I can."

"What would it accomplish anyway?" Nodi said.

"We need somethin' substantial we can take back with us to *prove* what we've seen here. We need to take the mechanic's body back with us and—"

"How are we even going to get back, Mal? The ship sank."

"What are you two saying?" Solomon said.

Trej spoke up. "My friend was hoping we might have something to take back with us. Perhaps something that belonged to this mechan—"

"No!" Solomon said. "If you're interested in truth, I'll send copies of the Bible back with you. What your people need is Jesus."

"Trade the bondage of one Messiah for another?" Nodi

said.

"I can't imagine the Lord Jesus is anything like this Tim you've been worshipping. The satisfaction you'll get from *our* Messiah can't be compared to that of yours."

Two guards entered the chamber. They slithered … slithered … and somehow, Nodi got the distinct impression that they, in spite of themselves, were in a hurry, panicked even.

"Sire, a squadron of strange ships is disembarking in the cove and they don't look friendly." He pointed at Nodi, "They're creatures like *that* one."

"You brought this here!" Solomon said, eyes widened to black ovals.

Trej stepped forward, hands in front of him. "They only want us. They are not looking for trouble with you."

"Well, they can have you." More soldiers oozed into the room, crossbows at the ready. "Send them on their way. Avoid conflict if possible. We can barely defend ourselves against the Northern kingdom without getting embroiled in a *new* war with an unknown enemy."

"Yes, sire."

The king's royal advisor and a contingent of heavily armed soldiers escorted them out of the city. Everywhere Nodi looked, Vespalids were pointing crossbows at him. They were perched on rooftops, at windows, in doorways. What they lacked in speed, they made up for in numbers. Their ability to mobilize so fast was almost incomprehensible.

The procession moved beyond the gates and up the path that led to the sea.

When Nodi crested the dune, he saw Persecutor Shirka standing next to the obelisk, her convoy just on the other side of it. She turned toward them, surprised.

Nodi was overcome with blind rage and charged her, but she stepped to the left and tripped him. He tried to stand, but she kicked him onto his back and placed her foot on his throat.

"Now Nodi, I know you're upset, but you're either going to be civil towards me, or I'm going to be *very* uncivil towards you. Do you understand?"

He tried to shove her foot off his neck, but that only made her push down harder.

"Do you understand?"

He stopped fighting, strained to take in some air, and then nodded. She took her foot off slowly to make sure he wasn't going to spring back up. As he stumbled to his feet and rejoined Mal and Trej, she observed the Vespalids. They were amassing along the tops of the dunes.

She motioned her convoy to take the fugitives down to the shore.

The royal advisor followed, looking out at what was left of the akigi squadron. The ships were battered—one sinking—but the catapults and slings along their flanks were loaded and ready for combat. Anxious soldiers rowed ashore.

The persecutor looked back at the Vespalids, stared at them as if to ascertain their intentions, and then took Nodi's pack from him. She pulled out the letter, the talisman, and *Holy Bible.*

The royal advisor spoke up. "What business do you have here?"

Shirka was surprised. She put the letter and the talisman back in the bag and threw it down, holding onto *Holy Bible.* "You speak English? These are fugitives from the Selidinian Empire. Our business isn't with you."

"Your arrogance is presumptuous, pagan," the advisor said. "You don't show up on our shore as if you have every right to be here. You'll pay allegiance to our king and hear the word of the Lord before you leave this place."

"I *know* the word of the Lord."

"We've heard about your lord, this Tim person. We represent the one *true* Lord, Jesus Christ."

"Jesus, you say? Is that the same Jesus mentioned in this book?" She waved *Holy Bible* in front of him.

"Have you heeded the words in that book?" the advisor said. "Renounced your silly religion?"

"This Jesus isn't fit to tie Tim's boots. Where is this lord of yours, anyway?"

"We await his return."

"Well *our* Lord is in Prontis *right now*, accessible to all."

"You can talk to him?"

"Of course."

The advisor narrowed his eyes, "Does he talk back?"

"Well ... yes, in a spiritual sense. His heart beats in the temple and tells us he is alive and hears our prayers."

"The heart *did* beat." Nodi said, always a stickler for clarity. "... *Did.*"

"*Did* beat?" The advisor said. "It doesn't beat anymore?"

"Well, no," Shirka said, "look ... this is all very complicated ... we'll just take our prisoners and go. We aren't interested in the affairs of snails."

"Affairs of snails?" The advisor's eyes darkened. "You'll not leave here before you confess Jesus as your Lord and take the gospel back to your kingdom with you."

About that time, even more Vespalid soldiers amassed along the beach to their left and right.

"They're pretty fast for such slow creatures," Mal said.

Shirka turned her back to the advisor and ripped as many pages from *Holy Bible* as she could, tossing them high into the air. The wind carried them north in a swirling gust. She threw the book at the advisor.

"Is it a Holy war you're looking for?" The advisor was afraid. "The Lord favors us, you can be sure of that." He motioned to the Vespalids on the dunes and they raised their crossbows.

"Are you denying us safe passage out of here?"

"For the time being, yes."

She swiped the eyestalks off his head with one deft stroke of her blade. He recoiled in stunned agony, dark blood spurting from the cut appendages. She yelled out to her troops, "Shields up!"

Nodi gasped and stepped back. *She's mad.*

Her troops moved up the dune like a single organism, shields in front. The Vespalids fired a volley of arrows at them. As the Vespalids reloaded, the akigi charged.

Nodi was left unsupervised and out of range. He picked up his bag and ran after Mal and Trej. They went around the obelisk until it stood between them and the battle. Vespalids swarmed the area.

A few errant arrows flew by, Nodi ducked—Mal took one in the ass and screamed. He rolled to the ground and fell through a thick patch of brush into a ditch underneath.

"Look!" he called out above the fray.

Nodi and Trej climbed under the brush as an akiga nearby took an arrow to the face. The ditch went uphill to the obelisk. At the end closest to it, Mal discovered a small metal grate with a tunnel on the other side of it. It led inside.

"Trej, can you pull this out?" he said, bent over and pointing at the grate.

Trej pulled the arrow out of Mal's ass.

"Owww. I meant the *grate!*" Mal said, straightening up, blood oozing onto the sand.

"I know," Trej said and handed him the arrow.

Trej pulled, but it wouldn't budge so Mal struck the hinges with a rock until Trej was able to pull it out. They crawled into the darkness, feeling their way along. It smelled like mildew and dust. The walls were fragile and crumbling.

"Nodi … the bag," Mal said, looking back. It glowed

faintly. Nodi opened it and looked inside.

"It's the talisman. It's active." He pulled it out. A white light shone on the disc-like surface of it.

"We must be close to the mechanic," Trej said.

Outside, the cacophony of battle played like hell's concert. The ground rumbled. They found a small square door above them. Mal sprung it open after some aggressive pounding.

They climbed into the obelisk. The top of it was open like a pyramid with its top lopped off. The red sky cast an eerie pink inside. The bottom was a crater covered in sand and soot from years of weathering. Metal twisted around the perimeter as if someone had moved the wreckage out of the way to make room for the tomb in the middle.

The tomb was cobbled together with stones of various sizes and shapes, held together by weak mortar. A crude inscription read:

JESUS IS OUR HOPE FOR THE AFTERLIFE. HERE LAYS ALL HOPE FOR THIS LIFE.

"Should we open it?"

"We have come this far," Trej said. He pulled a steel rod from the wreckage and began prying stones out of the tomb. Mal and Nodi joined in. The battle outside intensified, loud knocks and scrapes on the outside walls echoed through the chamber in fits and starts. The talisman in Nodi's bag glowed brighter as they opened up a hole in the side of the tomb.

In a rare appearance, the suns shone through the clouds above, casting long shadows in the obelisk and illuminating the inside of the tomb. Nodi climbed up the pile of rubble and looked in.

A body was there, naked, split in half, and pinned down by gnarled metal. Sinewy spools of cable poked out of punctures and tears along its midriff.

It looks nothing like Mada's body, Nodi thought. *Shouldn't it be more … decomposed?*

And then it opened its eyes as if the scant light had awakened it from its ancient slumber. Nodi fell back in terror—those eyes were locked on him, glazed, confused.

"Judas?" It said with a weak voice.

"Judas? No—"

"Who *are* you?" the body said.

The Akigi Bible

The Gospel According to Dumbass, 6:1-6

6 And the Lord performed many signs and wonders and would heal certain kinds of flesh wounds and infirmities if they were not too severe and if he was in a good mood.

2 One day, his disciples brought to him an akigo whose betrothed cut off his akigohood in a rage, accusing him of infidelity. 3 When they attempted to hand the Lord the severed organ, the Lord said to them, "I shall not touch that, for it is nasty," 4 and so they knew that it was unclean.

5 But some of them grumbled that he could not heal all wounds, only some, and so the Lord spoke to them saying, 6 "The deeper the wound, the harsher the judgment. There are some things even God will not forgive."

32

Y ou're not Judas," the body said, eyes adjusting to what little light there was.

Nodi was struck dumb, perched at the hole, looking in. Though it was dark, Nodi could see that this shattered person, Haley Mada's "mechanic," looked nothing like the Tim of his visions and dreams. The metaphysical lord of his mind's eye and *this* thing had nothing in common.

"I've known you my whole life," Nodi whispered, "and I don't have a clue who you are."

"Yeah, well I don't know you either, pal," the mechanic said, his voice getting stronger. "Listen, do you think you can get me out of here?"

Nodi looked at Mal, but Mal just looked perplexed.

"I remember you," the man said to Trej. "If I can't see a friendly face, a familiar one will do. Help me out?"

Trej chirped and sniffed to ascertain a clear picture of the man.

"The night I met you …," he said, "your device, it didn't finish. What … What's the missing piece? What did I miss?"

"Oh yeah, right. That always happens when there's a sudden influx of info previously unknown. It's natural. Get used to the mystery, pal, it's one of the more interesting parts of life. Now … can someone help me out of here?"

Nodi crawled into the hole and tried to pull the metal free, but it wouldn't budge. Trej was skeptical about releasing him, but reached in any way and pulled enough of it away that they were able to unpin him. His legs were severed at the waist, only his right arm was intact.

"What's going on out there?" the mechanic asked, hearing the battle noises.

"A holy war," Trej said. "You have been at the heart of more than a few of them. Who are you … really?"

"Sounds like you already know."

"What's he sayin'?" Mal said, not following the English conversation.

"We've always known you as Tim," Nodi said.

"Why would you think my name is *Tim*?"

"It said it on your clothes … on Terise Mada's clothes … we thought his body was yours and the heart was beating and the scriptures called you Tim and—"

"Jesus, man, you thought *he* was *me*? No one would have confused the two of us when he was alive, that's for *damn* sure. I guess all us *people* look alike to you. God knows you all look alike to me."

"Did you just call me Jesus?" Nodi said. "Is this what I'm to be called now?"

"You guys and your names. I have a bad habit of using the lord's name in vain," he said with a smirk. "No. The Jesus thing was funny for a while, but it got old. Before long, I'd say 'Jesus' and a hundred different akigi would answer. What *is* your name anyway?"

Nodi lifted the man's heavy upper half and handed it out to Mal.

"I'm Nodi and that's Mal and—"

"Trej," the man said with a wink in Trej's direction. Mal pulled him out and set him on the floor, propping him up against the tomb.

Trej was surprised the man remembered him.

"I have a very good memory." He tapped his temple with his one good index finger. "No name changes. Not anymore. Your ancestors called me things like 'Lord' and 'Messiah,' but my real name is Quentin Reese. Friends call me Q."

"Are we friends?" Nodi asked.

"I don't know. Are you? Fetch my legs, too."

"What's goin' on?" Mal said.

Nodi tried to pull the legs out, but they were stuck. "I ... uhh ... I don't think I can."

"Oh well, it doesn't matter." The man stared up at the sky as if it were a precious jewel. "Did you say something about a heartbeat?"

"Yes. It beat for over two hundred and forty years ... until it stopped recently." Nodi struggled to speak. His every reaction felt instinctual, emerging out of a life spent in spiritual servitude to this person. "That's part of what led us here ... you can imagine what ... what a miracle it is that you're here with us, alive and—"

"You're confused, I'm sure. Confused and looking for answers."

"Yes."

"We're *all* looking for answers, sport. Every last damn one of us, no matter what shithole corner of the universe we come from. Say, you think you can get me to Mada's body? I'd *really* like to see it."

"You murdered him," Trej said.

"Murder's such a strong word ... Look, I'm no saint," Q said. "I'm just looking for redemption like you are. Take me to Mada's body. Please. I'll tell you anything you want to know on the way, but Mada's body … it might hold the keys to the kingdom. I've gotta get there."

Mal was getting frustrated. "Would someone tell me what's goin' on?"

The talisman glowed brightly inside Nodi's bag. He pulled it out.

"I thought I sensed that thing around here," Q said. "Where'd you find it?"

"Judas buried it with *Holy Bible*."

"Judas. What a prick. What happened to him anyway?"

"He killed himself."

"Good."

"He left a suicide note written on Mada's sleeve," Nodi said. "That's how we found you. How did he get the sleeve?"

"I ripped the sleeve off in the struggle with Mada. Judas grabbed it out of my hands before he left the ship."

"Left … or was pushed?" Trej said.

Q chortled but didn't answer. He looked at the talisman. "Can I have it back?"

Nodi hesitated.

"You know what that thing is capable of, Nodi." Trej said. "And you know what horrors *he* is capable of. Think of his deeds as described in your scriptures and strip them of holy license. All that is left are the despicable acts of a very sad little man who deceived a lot of innocent akigi. Give him that device and you give him his power back. Judas knew it and you know it too."

"He's right," Q said, "I've done … questionable … things. But I can use it to put a stop to that battle outside and get us back to Selidin safely. If it makes you feel better, I'll give it back to you for safekeeping."

Nodi looked down at the talisman. The glowing screen on it flashed the words, "Standing By." The fighting was getting louder, harsh cracks against the outside of the obelisk growing more frequent. The sky clouded over again. It was too dark to see anything more than shapes and long shadows.

Q's eyes glinted. "Do you have a plan, some other way out of this? Do you have friends out there that can help you?"

Nodi looked at Trej, hoping for permission, but Trej didn't oblige. Nodi looked back at Q and placed the talisman on his hand.

"Curiosity killed the cat," Q said.

What did he mean by that? Nodi wondered.

The device lit up and Q's eyes went dead for a moment. Nodi thought he saw green numbers run across the man's pupils before he blinked and sighed in relief.

"It's getting worse out there," Q said. "Can one of you carry me?"

"What's goin' on?" Mal said.

"Oh for Christ's sake." Q pointed the talisman at him. Mal held his arms up defensively and gasped before the talisman lit up and held him in a trance. After a moment, he fell back, shook his head, and got back up.

"God*damn* it!" he said in English.

Q laughed. "Out of the mouths of babes. Now give me a lift, partner."

Mal struggled under Q's weight as he lifted him onto his back. Q clamped around his neck with his only arm and held on. The broken wires and sinewy bits of flesh dangled down and tickled Mal's back.

"Nice tattoos," Q said. "I used to have tattoos back when I had *real* flesh. They didn't glow, though. Had a stripper down the length of my back, a hot one, tits out, g-string. After the fact, I thought I should have put her on my chest so I could jerk-off to her in the mirror, but I was drunk and didn't really think about that when I got it."

They heard a fierce whizzing sound above them—a ball of spiked iron flew overhead.

Mal looked up. "They're firin' the catapults off the ships."

No sooner than those words escaped his mouth, the side of the obelisk burst in behind them and the tower collapsed in a tremendous cloud of dust. It thundered as the stone gave way. As the tower imploded, Nodi thought it was over, indifference had come to collect and none of this would matter. Q let go of Mal, held his arm straight up as he fell, and fired a powerful blast from his hand. The Shockwave sent the imposing stones rolling away from them in all directions.

When the air cleared, they stood in the open, amongst hundreds of Vespalid and akigi soldiers, living and dead. Many stopped fighting and stared at the rubble, confused. The akigi aboard the ships, having seen the blast, ceased firing.

For the first time, Nodi had a clear view of Q, at his pale flesh, black eyes, and square jaw. He was hairy in patches—arms, chest, face—and it made Nodi think less of him. Only wild, stupid things, had hair like that on Akigol.

Persecutor Shirka, bloody and bruised, was at the top of the dune looking down. In the fog of war, she couldn't see Q nor understand what had happened. She saw Trej's lumbering silhouette in the smoke and charged, battle hammer drawn. Mal tackled her before she could swing the hammer, and hit her repeatedly. The persecutor gained advantage and knocked him to the ground.

She got up, wiped the blood off her brow, and kicked him in the face as he tried to stand. He fell on his back. She picked up her hammer, placed her foot on his neck, and choked him. Mal saw his old dagger in a sheath in her boot. He grabbed it and slipped the knife into her upper thigh.

Even with the blade penetrating her leg, she had the strength to swing the hammer. Mal moved to the left, but the hammer crushed his right hand. It would have obliterated it had it not been lying in the soft sand of the beach. The damage was severe, though, and Mal screamed in pain. She kicked him in the face, again.

"Get the others!" she yelled at the soldiers standing by, watching.

They closed in guardedly. Q, still on the ground, fired a blast that incinerated them in a precise line that led down to the waterline. The ash that was their flesh blew into the wind.

Shirka, still not comprehending what happened, pulled Mal's dagger out of her leg and launched it wildly. It struck Trej in the belly.

He fell to the ground. Shirka charged Nodi, hammer overhead, when she spotted Q. Her eyes widened and her knees gave out. She skidded to a halt in the dust of the collapsed tower, staring at the half man in disbelief. It was as if the tightly wound threading of her soul came undone. Everything she thought she knew changed at the sight of him. Everything she feared most came to fruition. She tried to speak, but couldn't.

Mal wanted to kill her, but couldn't lift his hand. Nodi ran to Trej. Trej's breathing was irregular, strained. Nodi dragged Q to his side, close enough to touch the wound.

"Help him," he said.

"What do you expect *me* to do?" Q said. "It's too deep. Sorry."

"Try!"

"It's too deep, man."

Trej turned his face toward Nodi and muttered something. Nodi leaned in, but couldn't discern what he was saying. Trej kept trying to repeat it until his body went limp. Nodi held his ear to Trej's mouth hoping to understand, but he couldn't.

It wasn't just the last words of a single friend, but a whole species.

Nodi draped over him, holding his huge hand.

"I did your will, Lord," Shirka said to Q. "I think he might have been the last troogil."

Nodi pulled out the dagger and charged. He knocked her over, hit her feverishly, and held the dagger to her throat. The persecutor was terrified. Nodi lifted the dagger, poised to stab her in the upper heart when Q blew him back with a concussion blast. Nodi rolled to his feet, perplexed with the dagger still in his hand.

"I need her," Q said.

A group of akigi and Vespalid soldiers gathered around, watching what was happening. Shirka kneeled before Q, fearful and pathetic. Nodi couldn't move. He was so close to vengeance, but like everything else in this God-forsaken journey, he would come up empty.

"Who are you?" Q said authoritatively.

"Persecutor Erd Shirka, Lord, I command the armies of Prontis and I've served King Jesus the Fifteenth and Chief High Apostle Hinnoben the Eighth for many years. But if the truth be known, I've served you and you alone."

"Hinnoben the *Eighth*?" Q said. "The first Hinnoben wasn't worth repeating. Your ships look like they're in bad shape. Will they sail?"

"Two of them will, Lord, but I don't think we can make it through the cyclone again."

Q held up his hand and flashed Shirka's eyes. Shirka blinked as if something was in them, and then she regained her composure. She looked confounded by what she'd seen—her eyes were imbued with a maniacal spark.

"The numbers," she said, "What do they mean?"

"Give those coordinates to both captains. They have to follow that *exact* course. It'll get them through the cyclone safely. You go ahead with the first ship. We'll follow later. When I get to Selidin, I want a carriage, a covered one that can carry me and my new friends to the temple. Prepare the way for me. Make sure we get safe passage. Do you understand?"

"Yes, Lord. I will prepare the way for you. But what about the other things you showed me?"

"That's something special just for you," he said. "Prepare the way."

Q turned to Nodi and winked. It was a hollow, mocking gesture. Mal went to Q and held his damaged hand out to him.

"What do I look like, Mr. Fixit?"

"Please." Mal's hand was broken in multiple places.

"I help *you*, you help *me*, right?"

Mal nodded and Q grabbed his hand. Mal fell on his side, muscles stiff. He scratched at his arms and face as if something was crawling on him and then he went limp with relief. He held up his hand, flexed his fingers, and fell to his knees before Q.

"Bury your friend and get some rest," Q said to Nodi.

"Can I have the talisman back?"

"No."

33

Nodi didn't know what to think of Q. He was trapped in a nether region of ignorance and confusion.

Q decreed they remain on the beach overnight, and then move aboard the ship and stay there until repairs were complete. Shirka's soldiers granted his every request without question.

The half-man lay on the beach, relishing his newfound freedom even amidst the grotesque aftermath of the battle. He kept a close eye on the Vespalids who sat atop the dunes and watched, frightened, retreating into their shells at dusk. They made no effort to bury their dead. A few akigi soldiers remained, stacking their own fallen in piles to burn them.

It was low tide and the beach reached out into the water, white foam the only thing dividing black sand from black sea. The horizon burned with all the colors of an inferno.

Nodi found a spot on a hill to the south. Mal helped him drag Trej up there and they dug a grave with jumbo half shells they found on the shore. The sand was coarse and warm to the touch with cold, black clay beneath it.

They stared at the hole when they were finished. Mal squatted next to Trej, held his stiff hand for a moment, and walked away, shaking his head.

Nodi leaned over, rolled Trej's body into the hole, and shoveled the dirt over him. It was late when he finished and the ambient light from the Vespalid city cast an eerie orange glow. There were no stars, no moon, no aurora, just a rusty haze on the rushing clouds above. The wind was warm against his back as he sat next to the grave. He pulled out the cog Trej gave him—he forgot he had it—and turned it over in his hands.

"At least I got to bury *you*," he said. "That's more than I got with Aenna. Do you see her where you are now? ... Are you anywhere at all?" He scooped up some sand and let it run through his fingers. "I'm so sorry."

He looked down at Q who sat propped against some driftwood. The captain of the ship that would take them back to Sigate was there, and Mal too, a dim beacon of red light in the encroaching dark.

"I don't trust Q, Trej," Nodi said. "I think he intends to pick up where he left off, but how can he in his condition? He has a plan. I just wish I knew what it was."

———— ·!!═{•◑☒◐•}═!!· ————

"I'll prepare the way for you," Shirka had promised Q.

She stood on the bow of the frigate. Seafoam blew up and around her, tentacles rippling, body loosely conforming to the aggressive dips, rises, and sways. Since she first saw Tim's broken body in Prontis, she sensed something was amiss. Waves crashed, drenched her in hot, black water as she prayed for forgiveness. She realized she'd been on the wrong side of things.

The scribe was right.

The scribe was right.

The scribe. Was. Right.

God *chose* him and the ixaquoi too—they proved Tim's body was broken because he wasn't the Messiah.

The man on the beach was the Messiah all along.

She contemplated the lies, couldn't make sense of them, but had faith the answers would come. The man on the beach showed her things, things that enraged her, things that planted seeds of vengeance in her hearts.

She'd seen through his eyes, the night he was crucified.

He was tied up, missing his talisman, woefully weak. Judas was there, but not alone. Hinnoben was with him.

"It's your destiny, Judas," Hinnoben said. "No more excuses. He changed your name for this reason, we've talked about this."

They spoke Selidinese, and though they didn't know it, the man understood them.

"I don't know," Judas said. "It doesn't seem right. God will destroy us."

"You will be the greatest martyr who ever lived. What commitment it must take to sacrifice this life and the next one, too. God will not forget you, Judas, you must have faith."

Everything faded to black and when the man awoke, he'd been pierced and was unable to move. He couldn't see well, just shapes and firelight and bushes that appeared to shiver in his stupor.

"Why doesn't he die?" Judas said.

"He isn't flesh and blood like us."

"He is of the spirit. If it was God's will for him to die, he would have. We must take him down and beg his forgiveness."

There was silence awhile, but the man sensed Hinnoben's quiet fury.

"Hinnoben?" Judas said.

"*He is no Messiah*," Hinnoben hissed. "He is not God. There is no God. He used us, you idiot. He found the most powerful form of control there is—religious faith built on the impenetrable word of God. Who can question it? Who can question the logic of that which transcends logic? Who can argue morality to the author of it? Who can make appeals to he who controls all of creation? We cannot win, for this ... this *thing* ... has set himself up as the arbiter of such things."

"I don't underst—"

"Take this rock, Judas. Take it. Hit him. *Kill him.*"

"What will we tell the others?"

"We'll tell them what they *want* to hear. We'll make it gospel."

"Then what happens to me?"

"*Kill* him," Hinnoben said again and walked away.

The man passed out but was jolted awake when a rock crashed into his temple. A loud bass tone rang out, and then a screech and some static. He had white noise vision. The man could just make out Judas' silhouette ...

In the fury of wind and shattered wood, Shirka made her penance and vowed to make right what the Hinnoben's had made wrong. She was baptized by wave, consecrated by the man's command, reborn into a new faith she had no name for. The man's coordinates were an improvement over their previous trek across the sea, but the ship still sank before it docked in Sigate—the work of the evil one, she surmised. A dinghy carried her and a few others to the docks and they climbed onto the pier amidst a crowd who'd watched the ship go down off the coast.

Everyone knew the persecutor in Sigate—famous, infamous, it depended on whom you asked. As with every other part of the kingdom, the citizenry was on the cusp of civil war. The scribe and the ixaquoi gave the kingdom a hearty push in that direction when they violated the abomination that was in the temple in Prontis.

Shirka pushed through the crowd and climbed onto the roof of an old bait shop. She looked down at them like a sympathetic mother and took her armor off.

"I hereby renounce my post as persecutor," she shouted. "Ride with me, brothers and sisters, for today begins the first day of the new world order. The Messiah is coming. I have seen him and his name is *not* Tim. Prontis must fall in preparation for his glorious arrival. Ride with me!"

She climbed off the roof and mounted a runner they'd brought out to her. The mayor, a short, big-headed akigo was there, stunned at the persecutor's declaration.

"Gather every soldier, every runner, every able-bodied akigi willing to fight for me," She said to him. "We ride to Prontis. We must expose the treachery."

"What treachery?" the mayor said.

"It will all come to light soon enough. Spread the message. The Lord is back, resurrected, and coming to Selidin. Have a covered carriage waiting for him here. The scribe and the ixaquoi will accompany him—the ones we were hunting. They were right all along. We must prepare the way!"

———————•∺⊷◗◖●◖⊶∺•———————

Shirka rode toward Prontis joined by soldiers and the angry and the disenfranchised. She had a sizable army by the time she reached Kan Ludo and doubled it there alone. They swarmed the kingdom highway—now a one-way road to the capital—set afire with rumor, gaining momentum and personnel.

Shirka's forces entered Prontis without resistance. Neither King Jesus the Fifteenth nor Hinnoben the Eighth anticipated the act of aggression. They didn't even comprehend it as an act of aggression. Shirka emerged from the throngs of frothy-mouthed militia and stood near the doors of the temple. Hinnoben, adorned in his ornamental garb, stood on his balcony looking down, bewildered.

"Persecutor Shirka?" he said. "What happened in Sigate? Is there an invasion on the way?"

"I stand here," she yelled up, "humbled by the Lord. I'm here to tell you that he lives, he's on Akigol, and he's coming to the temple. He sent me here to prepare the way."

Hinnoben looked out into the distance. "What's happening at the palace?"

"Can I come up and speak with you, Chief High Apostle?"

"Yes, of course. Open the gates!"

Shirka went inside, marched down the corridor, and into the cloister. The tree still slouched from Nodi's escape and a strange sense of reverence coursed through her veins at the sight of it. She went into Tim's chamber and was disgusted to see the body reassembled with sticks and twine. On the far side of the room, an apostle beat a drum, simulating the heartbeat. Shirka pulled out her battle hammer and hit Tim's sarcophagus. The drummer ran out of the chamber and into the Great Hall, stumbling as he did. The case cracked and shattered with the seventh impact. The body collapsed, falling to the floor in pieces. Hinnoben burst in with the drummer peeking over his shoulder.

"You're insane!" he yelled.

Shirka retrieved the nearest torch and stood over Tim's shattered body.

"You'll burn in hell for this," Hinnoben said, through gritted teeth.

Shirka set Tim's tattered jumpsuit on fire then threw the torch at Hinnoben. Hinnoben ran out of the chamber and up the stairs. Shirka caught up to him as he tried to slam the door. She kicked it open. Hinnoben fell back on the bed, shocked at this sudden onset of violence.

"The Lord is on his way," she said, standing over him. "Physically. I saw him with my own eyes and he is *not* that abomination in the chamber down there. The scribe was right to search. If he hadn't, we might never have known this deceit. What was done in secret, God has brought to light."

"You're mad, Shirka," Hinnoben said, voice cracking. He clenched the sheets of his bed. Out of the corner of his eye, he saw smoke billowing into the sky. It came from the palace.

"The Lord showed me a vision," Shirka said. She put her foot on his chest and pinned him down. "I heard *your* forefather, Hinnoben the First, scheming with Judas, manipulating him. Hinnoben orchestrated the conspiracy and blamed everything on Judas. He deceived the akigi and seized power after the Lord's death. He twisted Holy Writ for his own benefit."

"How could I know that?" Hinnoben said. "I couldn't have known that. I'm not even related by blood. Kingdom elders chose me. I can't be held accountable—"

"We're *all* accountable!"

She dropped her hammer, pulled Hinnoben up by the neckline of his robe, and dragged him out onto the balcony. The crowds watched, shocked. Hinnoben begged for mercy, but Shirka picked him up by his feet and dangled him over the banister head first. He crowed and pawed the outside of the banister. The crowd roared, some in opposition, some in support.

Shirka let go.

Hinnoben fell and hit the ground, back first, blood spooling out of his mouth on impact. He clawed at the dirt with his dying hand, head pulling to the side until he fell still.

The dull thud of his body hitting the ground was like a trigger that set off riots in the streets of Prontis.

34

As he sailed away from Vespala, Nodi stood at the stern of the frigate and watched the Vespalids collect their dead. Solomon was alone on the beach near the water, watching them leave.

The island shrunk behind them while the swirling mass of chaos loomed up ahead. The captain directed everyone below when the water got rough. Mal sat Q on the bed, leaning against the wall in the captain's quarters. Nodi sat at the table absently spinning Trej's cog.

Q read the akigi scriptures as they sailed, devouring its words as if reading a secret diary. He shook his head sometimes and laughed. Mal stood by the door and watched him. Nodi felt like they were under siege.

"This is unbelievable," Q said.

Nodi stopped playing with the cog. "What?"

"Your scriptures. They're full of shit! I didn't do ... or say ... I don't know ... at least half of what it says I did, here. I mean ... God ... there's just so much wrong with this. And most of it claims to be written by people who were there!

Take this thing about me pushing the guys off the cliff. I didn't push them off the cliff. Here's what happened: Hinnoben and the others bring these two yahoos up to me who aren't wearing *pants*—turtle-tail dicks out for all to see. All I did was raise my hand to shield my eyes, y'know, and *Bam!* someone shoves them off the damn cliff. I say, 'What the hell did you do that for?' and they say, 'We thought you were trying to knock them over when you raised your hand like that." So I say, 'No, I wasn't trying to knock them over, I just didn't want to look at their creepy little cocks, that's all.' Jesus. This gospel by Hinnoben is a *real* piece of work. That fuckwit was the biggest damn con artist of them all. I can guarantee you he didn't write this himself. His hands were deformed. Bet you didn't know that. Hell, whoever jotted it down for him didn't even bother to refer to him in the first person. Like I'd appear to *that* prick after my death. It makes me look like ... like ... fuckin' Gandhi."

"Who?"

"Hinnoben was an arrogant asshole," Q continued, undeterred. "He was right about my return, though, huh?" He grinned and looked down. "Well, *half* a return's better than *no* return."

Nodi looked at Q's damages, at the wires and the black, bubbled edges of torn skin. "You aren't flesh and blood."

"I jumped the flesh a long, long time ago. Hell, you people were probably still ... I don't know ... running on all fours and throwing shit at each other."

"Jumped the flesh? What do you mean?"

"This isn't my first body, you know. Where I come from, we map our minds, our consciousness, and transplant it into artificial bodies. Body after body after body. We jump the flesh. Space is big and if you're gonna make it out here ... there ... you need longevity and you need to be able to survive the worst conditions imaginable."

"Built to last," Mal said.

"Hell, yeah."

"You have no soul," Nodi said.

"None of us do." He thought about it and added, "Still ... there's the question of whether I'm *really* me, whole and true ... or just a copy."

Nodi watched the cog slide back and forth. The ship hit a steep wave and it fell off the table and slipped through his fingers. He got down on all fours, put it in his pocket, and sat back at the table.

"Why did you come here?" he said as if nothing had happened.

"It was just a job. Reverend Mada hired me to be the ship's mechanic. Their other one absconded with some money or something. I was their only viable option at the time. Anyway, guys like Mada, religious nuts, don't believe in having artificial parts. People like me are cursed as far as he was concerned. That's why it's so damn funny that, apparently, he had an artificial heart."

"Artificial?"

"Yeah. He was a partial, mostly flesh and blood with a few machinations in the mix. Anyway, he hired me, but the whole crew treated me like shit, y'know. Do you know what it's like to be looked down on? To be treated like a second-class citizen?"

"I do."

"Yeah, well ... they set up these two away teams, one for the akigi and one for the Vespalids—hey, did you know, well I guess you *wouldn't* know this, but Akigol is tied for tenth in highest number of intelligent life forms on one planet? The word 'intelligent' is open to interpretation, of course."

"I ... uhh ..."

"They set up these away teams to try and come here and tell you all about the power and the glory. They assigned me to the team going to Selidin, but not to evangelize, I was just supposed to drop them off, but the ship went to hell on entry. I don't know what happened. She lit up like a firecracker. I ejected, but everyone else ... there was nothing I could do. I took a nasty shot to the head." He pointed to a hairless patch on his scalp.

"I'm not sure I understand—"

"Man, I was so out of it. Dazed and confused. My head wasn't right after that. I lost contact with everything. Something was dislodged in there." He tapped his temple. "I came to and there's these green, red, and blue fuckers with their tentacle heads and bug eyes, not a stitch of clothing on most of 'em—scared the shit out of me. I was so out of it all I could say was, "What the hell is going on here?"—scripture got that part right—but anyway, Judas knocked it loose. My brain, I mean ... somehow ... when he cracked me on the head during his half-assed crucifixion, the prick. That's how that jackass Mada found me." He shrugged as best he could with his one good shoulder. "It's funny. As a mechanic, I always said, 'when all else fails, beat the hell out of it.'"

"What happened to Mada?"

Q stared at Nodi awhile and then looked up at the ceiling contemplatively. "He showed up to rescue me, I guess, but Judas slipped aboard. Mada put two and two together and we got into it. I got the upper hand, kicked Judas off the ship and turned it around—went back the way we came. Mada slipped up behind me as I was trying to land, knocked me down, changed the coordinates back. I threw his ass out, too. Thought the fall killed him, but obviously it didn't. He had a direct link to Seraph in his brain, had to have, because he didn't have a transmitter on him. He had her run me into the rocks on the coast of Vespala. Didn't see that coming."

"Who's Seraph?" Mal said.

Q waved the question away and tossed the scripture book

on the floor.

"Why did you pretend to be the Messiah?" Nodi said.

"Who says I was pretending?"

Nodi looked down, exasperated. Q laughed. "I never claimed to be the Messiah, man. That title was put on me. I just went with it. Some of you akigi shits are savage, I thought they'd try and eat me, raw and wiggling, if I didn't play along."

"But in scripture, you knew so much about the *soul* of the akigi. Of the akigi condition. The sin and the longing for love and justice and—"

"Where I come from, sport, we call it the '*human* condition.' It's universal, man ... more or less. Life just *is* no matter where it is—there's only so many ways it can go. The themes never change. Take this boat, for instance. A boat is a boat, no matter what planet it's on. The variations are mostly cosmetic, all things being equal. The physics that make this particular type of design practical don't really change all that much." He snorted and added, "Except on Ugarbia Ten. Those fish head fucks have a whoooole other thing going on there."

Mal moved to the corner, just listening.

"What's with you, tattoos?" Q said.

"I've spent years tryin' to prove you were a fraud," Mal said. "To destroy the religion *you* started. But now you're here ... resurrected, as foretold ... The Timians claimed you'd come back from the dead and here you are. *I* claimed you were a liar and you were. Never thought both would be true."

"What are you saying?" Nodi said.

"What if he *is* a Messiah and isn't even aware of it? Or what if he knows and is testin' us?"

Q fought back a smile.

The waves were getting choppier. Nodi got up from the table and held onto a post in the middle of the cabin for support. The wind howled outside, waves thundered against the hull. The table slid against the far wall and back again, finally falling over.

"Think we'll survive the storm?" Mal said above the noise.

"Why do we need a Messiah?" Nodi said. "Why do we *need* to be saved?"

"Good questions," Q said.

They made it through the cyclone with only moderate damage to the ship and sailed into Sigate. Q's coordinates seemed almost divine. Word had spread about the resurrection of the Lord and his coming. Throngs of silent onlookers were on the beach, a makeshift shantytown erected, some waited on the docks and on the roofs of buildings. Nodi felt cold when he saw the pier where Aenna was murdered. He couldn't stop that moment from playing over in his head—the hits, the fall, the splash.

Mal fashioned a backpack and once the ship was docked, strapped the half man to his back. Q ordered the soldiers to bring the carriage to the pier, close to the ship so they could climb without trouble from the crowd. The carriage was faded purple with gray trim and thick wheels, inspired by Q's own designs two hundred and forty-three years prior. Four red spotted runners pulled it. Q was strict about not letting anyone see inside so the curtains were drawn. Up top, an old akigo held the reigns, snapping the runners forward once they were inside. The crowd parted in silence to let the carriage through.

Q let them open the curtains and look out once they were alone in the wilderness. Nodi stared up at the Mobo Mountains as they rode by at dusk, wondering where in that vast expanse Trej's observatory was. As night fell, the mountains became black silhouettes against the starry sky.

"Stop!" Q called out to the carriage driver as they rode past some brush off to the left.

"What is it?" Mal said.

"Carry me out to those bushes."

Mal carried him over. Q pulled some dried raptor leaves off a withered vine, licking his lips as if savoring it.

"Sit me down here," he said. Mal complied. "Now go tear some pages out of that holy book in the carriage."

Mal did and brought them back. Nodi watched from the roadside. Night bugs chattered and cricked, small animals scurried somewhere back in the woods.

"Tear some squares," Q told him, "... yeah, like that. Now crush these leaves and roll them up ... Too loose, roll it tighter ... Yeah ... Now twist the ends ... Roll as many as you can."

He put one of the cigarettes in his mouth, lit it with the talisman, and took a long drag. He went limp, spurted a stream of smoke from the corner of his mouth, and held it out to Mal.

"They're poison to us," Mal said.

"Just the thorns. The leaves won't hurt you."

Mal was wary and looked to Nodi for an opinion.

"I wouldn't," Nodi said.

Mal took it anyway and daintily sucked at it. He coughed, took a second drag, and his whole body relaxed.

"Keep it," Q said, lighting another one for himself. "Do you realize how many hallucinogenic plants are on this planet? It's a wonder anyone here keeps any semblance of reality, at all. God, I'm glad I sprung for the narco-effect implants."

"It's good," Mal said, nodding.

"Lay me down," Q said.

Mal laid him on his back and joined him on the ground. They looked up at the twinkling, pink-streaked expanse, billowing smoke into the air above them. Nodi watched the pulsing glow of their cigarettes, curious to partake, but too guarded to succumb.

"There she is," Q said, focused on something overhead.

"What?"

Nodi looked up and saw the dim star Trej had shown him, following its methodical path across the heavens. "It's Trej's star."

"*Star?*" Q said. "That's Seraph. She's what brought us here, still in orbit after all this time. I can't even begin to tell you how glad I am to see her. If you want a miracle," he said, and pointed up with the cigarette lodged between his fingers, "there she is."

"It's not like you can go there," Nodi said.

"You think?"

"What's it like out there?" Mal said.

"Beautiful ... Horrible ... Dead ... Spectacular ... Infinite. Words can't describe it." He took another drag and blew out a couple of smoke rings that drifted up and dissipated. "I wouldn't wish it on anyone ... but at the same time, it's sad so many have lived their lives having never been."

"There are a lot of others out there?" Nodi said.

"There's life *everywhere*. Not much of it is complex—even less that's intelligent. But as small a percentage of intelligent life as there is, it's still a whole *helluva* lot." He tapped some ash on the ground next to him. "And it's strange ... no matter where you go, you see the same *themes* over and over, y'know ... similar patterns, technologies ... crazy ass beliefs. They all have their own peculiarities, but most of it comes down to minute physical, mental, linguistic differences. At the core of it, though, it's all the same. There's only so many paths life can follow before it becomes unsustainable."

"If you *could* get up there, would you leave Akigol?" Mal

said.

"Not sure. What I've done here is illegal and ... man ... the explaining I'd have to do."

"What laws do you abide by?"

"Intergalactic law. Interference of any kind with primitive species is ... frowned upon. Obtaining deification on a primitive planet'll get you a slow, painful death. Still, no one's watching too closely ..." He flicked the cigarette away. "We'd better go. Mal, be a pal. Get me back to the carriage."

They rode to Prontis without any more stops, Nodi and Mal ate food the occasional citizen shoved into the hands of the carriage driver. Q never ate. The crowd was thick and unrelenting when they arrived. It was around noon and Q made Nodi close the curtains so they couldn't be seen. The carriage rocked from side to side in the swell of the multitude. The roar of the crowd subsided into a confused hush as they went. Sometimes rocks bounced off the outside—intentional or errant, Nodi couldn't say.

"That persecutor has a big fucking mouth," Q said. "How could she have stirred up this much chaos in such a short time?"

"The akigi were already on edge," Nodi said. "You've been the focal point of this city for over two centuries."

They rode across the cobblestoned bridge over the river Hyxl—the wheels clacked over the bumps. Shirka's soldiers pushed back the masses yelling, "Make way for the Lord!" As the carriage rocked, the curtain fell back a little. The sky was dark with smoke.

"What else did you say to Shirka?" Mal said.

"I showed her the truth. A truth long suppressed gets this kind of reception sometimes ... But I never imagined—"

The carriage came to stop. They had arrived.

"Is this it?" Q said.

Nodi peeked through the curtains. The temple gates were open but heavily guarded. "Yes."

"Mada's body's in there?" Q peeked out.

"Yes."

"Is there a way onto the roof?"

35

Nodi followed Q and Mal through the temple gates.

"It's gaudy," Q said of the temple.

Shirka was waiting in the cloister. She got down on one knee to greet her new Lord. The tree behind her was nothing but a charcoal trunk sticking out of an ashy patch on the ground. Hinnoben's crushed body hung from the tree, covered in insects, putrefying in the afternoon suns. Nodi turned away from it.

"Christ," Q said. "Who *was* that?"

"Hinnoben the Eighth," Shirka said, "spiritual successor of he who conspired to kill you, Lord. I've avenged you and seized Prontis. Your kingdom awaits its king."

"Bury him," Q said, wincing. "*Jesus.*"

"I am to be called Jesus, Lord?"

"No. Jesu—*fuck*—from this day forward, I'll never rename another akigi, okay? Now let us in and then bury that thing."

"Yes, Lord." Shirka opened the heavy door to Tim's chamber. As Mal passed her, he held up his restored hand, wiggled his fingers in front of her face, and slapped her. She remained subservient. Nodi felt some measure of petty vindication when Mal did that.

Broken pieces of Tim's sarcophagus were scattered on the floor inside the chamber. Among the shards lay pieces of Mada's charred body, black and twisted. The head and torso were there, the twine and sticks that held him together burned away. The stench of rot filled the place. Mada's heart—Tim's heart—a metal and plastic bean-shaped device, lay on the floor, crushed.

"Damn it! I …" Q was flabbergasted at Shirka's reckless destruction. "She's unhinged. Put me down near the head. I hope to God it's not destroyed."

"I could have told you she was unstable," Mal said. "Crazy even. Someone should rein her in or she'll destroy the city."

Q nodded, considering it.

"What are you lookin' for?" Mal put him down.

Q turned the head so that he could access the base of the skull. He poked his fingers through the now charred, petrified flesh and pulled it away to reveal a small metal panel. Three thin slots were under the panel, two empty, while the other held a black chip in it. Q poked the chip in and it released with a click. He pulled it out to inspect it.

"It's okay!" He laughed with relief. "Mada, you sonofabitch, you were a real hypocrite, but I couldn't be happier about that now. I could almost kiss you, man."

He looked up at Mal like a proud parent.

"I'd rather you not kiss me," Mal said.

"Ha! You're alright, man!" Q looked at the dagger sticking out of the top of Nodi's pants. "Now it gets tricky. Give that to Mal."

Mal took the dagger from Nodi and ran his fingers over the edge curiously. He looked down at Q, who was still inspecting Mada's chip with narrowed eyes. Mal caught Nodi staring at him and he disembarked whatever train of thought he was riding.

"Turn me over on my left side and cut a slit on the back of my neck," Q said. "It's in the same spot ... there." He tapped the area.

Mal did as he was told.

"Now take this." Q handed Mal the chip. "This is where things'll get weird. You're going to put that card in one of the empty slots. You'll hear three voices. Wait for the voice of the woman. She'll start counting. When she does, pull Mada's chip out. No matter what's happening, pull it out, understand?"

"Yes," Mal said. "But what is this thing?"

"It's Mada's consciousness," Q said. "His black box. His brain map. He was going to jump the flesh. It's complicated. Just do it, okay."

Nodi watched as Mal took Mada's chip and held it up. He wondered how someone's essence could be contained in such a small thing—what manner of abomination it could create.

Mal clicked the card into place. Q's eyes fluttered like a sharp blast of wind had burst into them. At first, Nodi heard gurgling vowel sounds in different vocal patterns, but no discernible language. The sounds synchronized and became clear. Q's mouth ceased to move, but voices emerged from his larynx anyway.

"Where am I?" It was Terise Mada speaking through Q's body. His voice was deeper, older, with an accent. "Who are you? The mechanic, Quentin Reese, he's trying to kill us."

"Mada, call the ship," Q said.

"Reese? Is that you?"

"Call the ship, Mada."

Mada resisted, groaning and yelling. Q's eyes continued to flutter—his skin grew hot.

"Call the ship, Mada!"

"Seraph!" Mada yelled.

The voice of a woman with perfect articulation said, "Systems rebooting. Access granted: Captain Terise Mada ... New administrator added: Quentin Reese ... Access granted: Quentin Reese ... Awaiting instructions."

Q went still, his flesh cooled, but his eyes fluttered again before locking open, staring straight up.

"I won't let you," Mada said. "I won't let you."

"Away ship preparing for launch," the female voice said. "Emergency rescue operation commencing in 10 ... 9 ... 8 ..."

"Pull it out," Q said through clenched teeth.

Mal pulled the chip out and dropped it on the ground. Q went limp and breathed deeply, recovering from the trauma.

"Get me ... to the roof," he said.

Mal strapped him to his back and they ran out into the Great Hall and up to Hinnoben's chamber. Shirka followed at a distance.

Hinnoben's chamber was ransacked, sheets strewn on the floor, furniture overturned. They stopped to look out of the balcony window. The palace smoldered in the distance and the city was aflame in patches. Fights were erupting again, between those faithful to Q by way of Shirka, and those faithful to their late high apostle.

Q stared out, calculating his next move. "Pass me over to chuckles there, Mal."

Mal complied. Q was painfully heavy for Nodi. Even at half his original size, Q was still almost as tall.

They crossed the room and climbed out of the window onto the roof. Nodi had to pass Q to Mal and then crawl out behind them.

The riotous crowds roared below them.

It's the end of all things, Nodi thought. *The apocalypse is here.*

Mal helped strap Q to Nodi's back again and said, "What now?"

"We wait. It shouldn't be long. You're about to get the ride of your life, Noodle!"

"Nodi"

"Whatever."

"What do you mean?"

"We're going up to Seraph."

"Trej's star?"

"Star*ship*."

"I … I don't *want* to go."

"I don't care if you don't want to go or not." Nodi heard the talisman hum, felt it warm on the back of his neck. "I can't do this alone. You don't get a choice." He looked at Mal. "I need you to stay here."

"What? Why?"

"I trust you more than this one here. Keep an eye on that crazy ass persecutor. See if you can help restore order. I'll be back—refreshed, recharged, and ready to rock. We're gonna have a ball!"

Mal furrowed his brow, probably wondering why he should be excited about a ball and what they were going to do with it when they got it.

Nodi looked around for any other recourse. *There's no way out of this*, he thought. There wasn't a tree to jump onto this time and Q's new lackey, Shirka, was crawling out of the window.

In the smoke-streaked sky above them, flashes of white radiated from a single point in the sky. A black dot emerged from the midst of it, getting bigger as it approached. The crowd hushed.

The almond-shaped ship arrived quickly and a gust of blue fire bellowed from below it as it slowed, coming to a gentle landing on the roof in front of them. The heat distorted its edges in squiggles and waves, smoke curled up and over the top. The upper portion of the ship was chrome, casting a reflection of the sky on its surface—the bottom was the color of brushed metal.

"Come on," Q yelled over the thunderous engines of the ship. He pointed at the back where an opening ramp led into the bowels of it. Nodi was cautious.

Shirka tried to follow, but Q stopped her. "Stay here with Mal."

"What shall I do, Lord?"

"Just wait. I'll be back soon."

She stepped aside and kneeled as the ramp closed in front of her. Mal looked confused and helpless.

The inside of the ship was lit red with grated floors, six tall seats on each side, and four in the middle, back to back. Up front, a screen flickered with numbers and symbols Nodi didn't understand. When the ramp sealed in place, all but the control panels and the floor became windows.

"Put me down in that seat," Q said.

Nodi struggled to lift him up and buckle him in and then he sat next to him. Bars lowered over their shoulders and secured them in place.

"Take us home, Seraph," Q said.

The ship lifted off the roof with a clap of the engines, pointed aggressively at the sky, and burst forward. Nodi felt like his organs were pressing into his back from the force. He clenched his eyes shut and gasped involuntarily, certain he was about to die. Hell, it seemed, was not below them, but above, and he was on his way there. He croaked and held his breath, vibrations rattling every part of him.

Q hit him on the arm and said, "Snap out of it, dumbass, you're the first of your kind to ride the chariot of the Gods, man!"

Nodi was brave.

He opened his eyes and looked to his left. Prontis was shrinking, fading into a tapestry of blues, greens, and browns.

As they rose, the width and breadth of the island of Selidin was exposed for the relatively small thing it was. They flew to the Northwest, over the swirling black cauldron of smoke and ash between Selidin and Vespala—what seemed so deadly from below was beautiful from above. A vast continent was beyond Vespala with great, snowcapped mountains and emerald seas beyond that. A semicircular horizon soon dominated their view and the cerulean sky faded into ultramarine, then violet, then orange tinted black. The aurora was below them now.

"It's beautiful," Nodi said. His heartsbeat lost rhythm, his eyes watered. "Who knew it could be so unimaginably beautiful?"

He tried to see the stars, but the luminescence of the planet blotted them out. A colossal ship—four dagger-shaped segments around a central hull, connected by tubes, no visible windows, and a series of thin pipes running the length of it—drifted in the darkness, dark gray and gleaming in the refracted light of Akigol. The side was peppered with cosmetic damage—dents, holes, patches. The word "Sera" was on the main hull in worn block letters, the last two letters illegible.

"Sera," Nodi said.

"Seraph, actually. That's the name of the vessel. She's a piece of shit, but it might as well be God's own throne to you."

As they floated closer, Nodi feared they might collide. He was weightless and let his arms drift out in front of him, thrilled and confused by the sensation. His tentacles wiggled like lethargic serpents in all directions. Their ship latched onto Seraph like a suckling calf, was pulled up and seated into a recess, and then stopped suddenly. The jolt frightened him.

A hatch on the ceiling opened to reveal a tube leading into Seraph's belly.

"Okay, we're good," Q said. "Let's go."

The seats released and Q floated into the tube, grasping onto the side with his one good arm. Nodi followed. They emerged out of the tube and into a chamber with slanted yellow stripes along the walls. The hatch to the tube collapsed into the floor, hissed, and then gravity was restored. Nodi fell on his side violently.

A thin green light surveyed the room and paused on Q.

"Grace and peace to you, Quentin," Seraph said.

"Hey, Seraph."

"All other crew members are registered dead. Is this accurate?"

"Yeah."

"You now have administrative privileges."

The light moved over Nodi and painted him red.

"Unidentified: akigo, Planet VIA 42.64b."

Nodi held his hand up marveling at the way the light danced on his fingertips. "It knows what I am?"

"He's clear, Seraph," Q said.

"Releasing. Grace and peace to you." The light turned green again until it locked on Q's talisman. He was clenching it in his fist.

"Please store in locker 5B."

A metal door opened out of the wall behind them. Q mumbled something and then gave it to Nodi so he could put it in the locker.

Nodi strapped Q to his back, the half-man's wiry midriff dragging on the floor. A gargantuan door opened top to bottom with a gust of warm air. It was dark beyond the door except for a few lights at the end of the passageway. Once they crossed the threshold, however, the lights flickered on. The walls were marred, the floor damp, and it smelled like mold. Pipes ran the length of the ceiling and beneath the grated floor. It looked like the walls once had murals of cloudy skies, crude trees, and religious iconography, but it was mostly worn away to mere ghost images.

"Welcome to Seraph," Q said. "Maybe she's a better ship than I gave her credit for. Over two hundred and forty years unattended and she's still in service."

36

When the ship began to lift off, Mal moved back, shielding his face from the hot wind. The roof beneath his feet cracked and bowed, the integrity loosening from the weight of the heavy craft. Shirka stayed on her knees, face toward heaven, eyes closed.

Mal kicked her in the stomach. She fell over and lay there. He kicked her again, but she didn't retaliate. It was as if she accepted it as penance. He straddled her and hit her four more times. Nothing. He stood up, breathing heavy, eyes full of hate.

"Forgive me, brother," she said without looking at him. "I have sinned against you and the scribe. I know that now … We must restore order for the Lord."

She was pathetic.

"Wait here," Mal said.

He ran out of the temple. Akigi fought in the streets, looting shops, throwing rocks, burning things. Dead and dying lay in pools of blood. He wove through back lots and alleys and went to the burrow where he and Nodi first escaped Prontis. Many ixaquoi were there, holed up inside its walls, storing provisions.

They looked at Mal, amazed he was still alive.

He grinned at them, eyes sparkly with mischief.

Q led Nodi to double doors at the far end of the bottom floor that opened automatically as they approached. The room beyond the doors was just a tiny little box. They got in and listened to the friendly music playing from somewhere in the ceiling.

"Third," Q said.

The doors closed and the box began to move upward. Nodi grabbed the sides to brace himself. When the doors opened again, he was surprised to find that they were somewhere completely different.

They went to the left, then down a hall to a door with Terise Mada's name on it. Nodi was tired of dragging the man around.

"Let me in, Seraph," Q said and the doors opened.

Mada's cabin was impeccably clean with wood cabinets, sleeping quarters, adjoining rooms, and all sorts of things Nodi couldn't identify. The walls and floor were magenta, the ceiling metal with recessed square patterns that met in the middle. A sharp, musty smell hung in the air.

"It's got to be here somewhere," Q said. He had Nodi take him to a large vault, but the door was locked. "Open it, Seraph."

The vault opened. A tall container was inside with frosted glass and the silhouette of a man inside.

"I knew it!" Q hit Nodi's shoulder to accentuate whatever it was he knew. "Take it to the chamber."

The container rose into a hatch in the ceiling and out of sight.

Q pointed Nodi down the hall and back through a set of doors that opened with a hiss. Nodi noticed everything opened with a *hiss* or a *swoosh* of some kind. They came to an intersection. On the wall in front of them, it said,

THEREFORE, GO AND MAKE DISCIPLES OF ALL WORLDS, BAPTIZING THEM IN THE NAME OF THE FATHER AND THE SON AND THE HOLY SPIRIT, TEACHING THEM TO OBEY EVERYTHING I HAVE COMMANDED YOU. AND SURELY I AM WITH YOU ALWAYS, TO THE VERY END OF THE UNIVERSE.

"Zealots," Q said, eyeing the message with disdain.

"They were missionaries?" Nodi said. "They came here to convert us?"

"That's right."

"My father was a missionary. How many religions *are* there?"

"Shit man, too many to count. Hell, each *adherent* to each religion has their own version of it. They *all* claim to know the truth or some part of it, but mystical revelation is no way to get at the truth. That's what science and reason are for."

"Science and reason are not the only ways to truth," Seraph said unexpectedly. "What about experience? What about the subjective? Can science categorize beauty, art, emotion?"

"Yes, in point of fact, it can," Q said. "God Seraph, not this again. It's like I never left." He pointed Nodi down the hall to the right. "Have you ever heard such a thing, Noodle?"

"Nodi."

"Whatever. A computer, a *thing* whose very existence is the product of *science*, that undervalues the importance of it? Isn't that rich? Seraph isn't true A.I., that part of her was inhibited. Mada believed A.I. is an abomination. She's *programmed* to respond that way. It's infuriating. Fucking quotes Bible verses and sings hymns on Sundays. It's enough to make you think about an airlock swan dive, man. Turn left at the end of the hall."

They went down to a brightly lit corridor that was white and sterile. Several long chambers were on either side, each with a clear door on the front.

"Here we are. Seraph, open the door."

The door opened to a room filled with harsh light, metal tubes, and boxes Nodi couldn't comprehend the uses of. The container from Mada's chamber lowered through the ceiling and latched into place with a *hiss* and a *clank*.

"Open it, Seraph." The chamber door opened with elegant precision, ready to embrace him. "Put me in, Nodi, near the top. The system will do the rest."

Nodi struggled to place him at the back of the chamber and then four metal arms clamped around him.

Q pointed. "Latch the container in place over there."

Nodi looked at the container as if he was a lutefish trying to do complex math.

"Christ. Pull up on the three little handles there around the top edges."

Nodi pulled the handles and they released a cloud of vapor from the edges that sent him scuttling to the other side of the room. A digital screen on top of the container flashed the words "DIRECTIVE 42" and then the word "ERROR."

"Clean slate the database, Seraph, make all amendments necessary."

"Yes, Quentin."

"This'll take a while, Noodle. Make yourself at home. When I come out, I'll be a *new* man. Seraph, grant him guest access."

"Yes, Quentin."

Q waved him out with a devilish smile as the chamber closed. As soon as Nodi left, the door closed behind him and a metal rod slid into place to seal it tight.

Nodi explored the passageways of the ship like a fish in unfamiliar waters, going floor to floor, peeking around corners, trying not to break anything. It was all so alien. He was frightened and amazed—felt like he was trespassing in the house of the Gods. He wanted to find a way home, but curiosity drove him on. He didn't think Seraph would let him leave, anyway.

He found a room that played a song by something called "Chopin." The name was on the wall, painted in light. The music seized him—a universal language, a language he understood—one not made of words, but rhythm and longing.

It spoke only of loss.

He left when the song ended, yet it played on in his mind.

He found another room down the hall and a floor down. It was hot and loud like a mighty waterfall. He watched lights draw diagrams across ghostly images of the ship rotating in mid-air—magic he couldn't comprehend. He tried to touch them, but the images had no substance. Everything was redundant, each piece seemingly inhabited by Seraph, every part built for longevity.

In the heart of the ship, he found a garden, three stories high, lit by fake sunlight. Half the lights were dark, though, so it looked more like a fake rainy day. Brownish trees were in the middle, scraping the vaulted ceiling, and vines grew on the walls all the way up. The plants that were still alive hung from gridded wires, roots and all, in long rows. Condescended water trickled from above, dripping off the roots and into drains in the floor. Metal arms moved about, pruning leaves and picking fruit. They sorted it out, casting refuse down a shaft. Intake and exhaust fans created a pleasant breeze and depending on where Nodi stood, he could smell things labeled with names like oranges, lavender, and cucumbers.

It smelled nice mostly, but foreign. Some of the unlit spots stank of rot

"I'm starving," he muttered.

A green light painted him for a moment, an analysis of some kind, and then either a green or a red light appeared in front of each plant.

"Eat only green," Seraph said.

He perused the room and poked at the fruits marked safe. He picked something called a "strawberry" off a plant and rolled it between his fingers, sniffed it, and took an exploratory bite. The texture was strange, the taste not *too* odd. He ate a few of them. He tried bananas, skin and all, before it occurred to him that he was probably supposed to peel it first. He tried an olive, but the pit made him gag so he moved to seedless grapes, and blueberries, and tomatoes.

He really liked grapefruit. "My God that's good. Similar to robus back in Kan Ludo."

He hadn't eaten a good meal in a long time and Seraph's hospitality made him feel a little better. Still, he wondered if he was eating his last meal. *When Q emerges from that chamber, he won't need me anymore,* he thought. *He'll be more careful now than when he first came to Akigol. I wear skepticism like a birthmark. I'm a problem for him and he knows it.* His stomach fluttered with dread. He felt trapped in a prison, as oddly luxurious as it was, and felt his life was no longer his own.

When he finished, he wandered some more and found a round, wood-paneled library on the top floor near the front of the ship. It contained only one paper book that sat on a pedestal in the middle of the room, a copy of *Holy Bible* identical to the one Judas had buried. A black mirrored panel was embedded around the circumference of the room, running from end to end and stopping at the doors on opposite sides from each other. Nodi looked into the dark mirror and stared deep into his own eyes. It was the clearest reflection of himself he'd ever seen.

He ran his fingers across the glassy surface and it came alive with three-dimensional words and pictures that suggested a variety of topics for his perusal. One of the topics was "Origins" and it branched into a variety of context-sensitive menus. He recognized a subset still bookmarked by whoever looked at it last:

Planet VIA 42.64b: Locally known as Akigol.

He touched the words and it was as if his brain changed frequencies. He was in a waking dream, consciousness merged with machine, synapses firing packets of information. All became light and sound and power and glory. He was out of body, floating in the heavens, witnessing the white-hot origins of his solar system's suns and the formation of the planets that revolved around them. Volcanoes erupted and he could almost feel the heat of their boiling hot temperatures. He saw desolation, floods, ice ages, primordial ooze, and single-celled organisms that erupted into complex life at multiple points along the chaotic timeline.

Primitives evolved into common ancestors that led to ixaquoi and akigi and troogils and he saw Vespalids and other things he didn't recognize, springing from the vast and complicated tree of life. Continents shifted, islands were born, the destructive power of erosion sculpted it all. He watched as the world changed and matured in ways he could never have imagined.

It's chaos, beauty, majesty, and indifference seized him.

How did all this happen? What of God?

He rolled the timeline back to the origins of the solar system and then to the origins of the universe. He saw the big bang explode, felt its subsequent and lasting radiation, saw the swirling births of galaxies and stars, saw black holes, quasars, atoms, and light, the fabric of space and time and how it all related to one another in ways he could never fathom.

He rolled the timeline back further. Everything dissolved into numbers and equations, branched into paths, some repeating the same or similar patterns over and over again, some leading to multiple universes, some to multiple dimensions, all to eternal regresses, and the contradictory juxtaposition of the finite and the infinite.

Chaos was at the core of it. Chaos that erupted into order and dissolved into chaos again.

All that is, is defined by what cannot *be.*

He stepped back and broke the connection, rubbing his eyes. He had a dull headache at the base of his skull.

What of God?

God seemed superfluous. Nothing he'd seen indicated there was no God, but nothing he'd seen *required* one.

A profound sense of loneliness washed over him. He threatened to lose his composure as he leaned against the wall, head hung low. It was the memory of his father and of Aenna that bothered him most. The glimmering hope of an ethereal reunion with them blinked out of the realm of possibility. It was as if they were irrevocably, hopelessly … lost.

"Curiosity killed the cat," he muttered.

Seraph displayed a quote from some ancient holy man, St. Augustine.

GOD FASHIONED HELL FOR THE INQUISITIVE

Nodi shook his head and turned away. He was angry— filled with righteous indignation. He punched the black panel as hard as he could, hoping to break it, but it didn't damage it, not even a little. His hand hurt, though, it would bruise soon.

"I know less now, than ever." He went through the open

door opposite the one he'd entered. It led to the bridge of the ship, the top half housed in a domed, artificial window. Akigol floated before him, blue-green and luminous against the velvety black of space. Lines and blips overlaid the image, displaying every conceivable piece of pertinent information about the planet in real time, moving with its rotation—sterile data vandalizing a mystical image.

He watched his planet turn, so gentle, so ancient, so wise. He wanted to save it, *needed* to save it.

Around the perimeter of the bridge, shiny displays pinged and chimed. He noticed movement in a bank of screens that cycled images of the ship. A man with wavy brown hair and an orange jumpsuit walked down one of the halls. Nodi poked at the screen. "Who is that?"

"Quentin Reese," Seraph said.

"Doesn't look like him."

"He inhabits Terise Mada's artificial body."

"Is this happening now?"

"Yes."

The man walked down the hall, running his fingers through his hair.

He'll kill me and no one will ever know, Nodi thought. *I'm trapped.*

Q left the frame and stepped into another view, one on an elevator. He cracked his neck and ran his hands over his pants to straighten them.

He's a monster. He'll never leave Akigol. He'll never die. He'll subject the planet to his every whim.

In another view, in another hall, drawing closer to the bridge, Q stopped and raised his arms over his head, the practiced pose of a triumphant Messiah returning to his subjects.

He must die.

Nodi looked out at Akigol and back down at the screen.

He clenched his fists, tightened his jaw, waiting for Q to come in.

Q grinned as he entered. "What do you think?" He primped. "Do I look ... Messiah-y?"

He stood by the door with his arms out, ready to resume where he'd left off, ready to usurp the throne of the hearts of the akigi, a throne he had no rightful claim to.

Kill, Nodi. Kill.

Nodi charged and fell into Q, grabbing his chin and smashing the back of his head into the doorjamb. Q fell sideways, shocked. Nodi kicked him in the face—wild-eyed, tentacles rigid, spit running over his lips. He kicked him for every committed believer who wasted his life following the lies, kicked him for every drop of blood spilled in his name, kicked him for love lost and shattered dreams and greed and desperation and shame—

"No more!" Nodi yelled. "No more!"

Q, impossibly strong, grabbed his leg and flipped him back, but Nodi was a tiny storm of quick, disorienting strikes. He rolled to his feet to resume the attack, but Q scuttled out of the door backward and fell on his ass. "Seraph, lock him in!"

The door sealed shut just before Nodi smashed into it, pounded it, raged in the window like a caged animal. Q got up and watched, breathing fast, face covered in synthetic blood. A piece of artificial scalp hung off the backside of his head—his hair was tousled. "You're *crazy*, you Goddamned primitive!"

"I'm done with you!" Nodi yelled. He was starting to cry.

"Don't let him out, Seraph. And don't let him ... y'know ... poke any buttons."

"Yes, Quentin."

Nodi's breath fogged the window in pulses, big eyes given over to tears and madness.

Q displayed his middle finger before walking away. It was a gesture Nodi didn't understand but took as an insult. He tried to display his own middle finger, but he only had four. He slapped the window with his palms instead and screamed.

"Let me out, Seraph!"

"I cannot."

Nodi punched the door, turned around, and slipped down to the floor. He wiped his eyes, pounded the door with his elbows, and then searched the bridge for a way out. He found a red emergency hatch with a manual lock below a panel in the floor. He tried to turn it, but it was too stiff. He struggled, pulling, pushing, kicking.

"Please don't," Seraph said.

"Shut up!"

Nodi gave the latch another kick and jarred it loose. He moved to the other side, pulled it down, and freed the lock.

He slipped into a crawlspace that led to a tube with a ladder down the length of it. He half climbed, half slid down the ladder from floor to floor all the way to the bottom. He burst through the door and it hit Q as he ran by. Q crashed into the opposite wall and tripped. Nodi fell out of the door and grabbed him by his pant leg as he tried to stand. Q stumbled but got free. Nodi chased him again, tackled him, thrashing, pummeling him with his fists until Q grasped his arm, twisted, and shattered it. Nodi screamed and fell on his back.

Q leaned over and put his finger in his face. "Fuck you."

He climbed on top of Nodi and started to choke him. Nodi grasped a piece of Q's dangling scalp and pulled down. A clump of hair came with it. Q let go and sheltered the stripped patch of skull with his hand. He seemed concerned about the diminishing returns of his own appearance if the abuse should continue. Appearances were everything. He got up, ran through the bay door at the end of the hall, and locked Nodi out.

By the time Nodi struggled to his feet and got to the door, Q was already descending the tube to the away ship.

Nodi fell to his knees when he heard him leave.

It was too late to stop him.

37

L et me in," Nodi said.

"I cannot."

"I just want to go home." He hit the door weakly with his good arm. "Please," he whispered.

"If you wish to leave, you must use Bay 2. I am sorry. I am under orders from Captain Reese not to let you into Bay 1."

"Bay 2?"

"Yes."

"I can get home from Bay 2?"

"Yes."

Nodi realized that Seraph was a stickler for specifics and Q hadn't been specific enough. "Well, tell me how to get me to Bay 2, then."

Seraph led him through a long, curved tube to Bay 2. He wrapped his twisted arm with a rag as he went. Bay 2 was a mirror image of Bay 1. He saw his ride through a window in the floor. It was smaller and sleeker than the one he came to Seraph on. Seraph disengaged gravity, lifted the floor hatch, and Nodi glided clumsily in and sat down. Seraph did everything else. The ship released with a jolt and blasted away, aimed at the planet. Akigol spun around making him dizzy. Orange and blue fire ripped across the front of the ship on atmospheric entry and Nodi thought about Q's original arrival on the planet.

How often do these things burst apart?

Selidin loomed larger and larger on the view screen. Dissipating vapor trails showed him where Q had already passed. Soon, he saw Prontis. The crowds moved insect-like through the streets, columns of smoke drifted over the city. The ship slowed on approach. The temple was there below him, Q's ship already on the roof.

Q stood on the temple's edge, a triumphant return that solidified an ancient promise, one that confirmed what so many of them already believed.

Nodi's anger burned even brighter.

The ship landed and the ramp lowered. Nodi ran out. An eerie hush was upon the crowd below. Mal and Shirka stood in front of Q, blades drawn as if to defend him. Nodi wondered what Mal was up to.

The wind and the heat blustered from beneath the ship.

"Mal," he said. "Please."

A mischievous glint inhabited Mal's eyes and he smirked. He stabbed Shirka through the abdomen. She fell to her knees as he swaggered over her.

Q was surprised. He'd been fooled by the ixaquoi's act. "Sonofa—"

Mal turned on him. Q lifted his hand, he had the talisman again, but Mal ran the dagger through it. The talisman sparked and went dead as black blood spurted through the back of Q's hand. He knocked Mal to the ground and Nodi lunged forward. Q kicked him in the stomach and withdrew the dagger from his ruined paw. He flicked the broken talisman away and held the dagger, weaving and jabbing it at

Nodi.

Mal got up, but Shirka stabbed him in the back. He collapsed, stunned—eyes going dark. Shirka fell back down, bleeding out onto the wood logs of the roof.

Nodi limped to the right. Q mirrored his movements while pointing the dagger at him. Nodi feinted left, but Q cut him on the forearm and again on the thigh. Nodi winced and withdrew. Mal crawled to the precipice and looked down at the crowd. His blood dribbled over the edge of the temple.

Someone threw a rotten vegetable and hit Q on the side of his head. He jerked violently and turned to see who threw it. Dissenters Guild folk were up on the cliffs overlooking the temple. They threw more, a rancid cascade designed to embarrass him, disgrace him, make him a laughing stock. No one worships a fool. Some in the crowd laughed and booed and hissed, others defended him. Q was confused, holding his hands up over his face to block the mushy strikes.

In the confusion, Nodi grabbed the dagger from Q and stabbed him in the thigh. He'd aimed for Q's heart but was too short to reach it. Q hollered and fell on his side. The crowd stopped and watched. Smoke drifted in black plumes from behind Nodi. Several ixaquoi ran out of the temple gates below, torches held high. The temple was burning.

Nodi lifted the dagger. Q held up his bloody hand, shaking his head.

"Nodi, stop!" Mal said. It took all his strength to say it. Nodi stayed his hand, but didn't take his eyes off Q. Mal struggled to speak. "Leave him be. This isn't about *him*." He pointed at the crowd. "It's about *them*. Don't give them a martyr. Give them a laughing stock."

Nodi lifted the knife, seemingly deaf to Mal's words. He stabbed Q again, but in the other thigh. It would leave Q hobbled but not dead. Nodi rolled him off the roof. Q was built to last, the fall wouldn't kill him.

"Now you can grovel at *our* feet."

The akigi closest to where he landed stared at the pitiful man. For a moment, Nodi thought the spell was broken, that Q held no more power over them until a surge of faithful broke the line and formed a defensive ring around their broken Messiah. They lifted him up and solemnly carried him down the street.

They understand nothing, but what they want *to understand,* Nodi thought. *"Tim" cannot be defeated. He jumped the flesh in more ways than one. He's an idea. There's no shame, no disgrace, no scandal that can destroy him. These events will be sewn into the narrative. This day will be counted as a glory, not a defeat, and I will be the new Judas.*

Nodi.

A bitter name on the tongues of the devoted.

Nodi spat at them. Mal groaned. Had all this been for nothing?

A horde of akigi chased after the faithful and a mighty swell of chaos broke out between them. The crowd became a mass of red and green static, fires bursting forth, temple businesses razed.

Mal smiled. "That's better."

The temple roof was giving way—wood splintering, stone breaking apart.

"We should go," he said, voice weak. He couldn't stand up.

Nodi dragged him toward the ship.

Shirka was lying in a pool of blood, looking over at them. "God gave *you* the strength," she said through weak breaths. "He gave *you* the strength. Forgive me ... Forgive me."

Nodi stopped and looked at her. Hate transformed into pity and a small kernel of forgiveness was born inside him. He didn't have the will to speak to her, but he nodded. It was the most he could offer. He didn't think she would survive.

The roof gave way as the ship lifted off it. The thick logs

fell in at an angle and Shirka slid down into the smoke-filled room below. He thought he saw her limp off, but wasn't sure. As they rose, Q's ship crashed through the collapsing ceiling, the dome falling in on top of it in a plume of smoke and ash.

Mal was bleeding, screaming as the force tore at the hole in his back.

"Hold on, Mal. Please, just hold on," Nodi said.

When they docked with Seraph, Nodi pushed his weightless friend up the tube and into the hangar. Mal's blood beaded and trailed behind them.

"Seraph, please help," Nodi said. A pallet quick released out of a wall and came toward them.

"Strap him on," Seraph said.

Nodi held on as the palette floated down the hall into a brightly lit room. The door closed behind them and the palette eased into a long chamber before gravity reengaged.

A white machine lowered out of the ceiling, scanning Mal's body from head to toe. It encased him inside and a screen displayed his vitals. Mal struggled out of fear but was too weak to put up much of a fight. His labored heart was audible through the machinery. Green squiggly lines ran across the chamber lid.

Bdump ... Bdump ... bump ... Bdump ... Bdump ... bump ...

I can't lose another one, Nodi thought. *Please, just this once ... Let him live ...*

After a quick injection from a metal arm with clear tubes running out of it, Mal fell asleep. A small window was near his head. Nodi could see him resting. The machine whirred and vibrated, Mal's heartbeat was getting closer together, more stable.

Bdump ... bump ... Bdump ... bump ... Bdump ... bump ...

"There's nothing you can do here," Seraph said. "You must wait and see."

"How long?"

"Until it is finished. Is Captain Quentin Reese dead? He did not establish a neural connection to me."

"It doesn't matter. He's not coming back."

"By the code of intergalactic salvage rights, you are the rightful owner of this ship until which time a more suitable owner is declared by law. All administrative privileges have been transferred to you."

"O ... Okay. I have no idea what that means, but okay." His shattered arm throbbed with pain now that the excitement was over. "Can you fix this?"

"Yes."

* * *

As Mal recovered, Nodi wandered about the ship and ended up back in the library by the bridge. For some reason, the obsidian wall read, "UPLOAD? YES / NO" with the word "Review" in small print under it. Nodi wondered what it meant. He touched the word "Review." Raw data about his life appeared before him. The machine had mapped his mind—dates and images of everywhere he'd ever been and information on everyone he'd ever known. His father was there, and Trej, but he couldn't take his eyes off Aenna.

She looked happy in the image, peaceful. He recognized it as his own enduring memory of her, a mental freeze frame he carried close to his hearts. He lifted his shaking finger and touched it. The words "DATA" and "SIMULATION" appeared. He withdrew his finger a moment and then touched the latter.

His mind melded with the system again. Aenna stood before him wearing a breezy yellow outfit, the one she often wore to the temple. She was in a green meadow, spring breeze blowing, looking divine.

"How is this possible?" He said, broken.

"I'm compiled from your memories."

Something about her wasn't right. "I wish ... I wish things had been different. That day at the dock—"

"Would you like to see what *could* have been?"

"What do you mean?"

She showed him a simultaneous series of scenarios. In one, she didn't walk away from him outside Judas' cave but was killed by the stickyfish in Hijoon. In another, she refused to go with him when he tried to free her in Kan Ludo. Yet another, the persecutor didn't kill her on the docks but took her back to Prontis where she was executed. Still another, she made it to Seraph with him but left for altogether unrelated reasons. The paths flooded in front of him—she died on the *way* to Vespala, she died *in* Vespala, she lived her life having never known him, she lived her life having rejected him, she turned him in, she protected him, she lived, she died, on and on ...

Very few of the scenarios included her standing there with him at the end of the journey, happy.

The ones that did crushed him with regret.

"This shows me what *you* could have done differently. What could *I* have done?"

Aenna looked at him with sympathy. "No one knows better than you. But why does it matter? You are the constant. What you did, you did. I'm just a variable in your mind. Maybe the universe *is* indifferent, but life dances to its beat anyway, Nodi. Sometimes it's timing is impeccable, sometimes it isn't. Call it divine will, fate, destiny, chance, it doesn't matter. If you want to know what you can do differently, look forward, not back."

"You loved Tim, more than me," he said.

"Of course." He thought there was a "but" coming. There wasn't. He was angry with her for that but realized she couldn't have helped her belief any more than he could help his *un*belief. He would have been willing to live with that reality, but he didn't think she ever could have.

"I miss you," he said.

"You have to move on, Nodi. I'm in a better place."

"Are you?"

She faded away.

He knew it wasn't really her. It was his perception of her, and maybe some things he *wished* were true about her. She lacked the essence of Aenna. That undefined, inexplicable something about her. This image didn't have it because he'd never really understood it. He wondered how much of anyone he truly understood.

He rolled his hand over the wall and brought it back to the words "UPLOAD? YES / NO."

He wondered if hitting "YES" wasn't his way of holding on to the past.

He hit it, anyway.

—— ·⊹═◖●◗◎◖●◗═⊹· ——

Later, he stood by the chamber in the infirmary, looking in at Mal who was asleep. He rested his head on the glass, fogging it with his breath. Mal's eyelids wiggled left and right and Nodi wondered what kind of perverted, drunken dreams he was having. His heartbeat was strong and consistent.

Bdump bump ... Bdump bump ... Bdump bump ...

Mal opened his eyes. At first, they swirled as if they'd forgotten how to operate. His brow furrowed and he focused on Nodi. Mal pressed his hand to the glass, wincing in pain. They stared at each other a moment and then Mal gave him a mischievous wink.

—— ·⊹═◖●◗◎◖●◗═⊹· ——

A week later, Nodi was outside of Trej's observatory. It was cold and fresh snow blustered around the dropship as its engines powered down. He wore a coat he'd found aboard

Seraph. He looked like a youngling in the oversized garment and he carried a metal marker Seraph had engraved for him.

Mal came out of the observatory, also in a coat. He held a leather pack, stuffing some of Trej's ale into it. When he saw Nodi watching him, he held a bottle out to him. Nodi shook his head and Mal shrugged. He latched the loose fitting flap over the bottles and tossed the bag over his shoulder.

"You sure you don't want to come with me?" Nodi said.

Mal looked up at the sky. "What the hell would I do up there?"

"Aren't you curious to see?"

"No. My life is here. I've already got what I dreamed of. To live in the aftermath, to breathe in the freedom, blow in the winds of change."

"The winds of chaos, you mean."

"Same thing."

"Do you really think anything will be different?"

"Absolutely."

"Better?"

"No tellin'."

Nodi nodded. "At least let Seraph take you back to civilization. It's a long way from here."

Mal pointed at the ship. "I wouldn't get back in that damn thing if you dragged me by the nose. No. I'll be okay."

He gave Nodi an awkward pat on the shoulder, paused to consider him a moment, and then started down the hill toward the path that led back to Kan Ludo.

"Mal. Thank you."

Mal stopped, turned, and smiled. It was the smile of a genuine friend. A smile that said "goodbye." A smile that said, "We'll almost certainly see each other again."

Nodi waved.

When Mal was gone, he searched for a perfect spot, one where the view of the mountains and the stars was just right, where the breeze from the north wasn't too harsh. Below him, a dense fog blanketed everything but the tallest peaks of the range. It smelled crisp and clean and he breathed it in.

He dug a small hole through the frozen tundra and put Trej's cog in it. He wished he could bury Trej there, and Aenna too, but the trinket would have to do. He struggled for the right words to say, but when he tried, his emotions overtook him. He filled in the hole and placed the marker on top of it. All it said was,

The suns were setting and he watched them fall behind the mountains. The sky changed from orange to pink and then star-pocked purple. Aqua strokes of the aurora glistened more brilliantly than he'd ever seen. He stared up at the sky awhile until he saw the small, slow light of Seraph drift by.

He knew more about the universe than he'd ever known before, and yet he knew far less. He'd found *some* truths, but not The Truth and he wasn't sure it would have made him any happier, anyway. He sat down on the ground and thought about everything. It occurred to him that ultimate truth is something no one is ever in a position to know. It's always one step away in an infinite regression of steps, like a dance partner that flits in semi-darkness, letting you see a little, but never touch, never seize. Nodi was okay with that. He'd keep dancing. What little his dance partner had let him see in this quest was something new, something wondrous.

He looked back up at the sky and smiled.

"You should see your star, Trej," he said.

The Nodian Testaments

The Gospel According to Erd Shirka, 22:14-20

[14] For I was blinded in my service to the pagan God, Tim, and was chief among those who sought to persecute the Lord Nodi. [15] But in His grace, Nodi spared my life and allowed me to witness His shaming of the evil one on the temple roof before He ascended to heaven. [16] If anyone deserved the Lord's judgment, it was I, but He spared me. How much more will He do for you, brothers and sisters? [17] I admonish you, in the Lord, turn away from sin. Reject the evil one.

[18] I tell you the truth, Nodi appeared to me in a dream saying, "Soon I will return. You must prepare the way."

[19] Woe to those who do not turn from their evil ways and receive salvation from the Lord and Savior of Akigol.

[20] Ah Lord Nodi, come soon!

Amen.

ABOUT THE AUTHOR

Ches Smith was born in 1974, spent six confused years in elementary school, three awkward years in middle school, four invisible years in high school, found Jesus, went to college, graduated, got ordained, got married, went to seminary, had a kid, dropped out of seminary, went back to seminary, had two more kids, became increasingly insane, dropped out of seminary again and then *lost* Jesus. He soon discovered there isn't much an agnostic atheist can do with a degree in Biblical studies and two-thirds of a Masters of Divinity and there isn't much *anyone* can do with a minor in philosophy. So, to kill time until his inevitable demise, he works to support his family and writes to support his mental well-being. He lives in Houston, Texas with his wife, Silvia, and their three children, Sarah, Cristian, and Max.

www.ingramcontent.com/pod-product-compliance
Lightning Source LLC
Chambersburg PA
CBHW051406170626
46809CB00006B/2048